J. W. Traphagan was born in Boston, Massachusetts and currently resides in Austin, Texas. He is a professor and Mitsubishi Fellow in the Department of Religious Studies and the Program in Human Dimensions of Organizations at the University of Texas at Austin and has been a visiting professor at Waseda University in Tokyo. He received his BA in political science from the University of Massachusetts at Lowell, his MA in religion from Yale University, and his PhD in social anthropology from the University of Pittsburgh. Traphagan first visited Japan in the late 1980s, and in the 1990s he conducted research for almost two years there as a Fulbright scholar. He has returned annually and spent a total of almost five years in rural areas and Tokyo.

After publishing numerous scientific papers and monographs describing and analyzing Japanese culture and society, Traphagan became disenchanted and bored with the jargon and theory-laden prose that typifies academic writing. He decided to explore ethnography by drawing on his fieldnotes as a basis for creating fiction intended to capture the richness and complexity of life in the rural area where he has lived and worked. *The Blood of Gutoku* is the first product of that endeavor.

His two most recent books are *Cosmopolitan Rurality, Depopulation, and Entrepreneurial Ecosystems in 21st Century Japan* (Cambria Press, 2020) and *Embracing Uncertainty: Future Jazz, That 13th Century Buddhist Monk, and the Invention of Cultures* (Sumeru Press, 2021). Traphagan is also host of a regular podcast on the New Books Network and performs as a jazz drummer regularly in the Austin area.

Balestier Press
Centurion House, London TW18 4AX
www.balestier.com

The Blood of Gutoku: A Jack Riddley Mystery in Japan
Copyright © J. W. Traphagan, 2021

A CIP catalogue record for this book is available from the British Library.

ISBN 978 1 913891 08 4

Cover design by Sarah and Schooling

This book is a work of fiction. The literary perceptions and insights are based on experience; all names, characters, places, and incidents either are products of the author's imagination or are used fictitiously.

The Blood of Gutoku

A Jack Riddley Mystery in Japan

J. W. Traphagan

BALESTIER PRESS
LONDON · SINGAPORE

CONTENTS

PREFACE

This book is the product of close to thirty years of ethnographic fieldwork in northern Japan. Although the story is fictional, the details, including those of the people (all of whom have been given pseudonyms to protect their identities), are taken from the fieldnotes I have recorded over the course of my career as an ethnographer. In several cases, the characters are not specific individuals, but represent composites of personality and other traits associated with people I have known. Other characters are based on specific individuals with whom I have interacted. Indeed, the setting is an actual village in northern Japan where I have lived and the town is a place to which I have returned and spent extended periods of time annually since the late 1980s. The characters set at Yale, however, are entirely fictional— any resemblance they have to real people is coincidental.

One of the more troubling aspects of ethnographic writing is the nagging feeling that one is writing fiction, despite having been trained (at least in my generation) that the ethnographer is doing social science. The goal, of course, is to accurately represent the lives of the people with whom one worked and lived during research; but there is a simple fact that the ethnographer as an author is always picking and choosing what he or she thinks matters most. And from those moments, conversations, interviews, and observations, the ethnographer constructs a story meant to inform readers about life in the place studied. However, regardless of how systematic any ethnographer attempts to be, it is important to recognize that all cultural representations are crafted by the researcher and, therefore, inhabit an interpretive space that lives at the threshold of fiction.[1]

---

[1]   Matt Jacobson & Soren C. Larsen (2014) Ethnographic fiction for writing and research in cultural geography, Journal of Cultural Geography, 31:2, 179-193 (DOI: 10.1080/08873631.2014.906851)

One of the difficulties in ethnographic writing is ensuring that the voices of one's interlocutors speak, rather than the scholarly product simply being a description of some other culture from the position of intellectual and scientific authority.

As I thought about this, I started to wonder, why not just write a novel? Maybe a good way to allow the voices and worlds of the people I've come to know over the years—many who have become some of my closest friends—to come to life would be to let them speak through dialogue. Of course, this still means I'm putting words in their mouths, but I think it also allows me to use the written form in a different way to dive somewhat deeper into my perspectives about the personalities of the people I know well. It also allows me to represent them through the story here in the ways I know them as individuals living out their lives in a small town in northern Japan.

Hence, this book represents an experiment in ethnographic writing. Of course, the idea of ethnographic fiction is nothing new; other scholars have delved into this approach to ethnographic writing. But as far as I know, this is among the first attempts at an ethnographic mystery novel, and certainly one set in rural Japan. My selection of the mystery genre is based on both my enjoyment of detective fiction (I'm a Sherlock Holmes fan) and a recognition that ethnographers have much in common with detectives. They are intensely trained in observational methods and most of what an anthropologist does when conducting ethnographic fieldwork involves piecing together and trying to understand the meanings of behaviors and symbols in a given cultural context. There is a great deal of puzzle-solving that goes on both in the field and when one returns to analyze collected data, which are mostly in the form of highly detailed fieldnotes. It is my hope that as the story unfolds, the workings of ethnographic research (at least as it operates in one anthropologist's head) will come through, along with the atmosphere of the setting and its people.

Another issue that I have struggled with in contemporary ethnographic writing is the overwhelming emphasis on theory over description. Current anthropology books can be very hard going for undergraduates in introductory courses who have an interest in other cultures, as well as for general readers interested in learning about life in parts of the world distant from their own. Quite a bit of writing in anthropology these days is dry or riddled with jargon that may leave those new to the discipline lost or turned off. One goal in writing this book was to create a volume that is ethnographically rich, but accessible to those not fully ensconced in the technical terminologies and writing styles of more theoretically driven works. Nonetheless, I see this book as having considerable potential for use in graduate seminars, particularly those focused on qualitative research methods and ethnographic writing, as a way of interrogating the approaches through which we can represent qualitative data. Indeed, this book is a conscious effort to challenge traditional approaches to the representation of ethnographic data.

There are a few basic conventions of ethnographic writing and romanization of Japanese words I have maintained throughout the book. One of these is an emphasis on describing context in detail and I have also focused on considering the symbolic elements of the things one sees in the field. It is worth noting that I use the term "cult" in the sense it is used as a technical term to identify a loosely organized lay religious group not directly connected with an institutional religion, rather than as a negative term for religious groups outside the scope of what is deemed normal.

All Japanese words are presented in Romaji, which is the romanized form used when writing Japanese in English. In general, I use standard romanization spellings but in a few cases I have made adjustments so that the pronunciation is clear. All romanizations and use of Japanese has been carefully checked by a native speaker of Japanese. For readers interested in the kanji characters, these are included in the glossary at the end of the book. I have also made use of the honorific -*san*, but the reader will notice that I do not always make use of this. In regular conversation, Japanese people normally use this honorific at the end of either family or given names. They use given names when they are relatively close to a person, but continue to use -*san*. However, family members don't usually use this when speaking to each other. Therefore, in cases when a name is spoken in dialogue without *-san* attached, it should be read as an indicator of a close relationship between the characters. Use of one's family name plus *-san* is an indication of a more distant or formal relationship. If the usage changes from family name to given name, that is a signal that the relationship is changing to becoming closer. The reader will find Japanese words throughout the dialogue and in these cases I have endeavored to always translate the term unless it has already appeared in the text. Finally, when pronouncing Japanese names when reading, keep in mind that the Japanese language works with a syllabary that consists of vowel/consonant pairs. Thus, the name "Abe" is pronounced ah-bay. Watanabe is pronounced wah-tah-nah-bay, Satō is sah-toh, and so on. A macron over a vowel, such as ō or ū, indicates a somewhat elongated vowel sound.

There are several people I wish to thank for their conversations related to the book and comments on various drafts. My graduate seminar on ritual at the University of Texas at Austin read a draft of the book, and thanks go to Julia Burgin, Frankie Summers, Nishant Upadhyay, and Jackson Walker both for their thoughts on the book and for a great seminar. My family have all either read portions of the book or discussed ideas with me. Many thanks to my father Willis, daughter Sarah, son Julian, and wife Tomoko. They have given me much to think about as I've worked through the writing. Thanks also go to Tomoko Hetherington for her outstanding editorial skills, and Kelly Smith, Rich Scaglion, and Keith Brown who read and commented on various drafts of the book.

This book is dedicated to the people who live in and around the village I am calling Tanohata in thanks for the kindness and generosity they have always shown to me and my family.

PART I

ENDING A CAREER

1
THE RETIREMENT PARTY

The room was loud. Jack sat in a corner trying to dissolve into nothingness. This goal was hindered significantly by the fact that the surrounding party was being held for his own retirement, the thought of which brought feelings of joy and relief, while talking about it with colleagues seemed at best tedious. Scattered throughout the reception space were his fellow professors. As Jack looked around, he observed the neatly dressed crowd eating hors d'oeuvres and blathering on endlessly about their research, views on politics, or the creative ways that students annoyed them. Thirty years in the academic world had left him tired of hearing the same, self-gratifying conversations that characterized every faculty gathering. He had long ago stopped going to departmental events, but he couldn't really pass on this one.

Just a few more days, he thought, and I'm off to the viridian rice fields of northern Japan. The good news was that Jack's retirement party represented the last public event he would have to endure as a professor. It was time to move on and start a new life on the other side of the world, remote from campus life. An anthropologist who had spent most of his career conducting ethnographic research in a small town north of Tokyo, Jack W. Riddley had fallen in love not only with one of the area's natives, but also with the village where he and his wife, Saori, had built a house in which to enjoy their later years. He trusted the down-to-earth natures of the people in the village of Tanohata and, as a result of spending many years doing fieldwork, the town surrounding the village was home to most of his closest friends.

Jack spied Ima Crabbe heading in his direction with a bright smile on her face. Ima was Chair of Religious Studies. She was pleasant and polite but had no patience for pointless debate or political posturing in faculty meetings. Her meetings ran efficiently and were completed in an hour, despite the extent to which colleagues strove to drift off topic. Jack attributed her skill as an administrator to the fact that she had spent several years in industry as a software engineer and then manager. She knew how to deal with people. As Jack rose from his chair to talk with Ima, he heard another colleague's voice from behind.

"Congratulations, Jack!" Black-haired political scientist Anais Martel approached, clothed in her typical dark green Brooks Brothers wool suit with an open, striped blouse in earthy hues. She reached out to Jack's hand and shook it briefly. Clammy, Jack thought. "I was a bit surprised when I got the invitation to your party. I thought you were too young to retire."

"I'm 64."

"That's too young."

"I have other things I'd like to do, and I have plenty saved in my 403b along with other sources of funds. So, I really have no reason to continue teaching from a financial perspective."

"I see. Well, we'll miss you! I'm sure you'll do great in whatever comes next." Martel always spoke to fellow faculty with an upbeat, but mildly patronizing tone that came through without any noise. There was little mystery in the fact that the professor was highly impressed with herself.

"Thanks, Anais," replied Jack, who then followed with a sardonic, "I appreciate the vote of confidence." The esteemed scholar floated off to chat up other faculty and administrators who mattered as she continued her endless quest to build an academic empire, one that Jack referred to as Martelia, at the university. Anais was always leading some new initiative, getting herself appointed to a directorship, or opining about the state of American politics as a CNN analysist, which made it easy to buy the expensive Porsche she drove.

As he surveyed the room, Jack wondered if he had made a poor choice in joining the Religious Studies department when he came to Yale. Trained as an anthropologist, he had always preferred the company of his own kind, as it were, and he never really liked most of his colleagues in religious studies. He often thought this discomfort was related to disciplinary differences. Anthropologists, by virtue of often spending years living in and studying cultures different from their own, have something of a basic resistance to broad generalizations and smug assertions of knowledge. Fieldwork is a humbling experience. It has a way of shaking up one's assumptions about the world, and the longer one engages in fieldwork, the clearer it becomes that no reality exists which humans can fully understand. Instead, there are many worlds humans create through their interactions with the social and physical environments in which they live. Scholars in the humanities, he thought, seem to be less uncomfortable with the idea that there is a truth that can be found, rather than numerous truths that all have a logic of their own if one simply understands the underlying assumptions that generate behaviors associated with that logic. That confidence allows for a certain smugness about their research, which is intensified by the fact that most of their work involves interacting with books that lack the ability to correct the errors and misunderstandings of scholars who interpret them—unlike anthropologists whose research involves the lived experience of another culture and society and constant interaction with people who have their own ideas about the reality they and others in their world construct. Anthropology is inherently uncertain, and a good anthropologist always carries a nagging feeling that every ethnographic work he or she writes is in some ways a piece of fiction.

Bored with the party, Jack slipped out the side door of the function room, terminating his stride at the entrance to the gender-neutral restroom down the hall. Unfortunately, Jack didn't have anything to do on the other side of the door, so he asked himself aloud, "Why did I leave like that? Oh right, I hate parties." At that, he turned and continued to the end of the hallway, darted out a side door of the building, and began wandering through the grassy quadrangles and stone walks of Old Campus, enjoying the cool, damp night air. "The party," Jack said with a satisfied smile on his face, "will go on just fine without me." As he strolled through the cast iron gates and ancient elm trees, Jack contemplated his years as a professor and anthropologist, and a few of the young minds he had challenged. The most memorable had always been Alex, a young man who grew up in the depths of rural West Texas and had no idea how brilliant he was until Jack and another professor simultaneously realized they had a genius in their respective classes. With their guidance, Alex emerged from the shy kid who drove a pedicab to make money for college to a star graduate student at Stanford and then a widely known anthropologist with a fine career. Of all the books, articles, conference presentations, and various accolades that had dotted Jack's career, it was being able to work with Alex that stood out as his most enjoyable and significant contribution to the field.

Standing in front of Battell Chapel, a chorale drifted into his head as he recalled a concert of Bach's organ music he had enjoyed there with his father many years earlier. As he listened, Jack realized this might be his last time walking across the campus where he had spent most of his career. As if on cue, the carillon of Harkness Tower began broadcasting Bach's 4th Invention over the gothic quadrangles as students scampered from place to place with intense looks on their faces. Continuing his stroll, he eventually pulled open the heavy wooden doors of the main library and took the elevator up to the book stacks, which was odd since he rarely had entered the library over the course of his career. Anthropologists don't necessarily spend a lot of time in libraries; they prefer to be out talking to people at their field sites—and electronic journal articles combined with Amazon had made trips to the library unnecessary. Why walk across campus when an article or book is only a few clicks away? Given his rather introverted personality, others often assumed Jack relished in the reclusive haunts of the stacks, but more than anything the books made him sneeze. How ironic it was that he became a cultural anthropologist, because the job necessarily entails interacting with strangers and a fair amount of small talk, something he had never liked when he was in the U.S. But for some reason, it always came easily in Japan. *Maybe I just don't like Americans much,* he thought, but that probably wasn't the reason, since he had known other anthropologists with similar anti-social tendencies at home that contrasted completely with their behavior in the field.

Back on the ground floor, Jack emerged from the elevator and wandered through the vast gothic nave that served as the main entrance to Sterling Library. He drifted in the direction of his most cherished campus locus. It was a narrow hall overlooking a small courtyard and had a series of corbels sculpted by René Paul Chambellan, depicting scholarship and life at the university. Jack stopped in front of a favorite corbel showing a young man reading a book on the pages of which was written U.R.A. JOKE. "Perhaps that's true," he said to himself. So much of academic life seemed to be a cruel joke as colleagues fought over insignificant "points," demanded to get their ways, and clamored for power in contexts where the stakes were remarkably low. He stared at the sculpture and contemplated the meaninglessness shrouding so much of what academics do with their time. Who really cares about some medieval text by an obscure monk who lived in the mountains of Italy?

"Jack! What the fuck are you doing here?"

"Hey, Sam."

"Aren't you supposed to be at your retirement party? I was just heading over there."

"Oh, right, well I was there, but it was boring, so I left."

"You're incorrigible. You ditched your own retirement party?"

"Yeah. But I don't think anyone will notice, they're all busy telling each other how great they are."

"Mmm… You're in a foul mood tonight. Depressed about retirement?"

"Hah! You know I'm overjoyed about retirement. No, I'm just wondering about the value of what we do for a living. How many people actually read an ethnography? Have I really produced anything of lasting value in the three decades I've been collecting data and writing about Japan? Then there are the endless attacks on higher education and so little interest among the general public in knowledge that isn't aimed at getting a job. Oh, and the morons in university administration who get a choice between the blue pill, which makes you stupid, and the red pill, which makes you amazingly stupid, before they take their jobs."

"You're repeating yourself—I've heard you whine about all of these things before, and the blue pill, red pill trope is getting old. We keep the flame of critical thinking and intellectual exploration alive for future generations who might someday realize that there is more to life than a paycheck."

"Right you are, my friend. On all counts…"

His smart phone started to vibrate. It was Saori calling from Japan. Jack answered, "Hey," with his usual curt response to a phone call.

"*Konbanwa.* How's the party?"

"It was nice. Pretty much the usual. I got tired and ducked out for a walk and now I'm talking with Sam at the library."

"Right, somehow I knew you wouldn't last long."

"How are things over there? How's work?" After several years employed in government in the U.S., Saori had taken a job back in Japan as a statistical analyst partly to be closer to her mother, but also because she had tired of life in the U.S., with its incessant conflict and political debate and endless fear over mass shootings. She wanted to return to the safety and comfort of her home. Jack looked forward to joining her in a few days and settling in to the new house they had built in Tanohata.

"Work's good. I've been busy, but now have a few days off, so I'm on the bullet train heading to Tanohata. I'm going to unpack some of the book boxes you sent over and get things in order so that we can start living there comfortably. At the moment, it's a mess."

"Thanks. I'm looking forward to getting to our new home, enjoying some peace and quiet, and having time that I can devote to writing and music."

"You'll have to set up the music studio yourself, but the rest of the house should be in order within a few days. When do you get here again?"

"Next Monday. Will you be back in Tokyo?"

"Nope. I'll be in Tanohata all next week."

"Okay, I'll just head straight up there in that case."

"I should let you go, since Sam is waiting. We can talk over the weekend. Say hi to Sam for me. Tell him I miss him! Can't wait to see you!"

"Will do!" They disconnected and Jack looked at Sam.

"Wanna get a drink and a smoke?" said Sam.

"Deal. Let's head over to The Owl Shop."

They took a right after exiting the library doors and headed down High Street crossing Old Campus as a shortcut to their destination. Dating back to 1934, The Owl Shop was a smoking bar that carried pipe tobaccos, including its own blends like Harkness Tower, as well as fine cigars. Decorated with dark wood, ornate tin ceiling tiles, and amply padded leather chairs, it was a haven for those longing for a bit of the elegant and elitist past of Ivy League life. In recent years, it had also become the best venue for live jazz in town, which bolstered its privileged, smoke-filled ambience. Business was booming.

Jack and Sam settled into a pair of comfortable chairs. Sam purchased a Macanudo and Jack pulled out a Dunhill pipe, into which he began to stuff some tobacco. They lit up and sat quietly with their smokes and drinks; bourbon for Sam, scotch for Jack.

"I still don't see how you can drink that dirt water," teased Sam after a few silent moments.

"It's better than that moonshine you drink." They laughed, having had this exchange hundreds of times over the years, and Jack thought to himself that this was the one truly difficult aspect to moving away. He was going to miss Sam, his best friend and intellectual companion for over twenty-five years. Sam was the exception that tested Jack's rule, that colleagues and friendships should always be separate. Colleagues should be colleagues, not friends. That ensured relationships remained professional and held the people he spent his days with at something of a distance, which was Jack's preference. They had both come to the university as associate professors in 1999 and neither had ever had much interest in moving on. Over the years, they raised families together, their wives became good friends as they pursued their careers, and the families purchased houses in Hamden not more than a mile apart.

Samuel Jones, a philosopher of science and ethicist, routinely challenged the logic and structure of Jack's thoughts related to human behavior and Jack responded in kind to Sam, accusing him of ethnocentrism every time he made some grand, universalist statement about moral principles or metaphysics. Sam would then remind him that the commonality of multiple truths Jack so cherished should never be taken as indication that anything goes, as there are multiple stupid positions as well. They had forged a close friendship not only on the basis of their intellectual interests, but also because they had similar personalities. Both tended to swear quite a bit, although Sam had the upper hand on that one to the point that once, when being interviewed on NPR, he put a sign on the desk reminding himself not to curse in front of a national radio audience. Both were inveterate punsters. And both enjoyed a good smoke. Another trait they shared was that neither, despite having made careers in academia, had any patience for the pompous proclivities of intellectuals.

In the repose of the grey-blue haze that emerged from their respective smokes, the two men remained silent. Both knew what the other was thinking with little need for conversation. It wasn't as though they would never see each other again. Sam would be heading to Japan in a few months for a conference, so they'd be able to get together in the near future, at least. There was, of course, always Facetime or Zoom. Moving halfway around the world didn't mean what it had just a few decades earlier when places like northern Japan were isolated and represented expensive destinations for a phone call. That's the way it had been when Jack did his dissertation research—he was far from the mainstream of American life, with limited means to communicate with family and friends back in the U.S. He basically disappeared from his normal world for two years. Email existed, of course, but it was cumbersome due to the slow dial-up service. And "the Internet" really hadn't become a reality when Jack left for the field. When he got back to the University of Pittsburgh to write up his dissertation, there was this new thing called "the web" that had erupted in the U.S. that he had completely missed while in northern Japan. Now, only a few decades later, even the most remote parts of Japan were just as connected as anywhere in the States, and perhaps even more so than most, due to the ubiquity of smartphones and Wi-Fi access.

As both men smoked in silence, Jack's thoughts drifted back to the retirement party. "Sam, why do we celebrate retirement? What's the point? We don't celebrate when someone takes another job and leaves the university. Why should this particular transition matter?"

"You're the anthropologist. You tell me, Jack."

"I know. I'm asking stupid rhetorical questions. But I do find myself somewhat fascinated about the meaning, or meanings, of the party I just left. By the way, hanging out with you and smoking is a lot more fun..."

"Um, thanks? I also prefer this venue and your company to academic parties. And I feel a Jack Riddley lecture coming on..."

"Yeah, probably. But it's damn interesting from an analytical perspective. Everyone at that party knows that I basically don't like any of them. I respect some of them as scholars, but I largely dislike them all as people. And the feeling is mutual. I've always been the sort who says exactly what I think, which means others often don't care much for my presence, particularly administrators who hate hearing anything that contradicts what they already think and know to be true—even when they're wrong."

"In other words, you're an asshole..." Sam took a long draw on his cigar.

"Right. But we have that in common." They both raised their glasses with a nod. "So why would they hold a celebratory gathering to mark my retirement?"

"They're celebrating the fact that they finally got rid of you."

"Yes, that's one possibility."

"I was joking, Jack. Don't you think it has to do with a general concern or fear about transition and death? Most of the people in that room are facing retirement in a few years. I think you tend to view retirement as an opportunity to do more research or at least to keep learning—I mean, shit, you're moving to your field site. And you've also always had a lot of other things going on in your life, like playing jazz drums. You never really settled in on the academic persona. In fact, you've always resisted it a bit. But for most academics, and probably people in other professions, much of their identity is wrapped up in their position within their workplace and larger professional circles. Retirement is not so much a transition, but a precursor to death. First, one's identity dies and then one's body dies a few years later."

"That's darkly philosophical and cynical, Sam, but I think you may be onto something. It's interesting that in Japan they actually mark retirement as a transition to old age and a rebirth into a second life. There's a ceremony called *kanreki* that people do when they turn sixty. They're given a red hat and red sweater. It symbolizes a rebirth into a second childhood."

"Why red?"

"Oh, yeah, it has to do with the word for infant, *aka-chan*." Sam pulled out a note card and wrote a kanji character on it—赤. "It's the character for the color red, but is also the character used in the word *aka-chan*. You know, babies are kind of red when they are born. So, the red hat and sweater are symbols of rebirth, and old age is viewed as a time when, like in childhood, a person can legitimately be, in some ways, dependent on family members for care, finances, housing, and so on. Of course, in the modern world it rarely actually works that way. Most older Japanese nowadays live alone or as elder couples. But there's still a sense that retirement opens a door in which men, in particular, who have toiled at office jobs for their entire adult lives, can pursue things that interest them without inhibition."

"Okay, but you've also told me that men in Japan often struggle with retirement. They have some sort of identity crisis."

"True. Sometimes newly retired businessmen are called wet leaves because they stick to their wives and are difficult to peel off. They don't know how to cook, do laundry, clean. Their wives did all of that for them while also developing lives of their own with friends as they found interests to pursue once the kids moved out. Men sometimes end up with an identity crisis when they feel like they're just appendages to their wives and can't find meaning in life outside of the workplace. It's one of the reasons suicide rates spike for men around that age."

"In other words, the symbols don't do much work."

"Maybe. But I think more important is that the symbols are not uniformly interpreted by people who are in the middle of the transition or who are approaching it. One person might see retirement and its symbolic elements as a door to a new life; another might see it as you describe—a precursor to death—or a transition into a future of meaninglessness. The same symbol can be interpreted in many ways."

The two men became quiet and returned their attentions to their smokes. It was ten o'clock and they had passed the evening in contented friendship for close to two hours. Jack stretched, tapped out his pipe in the ashtray, and told Sam he needed to get back to the hotel. Still some things to do before the flight to Japan on Sunday. Sam had just finished his second cigar. He stood up, left a few dollars on the table, and they strolled out of the shop.

"Dinner tomorrow, right?"

"Sounds good," replied Jack, "is Emily coming?"

"Indeed, she is."

"Great! We can text tomorrow to figure out details."

"Think about somewhere you want to go for your last supper..."

"Thanks..."

The friends parted as the mist morphed into light rain. Jack hurried in the direction of his rental car, having forgotten to bring an umbrella, as usual. Fortunately, it wasn't far. As he drove to the hotel where he was spending his last few nights in New Haven, he thought about how enjoyable the serene and pastoral qualities of rural Japan would be, but there was no question he would miss Sam deeply.

2
NARITA

Dinner with Sam and Emily was bittersweet. The trio enjoyed a typically pleasant evening of interesting conversation and light-hearted banter, despite missing Saori, although they did manage to facetime her at one point in the evening. Emily gave Jack quite a bit of ribbing about cutting out on his own retirement party, but much of their time was spent planning for visits in the future and imagining the possibility that Emily and Sam might someday themselves retire to the quiet life of northern Japan. Of course, they all knew that would never happen. Ever adventurous, Sam might consider it. But Emily was an East Coast city person at heart and would not be able to live far from a major metropolitan area like New York or Boston.

They laughed and drank. And the evening ended all too soon.

As Jack looked out the window of the taxiing airplane he would inhabit for the next fourteen hours and thought about his friends, he held back a few tears. Life's transitions always involve a combination of gain and loss, joy and sorrow, precariously balanced on the pendular embrace that formed a life.

Many trips across the Atlantic and Pacific oceans and one circumnavigation of the planet had taught Jack how to prepare for the misery of air travel. He had his Bose noise cancelling headphones to block out the sounds of his fellow passengers, melatonin to help him sleep, and a carefully curated icy stare to dissuade conversation. Over the years, he had become adept at creating a cocoon inside the tiny airline seat that signaled to his neighbors to leave him alone. Never being able to work on planes, he usually passed the time watching movies or reading a book until becoming too tired to stay awake.

This particular flight to Japan turned out not to be abnormally unpleasant. The seats were too small, there was no legroom, and the person next to him snored, but at least the service was good since it was a Japanese rather than American carrier. Still, Jack wondered to himself if airline executives, particularly in the U.S., were basically sadists who sat around boardroom tables conjuring up new ways to torture innocent travelers. Double, double toil and trouble/Fire burn and caldron bubble/Passengers cause all our troubles...

After two movies, Jack passed out and enjoyed an unusually deep sleep for an airplane trip. The past few weeks preparing to move had clearly tired him out. Jack awoke to the pungent aroma of plastic omelets being microwaved and knew there was a little over an hour until they landed at Narita Airport outside of Tokyo. Like many other parts of Japan, Narita had changed a great deal since Jack first started visiting in the 1980s. The large signs posted by famers protesting construction of the airport on their land were long gone. And, in almost an affront to the protesters, the airport had expanded considerably, with the pandemic-delayed 2020 Tokyo Olympics stimulating construction of a new terminal and an ever increasingly international atmosphere.

"Flight attendants, prepare for landing."

Once on the ground, Jack followed the parade of travelers through customs, had his photo and fingerprints taken, and headed to baggage claim, after which he cleared the final rite of passage to enter the country without incident and headed to the Narita Express, which would take him to Tokyo Station. As soon as he entered the jetway, he knew he was in Japan. He could smell it. Different countries have different aromas, which was something Jack had learned from travelling around the world. Japan was no different. It had its own distinct odor and Jack noticed it immediately, which was probably more than anything, a product of his training as an ethnographer that made him a careful observer of the sights, sounds, and smells of everything happening around him. Indeed, ethnographic methods of observation were never far from Jack's mind and constantly shaped his behavior. He always noticed, and noted, when someone changed glasses or put on different colored nail polish. He picked up on new ties, changes in speech patterns, and whether others looked tired or energetic. And his brain never stopped analyzing what he saw. There was a reason for every behavior, Jack often thought; the key is to carefully observe and try to understand the logic behind that behavior. Years of ethnographic research had also trained Jack to have a keen awareness of detail. His sartorial style always included a shirt with a breast pocket, in which he kept notecards and a pencil. Regardless of where he was, at some point the pencil and notecards would be pulled out and a few quick jottings recorded. This practice had started in graduate school when conducting his dissertation fieldwork in northern Japan. He had picked up the habit from his graduate advisor. Jack would use the notecards to write jottings that he would use later to generate detailed fieldnotes about everything he observed throughout the day. Sometimes this amounted to only a page of text, but if there had been an interesting event or conversation, he might write long, detailed accounts of what he saw, tasted, heard, and smelled. When he returned to the University of Pittsburgh after two years of dissertation fieldwork, he had accumulated over 3,500 pages of typed fieldnotes.

Jack was among the most well-known ethnographers of Japan in his generation of anthropologists and had been invited to many parts of the world to give talks about his research or to spend time teaching and collaborating with other professors as a visiting scholar. A large part of his international reputation was based on the care and detail he put into his written work, which by the time of retirement numbered six books and over a hundred journal articles. That care and detail were entirely grounded in Jack's tendency toward obsessive observation of his surroundings and an exceptionally precise and powerful memory that recorded what he observed in considerable detail. Both traits also made Jack somewhat impatient with others, who he felt often failed to see minute aspects of behavior, were usually oblivious to motivations, or misremembered the content of conversations and events that seemed so obvious to him. At times, the impatience ventured into arrogance when Jack was particularly certain of his perspectives. However, along with powerful observational skills, Jack also had a knack for tunnel vision. He focused both his memory and observational abilities on those things that interested him and tended to completely ignore those things that didn't. Departmental administration was one of the things that did not interest Jack and he had largely excused himself from administrative duties as soon as he became tenured—his behavior stemming from a complete lack of interest in anything that smacked of tedium.

Stopping at a ticket machine he purchased passage all the way to the station where he would disembark in Iwate Prefecture and headed directly for the platform, since the train would depart in only twenty minutes. Lining up at the color-coded spot on the platform, he waited a few minutes and then the large red, white, and black train pulled in. When the doors opened, Jack and the other passengers neatly filed into the compartment and found their seats. Jack threw his bag on the overhead rack and sat down next to the window.

The trip took an hour from Narita to Tokyo Station, followed by an hour of hanging around at Tokyo Station, and then two and a half more hours to get to Kanezawa Station, where Saori would be waiting to take him to their new house a few kilometers away. Jack was tired, having spent a seeming eternity on the plane from JFK, but also energized to be back in Japan. As he watched his progress to Tokyo Station displayed on the screen in front of him, his gaze shifted to the mantis green rice fields surrounding the rail line, interspersed with occasional concentrations of buildings forming a concrete forest that became increasingly dense as they approached the city. Eventually, the train moved underground and Jack heard the announcement— in Japanese, English, Chinese, and Korean—that they were about to arrive at the terminus.

To describe Tokyo Station as a maze would be to dramatically understate the challenge of finding one's way through the complex of corridors and platforms. Jack had lost more than one student in the station when leading study groups to northern Japan, but fortunately they had always found their way to the bullet train track that headed to his field site before the train departed. At least he had never been forced to make an awkward intercontinental call to some parent explaining that he couldn't find their kid but was sure that they were somewhere in Japan.

With a few minutes to kill, Jack walked up to one of the station's numerous confectionary shops and purchased some sweets, which he would give to his in-laws; it was customary in Japan to always bring some sort of gift when returning from abroad or just traveling within the country, and the cakes would add a little extra to the gifts he had brought for family and friends from the States. Those gifts were a bit lame at this point because after decades of going back and forth, there just weren't many interesting American goods and anything available there was also available in Tokyo or even in the area around Tanohata. There were no surprises and few unusual gifts anymore due to globalization, at least when moving back and forth between similar post-industrial countries like Japan and the U.S.

Jack looked around at the kaleidoscope of signs pointing tourists and commuters to different tracks and was reminded of the first time he came to Tokyo and couldn't read anything because there was no romanization and he had yet to study Japanese. The experience proved to be a minor foray into participant observation that provided a clue about what it means to be non-literate in a highly literate society. It was impossible to find his way anywhere. Nowadays, signs throughout Japan were romanized so it didn't actually matter that he had learned to read Japanese characters. In any case, Jack knew exactly where he was going. Track twenty-three. Follow the green bullet train signs to the Tōhoku Shinkansen and you end up at the tracks that lead to the northernmost six prefectures of Japan's main island of Honshu.

Collectively, the area known as Tōhoku, or the Northeastern Region, includes Akita, Aomori, Fukushima, Yamagata, Miyagi, and Iwate prefectures. In the distant past, the region was known as Azuma and formed the frontier in which native people called the Ezo lived. They were ultimately pushed north by the invading Japanese who descended from the flow of mainland East Asians that had started entering the islands around 300 BC and gradually took control of the entire archipelago, displacing, killing, or interbreeding with the Ezo and other native peoples who had lived in relative peace for several thousand years prior. Tōhoku's historical settlement began between the seventh and ninth centuries, and after numerous battles the region became a northern stronghold of Japanese culture and society while retaining a fair amount of independence from the power center in distant Kyoto for centuries. That independence continued to be reflected in the attitudes and behaviors of locals even into the 21st century. Many spoke with dialects that distinguished them as peripheral to the economic, intellectual, and political center that is Tokyo, as well as other metropolitan areas like Osaka. Somewhat disparagingly, the region continued at times to be referred to as the Tibet of Japan, a moniker that conveyed a sense of traditional backwardness of both people and place.

Despite images of agricultural work and obsolete ways of living many in Japan used to stereotype the region, to speed on the bullet train north from Tokyo into Tōhoku no longer presented a transition from urban/industrial to rural/agricultural society, but formed a passage through a mosaic of cities, rice fields, and forested mountains linked by limited access highways, rail lines, and communications networks. As he sped north, amidst the ubiquitous checkerboard rice fields Jack could see the occasional red and yellow McDonald's sign, 7-Eleven convenience store, high-rise hotel, and shopping mall with large parking lots necessary to accommodate the automobile-centered lifestyle of the Japanese countryside. At one moment, he saw farmhouses that looked as though they floated on their surrounding water-filled paddies. A few kilometers later, the landscape would morph into a maze of prefabricated houses planted like multi-story onions in tightly packed rows. And then the scene would shift back into verdant rice fields. The landscape blurred in a beautiful and strange dance of manufactured agricultural and urban spaces enveloped in shades of grey and green.

Gazing out the window, he remembered the comment made by a prominent scholar of Japan when Jack was a mere postdoctoral fellow helping at a seminar the senior professor had organized in Tokyo. "Jack," condescended the pompous political scientist as Jack was about to depart for the north country, "just remember that the *real* Japan is here in Tokyo. Nothing is going on in that backwards place you study. If you are going to study Japanese culture, you should focus your research on the city. It's an urban society." At the time, Jack wondered silently how all those people living in the countryside would feel about not being part of the real Japanese culture. Thirty years later, having gained the confidence of age and a career, he would have let the blowhard have it.

Feeling financially flush, Jack chose to ride first-class on the *shinkansen*, which meant he would get exceptionally polite service and a meal. Impeccably dressed in her pastel pink uniform, the attendant stopped at his seat, offered him a multi-lingual menu, and asked what he would like to drink. She didn't try to use English, as some service people did in Japan, and smiled brightly when Jack responded in fluent Japanese. He asked for a beer and chose the bento box on the menu for his late lunch. Before his food arrived, he was fast asleep.

A few hundred kilometers to the north, Saori was putting finishing touches on their new home. The Ginori dishes they shipped back from the States, her favorite, were stored in their cupboards, some of Jack's endless boxes of books had been unpacked, and enough of their new furniture had arrived so they could be comfortable. Saori scanned the living room and thought to herself that the home was beautiful. They had chosen to build in a modernized version of traditional Japanese housing architecture. Simplicity ruled. There were large, wooden beams, hardwood floors, and sliding doors that gave the main living space a traditional Japanese feel with a Western twist. The couple had splurged on a live edge wooden breakfast counter that separated the kitchen from the living room and the stone fireplace looked like something out of a New England cottage with a Jøtul woodstove jutting out of it. A hallway at the front of the house had sliding glass doors that overlooked a carefully tended Japanese garden. Two of the rooms off the hallway were of the sparsely furnished tatami-mat décor to be used for sleeping or sipping tea while enjoying the garden. One of them had a *kotatsu*, the low table with a blanket and heater attached to the bottom that would be a locus of warmth in the cold winters or even in cool, damp early summers. Too warm for that soon, so I should put it away for the summer, thought Saori. The third room was Jack's study, lined with bookshelves and sporting a bird's eye maple built-in wooden desk situated beneath a large window that overlooked the expanse of rice fields surrounding the village. The plot of land where they chose to build was at the outer edge of the village, giving them a sweeping view of nearby rice fields and mountains in the distance, framed by several cedar trees that ringed the edge of their property. Saori was especially proud of the eco-friendly approach they had taken with the design. The house sported solar panels, geothermal heating, and a solar hot water heater. Although the living space was small compared to their house in Hamden, they had spared little expense in construction materials to make the home comfortable and aesthetically pleasing, also in the hopes that their kids, Irene and George, would enjoy visiting and ultimately make use of the house in the future when they were both gone. Property values were so low that the house didn't represent an investment—it would prove difficult to sell unless the economy of the area unexpectedly changed for the better.

The couple had chosen to build on a lot occupied by an abandoned, collapsing house at the southern edge of the village where Jack had done his dissertation fieldwork thirty years earlier. Too broken to restore, they removed the old house, but kept the *kura* or traditional storage building, which they refurbished as the music studio. Although it had the feeling of a countryside retreat, their new home was convenient to the neighboring city of Kanezawa with its strip malls, a Baskin Robbins ice cream store, hotels, and eating establishments ranging from an Italian family restaurant to ramen shops. Many of the houses in the village were spacious buildings with lush gardens occupied by descendants of the samurai Lord and vassals who centuries earlier had guarded the border between the Nambu and Date feudal domains. Nestled on a hill that overlooked sprawling rice paddies, most of which were owned and farmed by older residents from what was left of the former samurai households, one rarely heard more than a gentle wind whispering through the tall cedars that engulfed the houses, punctuated by the occasional caw of a crow. A few years earlier, Jack had done a brief survey of the village and found about forty percent of the houses empty, following a pattern of depopulation that was common throughout the Japanese countryside. Some of the empty structures were collapsing with the weight of time, combined with neglect and the relentless advance of nature, while others conveyed an eerie tended emptiness—the gardens carefully trimmed in front of windows whose drapes remained perpetually immobile. Decades of low fertility and out-migration of young adults had created a situation in which the population was experiencing a precipitous decline. It was one of the reasons property values were so low. The village that, when Jack completed his dissertation research was home to 450 people, was now home to only about 220.

Saori looked at her smart phone to check the time. Jack would arrive in about thirty minutes, so she needed to depart for the station. Early evenings in June were often damp and chilly. She put on a grey sweater and headed for the dark-blue Tesla 3 she had purchased from a dealer in Tokyo, hoping that it would rarely need service, given the distance to bring it back. She navigated smoothly until reaching the shopping district of Kanezawa where large trucks slowed her progress, but the traffic cleared quickly and a few minutes later she arrived at the station shortly before Jack's train. Saori was looking forward to seeing him. It had been six months since they were last together and, finally, they could enjoy creating a new phase of life in the tranquil and friendly climes of Tōhoku.

Saori exited the car and hurried into the waiting area in the station where Jack would soon arrive. At five feet in height and with a diminutive physical structure, she was slightly under the average for a woman of her generation and, unlike many, her hair shined jet-black with a few streaks of grey—Saori had always refrained from converting her hair to the orangish color so many in Japan chose to adopt. "Attention. The Yamabiko 485, bound for Morioka, will soon be arriving on Track Two. Please be careful," announced the calm, nasal, stylized male voice reproduced over station sound systems throughout Japan. She could see on the overhead monitors that the few passengers disembarking at Kanezawa Station were headed her way, and then caught a glimpse of Jack pulling his wheeled suitcase in the direction of the escalator.

Jack placed his rail ticket in the slot on the exit gate, which inhaled it silently, and he strode in Saori's direction. They smiled and then hugged. Saori welcomed him with the traditional greeting used upon returning to one's home, *"Okaerinasai,"* and the couple headed for Saori's Tesla waiting patiently nearby in the small parking lot.

"It's good to be back in Kanezawa," said Jack.

"When we get to the house," responded Saori, "you can take a hot bath while I make *katsudon* for dinner." The dish, consisting of pork cutlet, egg, and onions on white rice, was one of Jack's favorites. They loaded his luggage into the back of the car and exited the parking lot. Just before they arrived at the intersection, Jack said, "Can you stop at Lawson?" Saori laughed and simply replied, "Right." She knew exactly what Jack had in mind. Both Jack and their daughter, Irene, were obsessed with Japanese convenience stores, which usually represented one of the first places they visited whenever they got to Japan. "Let me guess," as she smiled, "you want a chocolate parfait."

"You know me too well."

With the parfait and a few other items happily acquired, they sped through open green rice fields and after a few kilometers turned into the narrow streets of their village. Winding around a sharp bend up a hill, Jack saw the vast, empty house of Torisawa Takanobu, with its tile roof constructed in traditional Japanese style. The house was roughly 250 years old, but remained in good condition, despite being vacant. Jack had spent many hours inside drinking tea with Torisawa amidst his somewhat creepy collection of antique samurai armor, swords, and other objects, some of which had been used by his own ancestors. Another sharp turn took them past the large, wooden gate in front of the Yamaguchi house, which the town government had renovated and repurposed as a gift shop and restaurant serving local cuisine after the village was designated a national heritage site due to its samurai past and historical buildings.

Saori carefully avoided an electrical pole on the side of the road and turned right onto their nameless street, at the end of which was their new house. Jack had not yet seen the completed building and was pleased with the exterior aesthetic, which blended nicely into the traditional architecture of the village. They stopped in the car port, grabbed his luggage, and hurried inside as the cool air started to become misty.

"The place looks great!" said Jack, "you've done a lot of work."

"Yes, I have."

"Don't be so humble…"

"Your bath water is already poured, but you may need to heat it a bit."

"Sounds good. It'll feel great to get the travel grime off my body." Jack dropped his bag in the bedroom, threw off his clothes, and after washing, settled into the hot bathwater for a long soak. A few minutes later, Saori called out that dinner was ready and he reluctantly pulled himself out of the bath, dried off, and put on some warm clothes. The sweet aroma of cooked soy sauce and egg wafted in his direction as he padded into their dining area.

"Yum," said Jack upon entrance to the kitchen with a large smile on his face. As they ate, Saori caught Jack up on village news, which didn't take long, and they talked about friends he wanted to see.

"How is Taitsu-san?" asked Jack, "I think I'll drop by the temple tomorrow morning."

"I think he's doing fine. I haven't actually seen him yet on this trip. You know…, he's always busy with funerals." The comment reminded Jack of how different the lives of Zen Buddhist priests in Japan were from the stereotyped images of endless meditation and arranging stones with a rake that most Americans assumed was the norm. In fact, like many of his peers, Taitsu rarely meditated. His job, as he put it, was taking care of the ritual needs of his parish, which for the most part meant leading funerals and other death-related rites.

Jack and Saori spent another couple of hours talking, drinking wine, and listening to some music. Travel fatigue finally caught up with Jack and they retired to their bedroom, where they unfolded the futon and cuddled under the thick, warm covers as they drifted off into a long sleep. Saori awoke at five, as usual, but Jack slept until about nine the next day, when Saori came in to wake him. "Jack, you should get up. You won't be able to sleep at night and it will take forever to get over the jetlag if you stay in bed all morning."

"Mmmph." Jack was blissfully dreaming under the covers, but eventually managed to pull himself up from the futon. He shaved, dressed, and walked out to the kitchen, where Saori was making rice and miso soup—another favorite—for their breakfast. "I'll cook something tonight," he said.

"I thought we might go out. There's a new French restaurant in Kanezawa that I want to try."

"Sounds good." After finishing their breakfast, Jack washed the dishes and opened his laptop to check his email and catch up on world news—a now decades-old morning routine. Saori had arranged a lunch date with some high school friends and headed out the door at around eleven o'clock. Since they didn't yet have two cars, this meant Jack was confined to the village, which suited him well. As Saori backed the car up, Jack started walking in the direction of Taiyō-ji, Taitsu's temple, avoiding a direct path so that he could wander around the locale in which he had conducted research for several decades. The tall cedar trees and fragrant flower gardens recalled images from the past. Thirty years prior, the same walk would have included several conversations with locals out working in their gardens or taking care of a grandchild. He remembered the kind, warm smile of Satō Keiko, whom he met for the first time on a similar walk. Keiko's granddaughter was strapped to her back with an *onbuhimo*—a long, narrow cloth sling traditionally used to carefully tie an infant to a mother's or grandmother's back. As Jack remembered their meeting, he thought of the baby snoozing quietly to the warmth of her grandmother's body and the rhythmic beating of her heart. They chatted about the cool weather, a polite conversation that led to many deep and important discussions as Keiko became one of Jack's key informants—a term anthropologists sometimes use to identify particularly engaged local interlocutors with whom they spend significant time learning about life in the place being studied. Keiko had taught him much about the meaning of growing old in Japan, or at least in the village of Tanohata, as well as sharing many discussions about the relationship between mind and body, a topic that had long fascinated Jack. He could almost see her standing on the road, baby strapped to her back, large straw hat shading her face, and red-stripped apron keeping away the dust and dirt of the day. The image dissolved and Jack drifted westward in a melancholy stroll toward the temple. So many of the people he had known when he first arrived in the village had passed on.

Immersed in thought about the past and his many years of fieldwork in the village, Jack had no idea how he arrived before the large, uneven stone steps to the temple. He gazed up toward the temple gate and remembered an old black-and-white picture of the exact same steps with people dressed in festival costume taken in the 1920's that an informant had given him. He started the climb. At the top was a tall, roofed gate constructed of wood that had greyed with the weather of decades. Just inside the gate to the left, stood five granite statues of Jizō, the Buddhist protector of children and travelers, with their round, serene faces, prayer beads, and bright red beanies and bibs. Directly in front of the statues were flowers and offerings, which typically were presented to memorialize the deaths of young or stillborn children and aborted fetuses. Directly across from the Jizō statues was a rack holding numerous buckets and ladles to be used by visitors to clean their family graves, typically at the autumnal and vernal equinoxes or at the summer festival of the dead known as *obon*.

From the top of the stairs, Jack could see the large temple building, which was relatively new compared to many others in the village. The older structure it replaced had burned in the late 1990s, leading to the construction of a modern building that reflected traditional architectural styles, but included amenities such as an alarm system.

Unfortunately, security had become a necessity because of the increasing burglaries of temples in rural parts of the country. Easily accessible ancient artifacts kept in many local temples had been stolen to be sold to collectors, mostly in China. When Jack first arrived in the village in the early 1990s, the main temple hall was always open and few people kept the doors to their houses locked. He remembered asking one person where the key to her front door was, and she admitted to having no idea. Those were different times.

Jack turned left into the cemetery. The long rows of tall, rectangular family gravestones gave the cemetery the appearance of a strangely symmetrical city skyline of black and grey obelisks. Gravesites were bordered by low curbs, creating plots of various standard sizes, each of which represented a single family whose name was engraved vertically in large kanji characters on the front of the gravestone. Behind the main stone, there was usually another flat, horizontal granite stone plaque facing front on which was engraved the posthumous names of all deceased family members—in Japanese Buddhism, the dead typically receive a new name commemorating their status in life. Directly in front of each vertical stone, there was an altar where one could burn incense, make offerings of food or drink, and place flowers. The altar areas opened, if one knew how to do it, to a pot buried in the ground where the cremains of all the family dead were mixed together for eternity. In contemporary Japan, virtually everyone was cremated after death and their ashes, which consisted both of bone dust and complete bones, were placed carefully into the pot under the family grave to form what were collectively known as *gosenzo-sama*—The Ancestors. The most important part of religious life for many Japanese was making sure that one's ancestors were properly cared for through regular rituals that included incense burning and offerings of rice, water, *sake*, or other foods. Jack was thinking about this when he rounded the corner and found himself in front of the most unusual grave in the cemetery.

Like other Buddhist cemeteries, the one at Taiyō-ji had a single grave that looked different from the others. It had no stone, instead being constructed of a dirt mound, with a low curb surrounding it like the other graves. The plot was somewhat larger than others and placed at the northeast corner of the cemetery, slightly remote from the other graves. Because it was important for all dead to be memorialized, this grave had a special function, which was to provide a place for memorialization of those deceased who had left no-one behind to provide care. After death, if regular rituals for the dead were not performed, the deceased was at risk of becoming a *muenbotoke*, or a wandering, unattached spirit who was lonely and, therefore, might cause troubles for the living. Jack had been told by a few local priests that the problem of wandering spirits was increasing as a result of the population decline in the area and the lack of younger family members left behind to care for graves. In response to this, many temples had created, or resurrected, single grave sites at which priests could provide ritual care all at once for the deceased who lacked nearby family members—or any family members at all. This prevented those deceased from becoming sad and lonely wandering spirits.

"Jack-san!" It was Taitsu. Jack smiled and the two headed for each other quickly, shook hands, bowed and then laughed a bit. "Saori texted that you would be in town soon. Tea?" Slender, tall, and having very large feet that his wife often teased him about, Taitsu towered over most of his neighbors and parishioners. His head was shaved and bespectacled and he stood with a mildly hunched posture. Having come out to clean the area around the temple building, he was carrying a broom and was dressed in the simple pajama-like grey, cotton pantsuit typically worn by Buddhist priests when working around the temple or just relaxing. On his head, he wore a straw hat with a wide brim to shade his face from the late morning sun. Taitsu's voice was low and melodious, which suited him well for the frequent chanting he was required to do as part of his work as a priest. And work was how he viewed it. He had once told Jack, in confidence, that he didn't believe humans actually had spirits that persisted after death; he saw death as an off switch. But because most people did believe this, it was important to have priests to lead the rituals for the ancestors.

People needed the consolation and comfort of the rituals to help them deal with the loss of loved ones. Educated as a sociologist in college, Taitsu saw the temple, its priest, and the rituals as social structures that contributed to maintaining group cohesion in the village. It was likely this academic approach to his work as a priest that had brought Taitsu and Jack together and led to their long friendship. Taitsu's wife, Etsuko, had once intimated to Jack that Taitsu was always excited when Jack would return to the village, because he had few people around him with whom he could hold long, intellectual conversations. The two had spent many evenings talking about sociology, anthropology, philosophy, Zen, and so on and had become the closest of friends over the years of Jack's regular trips to the village. Etsuko and Saori were equally close and often spent time together visiting local restaurants or sipping tea. Their friendships were the reason that the temple always formed Jack's first stop when returning to the village for research; and now was no different when he had returned to retire.

The two chatted about the weather as they headed for the main hall of the temple. Taitsu needed to pick something up and then they would head to his adjacent residence for tea and cakes. Walking past the concrete circular path in front of the building, which was used to confuse evil spirits by walking in circles before entering the temple building with cremains as part of a funeral, Taitsu pulled out his keys and unlocked the sliding doors to the large room where most religious rituals were performed. He opened the door, but then quickly bent down as he dropped his keys. As soon as the door opened, Jack's eyes followed Taitsu as he bent over to retrieve his keys, and then he noticed a faint scent that seemed out of place for the temple hall. Jack looked up and stared through the open entryway door and with an initially quiet, but increasingly alarmed voice said, "Taitsu-san, Taitsu-san!" Taitsu stood and they stepped into the entry area, known as the *genkan*, equally shocked and dumbfounded by the gruesome image they beheld.

In front of the Buddha statue, with its intricate gold leaf that sat at the back of the main hall and directly above the altar, where incense sticks were burned and sutras chanted by Taitsu for funerals and post-death memorials, a body dangled from what appeared to be a rope tied to the main wooden support beam that crossed the entire hall. The flat, purple pillow on which the priest would sit to lead rituals had been pushed aside and in its place was a chair, knocked over so that its back was facing upward toward the ceiling and the body directly above. As it hung motionless from the rafters, the body's back was to the *genkan*, so Taitsu and Jack could not see the face of the victim. Jack noticed that the cup-shaped bell rung by Taitsu in rituals was on its side, about two meters from the spot where it was normally placed at the altar. It looked like it had rolled across the tatami mat floor in an arc to the spot where it now rested.

The two men removed their shoes and stepped up from the *genkan* onto the tatami mat flooring in the main hall. They carefully inched toward the body and Jack reminded them both to avoid disturbing anything for the police. As they neared the dangling body, Jack noticed it was an older male and he clenched a white candle that had burned and appeared to have extinguished when it reached the victim's left hand. They circled the body and Taitsu said, "It's Takahashi Eizo." This was not a person familiar to Jack. "He's a member of the parish, but one I don't think you've ever met. He doesn't…didn't…live here in the village. His house is about ten kilometers to the west, out in the middle of the rice fields over near the mountains." Jack didn't respond for a moment, and then said, "That's odd, why would he be holding a candle in his left hand?" Taitsu looked at the body again and said, "*fushigi desu nee.*" Strange, indeed.

"There's something else really strange, Taitsu-san."

"Mmm?"

"Look at the ligature. It's not a rope." Jack spied the long, narrow piece of cloth from which Takahashi was suspended and said, "It looks like an *onbuhimo*, doesn't it?"

"Yes, it does, actually. Why would someone use that to hang himself? Rope isn't exactly difficult to come by. I wouldn't have thought it strong enough, although Takahashi-san is rather small." Indeed,

Takahashi was a slight man of seventy years, who barely passed five feet on the height chart. Looking at the body, Jack thought he couldn't have weighed more than 120 pounds. If the cloth were the right type, it would probably hold, he thought to himself.

The anthropologist, the carefully trained observer, in Jack continued to function as they talked. He carefully looked around the room at every object, in addition to observing the location and condition of the body. The face of the deceased had turned somewhat ashen blue. And he quickly realized that the smell he noticed upon opening the door was a result of the victim's reflex defecation at the moment of death. He also noted that under his pants, the man appeared to have an erection, which he later read was not unusual in this type of situation. The deceased was dressed in a dark suit with a black tie, black socks, and was not wearing shoes. Jack thought to himself that only a Japanese person would worry himself about removing his shoes before entering the building in which he planned to commit suicide—ever polite. He walked back to the *genkan* and noticed that there were three pairs of shoes, including a pair of black wingtips that did not belong to either Taitsu or Jack. They were far too small. Those must have been Takahashi's shoes, which should mean he came in through the *genkan*, thought Jack.

"Taitsu-san, is there a back door?"

"Sure. Down that hallway to the left."

Jack headed toward the back door and looked down into the back *genkan*. "No shoes." He returned to the main hall where Taitsu was checking around to see if anything was missing.

"Taitsu-san."

"Yes."

"The front door was locked when we came in, right? It was latched and you had to turn the key to open it."

"Yes."

"You're sure about that."

"Yes, I pulled the doors slightly before unlocking them and could see that it was locked. Why?"

"Why indeed. Come over here. There are no shoes at the back door. There's no other entrance, right?"

They looked down into the *genkan* and Taitsu immediately realized what Jack was concerned about, "that's right, no other entrance and I am sure I locked the front door last night. So how did the shoes get here?"

"Exactly. Who in their right mind would enter a building by the back door, pick up his shoes, carry them to the front door, set them down, and then proceed to hang himself?"

"Someone who commits suicide isn't in his right mind," replied Taitsu.

"Mmm...yes... Or maybe it wasn't a suicide..."

3
THE POLICE

Saori enjoyed lunch immensely. The group of women consisted largely of friends from her high school archery club. Several of them had spent most of their adult lives living and working in the area around Kanezawa, although five of the seven had attended college in Tokyo and two of them, other than Saori, had lived in Tokyo or other major cities for several years, moving back only after retiring. As the Tesla silently sped toward home, Saori thought of how happy she was to be back in the Kanezawa area and to be able to spend time with her friends regularly after so many years away. Just a few more weeks cleaning up some projects in Tokyo and then she could move permanently to Tanohata, where she planned to work in statistical consulting remotely. She didn't actually need the money, since she had a government pension, but Saori was incapable of sitting still; therefore, she was always compelled to be working at something. Her brain was simply too sharp and active to allow for time off.

She depressed the blinker stalk and turned right onto the street that passed Taiyō-ji, where she noticed an ambulance parked in the lot across from the temple. Without giving it any thought, she drove on; the population in the village was elderly and ambulances were not an unusual sight. Two minutes later, she pulled into the car port. The morning's blue skies were giving way to grey clouds and the temperature was dropping. We'll probably need a fire tonight, she thought. Saori carried in some groceries she picked up on the way home, stowed them in their appropriate places, and then opened her computer to do some work. In the distance, she could hear the bee-bah, bee-bah of sirens.

Shortly after discovering the body, Taitsu pulled out his smart phone and called the police. The ambulance arrived first, followed by two police cars, one of which had to travel from the station on the other side of Kanezawa. There were no detectives in the town where Tanohata was located, since most temples now had alarm systems there was virtually no crime other than the occasional petty theft, and that could be handled by the local police. Suicide, however, was common particularly among the elderly and the routine when there was a hanging or other suicide was to get the ambulance to the scene as quickly as possible just in case there was any hope of a rescue. From what Taitsu described on the phone, the local police officer didn't think there would be much to investigate. Northern Japan had long been known for its high suicide rates and men over the age of sixty were the most likely to succumb to the vicissitudes of aging that caused loneliness and despair. Years of work ended abruptly at the mandatory retirement age, leaving some men feeling irrelevant—identity and purpose in life lost to the inevitability of growing old.

As Jack watched the pendular sway of the body dangling in the gentle breeze that wafted through the room after the police opened the doors to remove the growing stench. Inspector Matsumoto entered the *genkan*, removed his shoes, and proceeded in the direction of Jack, Taitsu, and the corpse.

Inspector Matsumoto surveyed the body, circling it as he carefully observed the scene. After about five minutes of examination, he turned to one of the other police officers and said, "Cut him down." As they gently removed Takahashi from his noose and set his body on the tarp that had been laid out on the floor, Matsumoto called out to his assistant, "Suicide. Take care of the usual paperwork and processing and then you can release him to the crematorium and call the family."

Jack overheard and walked in the direction of Matsumoto. "Inspector, you're not going to do an autopsy?"

"Why would I order an autopsy? It's obviously suicide."

"I'm not so sure. If you come to the *genkan* I think you'll notice something strange about this."

Turning to Taitsu, Inspector Matsumoto said in a gruff tone, "Um, who is this?"

"Inspector, this is Professor Jack Riddley from Yale University in the United States. He lives around the corner, just moved in." Jack pulled out his business card to do the usual exchange, but the inspector continued to converse with Taitsu and ignored him.

"And why is he here?"

"He's my friend and was visiting when we found the body."

"Has he made a statement?"

"Yes, Inspector, I did to the sergeant a few minutes ago," interjected Jack with little notice from the inspector.

Without acknowledging Jack's response, Inspector Matsumoto asked Taitsu if Jack understood Japanese, to which Taitsu responded, "Actually he just responded to you in Japanese." Matsumoto turned to Jack and in the rather low, blunt tones that Japanese males sometimes used, blurted, "I suggest you leave the police work to us and go home. We can handle this just fine."

"Of course, but I thought…"

"Did he understand that?" turning to Taitsu.

"Yes, he is fluent in Japanese, Inspector."

"I see," and then turning back to Jack, "this is not your concern, go home."

Taitsu grabbed Jack by the arm, pulling him away from the inspector. "Jack, you need to mind your own business. Inspector Matsumoto doesn't need our help."

"Taitsu-san, you saw the same thing I did. This is strange. The shoes don't make sense." Taitsu continued to pull Jack farther away from the inspector and suicide scene and said, "Let's go outside." They put on their shoes and stepped into the cool air.

"I'm sure Inspector Matsumoto knows what he's doing. He has a lot of experience with these things."

With a mild note of frustration, Jack responded, "I'm not questioning his ability, but he doesn't seem to be interested in any explanation other than the obvious one."

"Jack, you've been coming here for a long time. You've done research on elder suicide. You know that this is common."

"Yeah, but this doesn't look like a suicide."

"So, the shoes are weird, but other than that, it really does just look like the run-of-the mill elder suicide, even if the choice of location is on the dramatic side."

Jack pulled his pipe out of his pocked and began to turn it over in his left hand. "*Moshikashi.*" Maybe, replied Jack, and then he lowered his voice as Inspector Matsumoto came out of the building. He started to walk toward the cemetery with Taitsu close by his arm. "Did you see the chair?"

"What about it?"

"It was facing forward, with the back toward the ceiling."

"So..."

"If you were going to hang yourself by kicking a chair out from under you, which way would you kick the chair? It falls over easier if you kick it backwards."

"Hmm." Taitsu's face began to grow dark in thought. "Maybe he was flailing around trying to get the rope off his neck as he choked and knocked over the chair in that direction. No, the chair would already have been kicked out from under him."

"Right, and if he were doing that, he would have dropped the candle."

"Hmm."

"They need to do an autopsy," Jack insisted.

"I'm beginning to think you may be right. But you need to stay out of this. It's a touchy area and you are not Japanese."

"What's touchy about doing an autopsy?"

"The police rarely order autopsies in Japan. Didn't you know that? Even in high-profile cases. Remember the suicide of Agriculture Minister Toshikatsu Matsuoka back in '07? They found him hanged in his Tokyo apartment just a few hours before he was supposed to appear before a parliamentary committee investigating the financial scandal he was implicated in."

"Misappropriation of funds, if I remember right."

"Yes. And the scandal was destabilizing the government. It

seemed like a situation in which foul-play could have been a possible explanation, at least, but no autopsy was conducted to confirm that he hadn't died from anything other than hanging. A day later, Shinichi Yamazaki, a businessman implicated in the same scandal, jumped off the balcony of his Yokohama apartment. No autopsy was conducted in that case, either. The police called it a suicide because he had apparently left his shoes placed neatly on the balcony."

"Why would his shoes be on the balcony? They'd be in the *genkan* at the entrance to his apartment. If anything, there would be sandals on the balcony."

"Right." Taitsu gazed intently at Jack. "I'm not saying the police are corrupt, Jack. But the culture is different here. In America, they use autopsies to determine the cause of death if there are any questions at all, if what I see on TV is right."

"Yes, that's right."

"In Japan, investigations are focused on determining whether or not a crime has been committed instead of finding the cause of death. Without obvious signs of a murder, the police are unlikely to order an autopsy. Murders are rare here, so the police don't see autopsies as necessary unless there is very clear evidence of a crime."

"And that's not the case here..." responded Jack with a frustrated tone, "it just looks like another of the long line of suicides by hanging the police encounter routinely in their work, even if more dramatic because it was done in the main hall of a Buddhist temple."

"Correct."

"But things don't add up this time, Taitsu-san."

"I know, but you aren't the one to point that out. To us here in the village, you are family, but to everyone else, you are an outsider who shouldn't stick his nose where it doesn't belong. Put on that anthropologist's hat of yours and remind yourself that you're not Japanese. Go home and spend some time with Saori."

"Taitsu-san, you can be annoyingly blunt at times, but you are also a good friend. And you are right. It's not my place."

Taitsu smiled. They knew each other so well, he thought. He had never met another foreigner with whom he felt he could be as honest and direct as with Jack. It was almost like they were brothers.

"It's getting cold, do you want a ride?"

"No," Jack paused, "I think I'll walk. I need the air."

"Okay. Don't worry. It will work out. And in the meantime, I will carefully try to talk to Inspector Matsumoto and point out some of the discrepancies we both found here today. You know that I agree with you completely. We just have to handle this in a Japanese, not American, way."

"*Arigatō*, Taitsu-san." Jack bowed slightly and started toward the stone steps he had climbed to start this peculiar day. He lost himself in thought as he wandered in a direction away from home.

4
A PIPE FULL

An hour later, after a walk that should have taken no more than seven minutes, Jack appeared in front of the house where he had only spent one night, slid open the front door and quietly removed his shoes, stepping up from the *genkan* into the living room. He could hear Saori in the kitchen chopping something, which no doubt was in preparation for dinner. He padded into the kitchen area as Saori looked up from the frighteningly shiny steel knife she held in her right hand.

"You're soaked!"

"It's raining."

"I kind of guessed that. And you're dripping on the floor. Why didn't you ask me to come and get you?"

"I needed to walk."

"In the rain?"

"Yeah, in the rain. You haven't heard what happened at the temple?"

"No, after getting home, I've been working on the computer. I did hear a siren; did someone get sick?"

"Not exactly. When I arrived at the temple, Taitsu-san and I went to get something from the main hall. We opened the door and found an old man named Takahashi Eizo," he paused as his voice choked slightly, "hanging over the altar."

"Oh, my goodness. Suicide?"

"That's what the police think."

"Well, it's pretty common around here with old people, but in the main hall of the temple? I don't think I've ever heard of anything like that before."

"No. And I'm not at all convinced it was a suicide. There were some strange aspects to the scene. I was walking and thinking about what I observed. I'm increasingly convinced that it was murder...will do some poking around tomorrow."

"Jack! Stay out of this. That's what the police are for—I know you've done some amateur sleuthing back in New Haven and even consulted for the police a few times, but you're an anthropologist, not a detective."

"I suppose you're right..." Jack's voice trailed off as his body drifted into the bedroom where he could change into dry clothes. Saori watched him heading down the hall and knew he was going to ignore her advice. Once Jack got it in his head that there was a puzzle to be confronted, which normally meant some sort of complex cultural problem, he focused on little else until satisfied all was at least reasonably understood, if not solved. Cultural anthropologists rarely arrived at solutions for the puzzles they studied. Saori thought to herself that his anthropological mind—the willingness to see things from many different perspectives and try to understand human behavior on its own terms—was one of the things she had always loved about Jack. It was also one of the things that had made him a well-known anthropologist of Japan. But that same inquisitive mind had a tendency to stick its nose into the business of others while trying to understand the reasons behind the behavior it observed. Jack was, indeed, tremendously observant; he saw things that seemed completely hidden to others. Little behavioral tics, the subtle semiotics through which a wink was distinguished from a twitch, and the complex ways in which words were used to convey deep meanings even in the most routine elements of daily life. As she watched, she recalled a research project he had developed with a colleague on fast food in Japan. Jack had spent hours sitting in McDonald's and other fast-food restaurants watching how people consume their burgers and fries, as well as interviewing people on their conceptualizations of what constitutes fast food as opposed to other types of food. It seemed like a silly research project, but Jack ended up co-authoring an article that led to interviews on NPR and other major news and business outlets. That was always the way with Jack; he saw the deepest of meanings in the most mundane of things and behaviors. He knew how to read the public, acted narrative that people referred to as culture. Maybe he *would* have made a good detective, she thought.

"I'm dry," announced Jack as he re-entered the kitchen and dining area of their house.

"Good. Dinner will be ready in a few minutes. Could you set the table?"

"Sure, where do we keep the tableware?"

Saori chuckled and pointed to the drawer in the kitchen's center island. Jack dutifully set the table, asking several times where necessary items such as plates were stored, and they settled in for a dinner of spaghetti with seaweed sprinkled on top and a salad, accompanied by an inexpensive bottle of Italian red wine. Conversation largely avoided the events at the temple, as Jack didn't want to talk about it and Saori didn't want to hear about it. Saori told him about her lunch with friends from the archery club and some of the new shops she noticed while out in Kanezawa. Jack didn't talk much, since his mind continued to process the day's tumultuous events in the background.

"You're quiet," noted Saori with a concerned look on her lovely face that appeared more like it had forty rather than over than sixty years of experience.

"Sorry. I'm still thinking about what happened today."

"Get some sleep and in the morning, I'm sure things will be less troubling."

"Perhaps…" Jack's voice was gentle as he thought about her words. And then in a much more energetic tone, he said, "*Gochisōsama deshita*," the customary invocation at the end of a meal in Japan thanking the cook for the feast, as he pushed himself away from the table. As was their custom, he began clearing the table and then washing the dishes. For decades they had an understanding, never really stated, that whoever cooked was relieved from doing the dishes. Saori cooked this night, so Jack did the dishes. As he put the last of the glasses in the dishwasher, he dried his hands and headed into his study to find a pipe. Jack didn't smoke often—only when he needed to think deeply or was feeling stressed—but Saori hated the habit anyway. She was always concerned about their health and tobacco was certainly not conducive to enhancing longevity. But the pipe helped Jack think. And thinking mattered to Jack more than just about anything.

The rain had stopped, which meant Jack could successfully smoke a bowl. Saori would not allow him to smoke in the house, so his only options were to use tobacco either on a walk or on the porch behind their house. He elected the porch. With pipe and tobacco pouch in one hand and towel to wipe down the chairs in the other, he headed out the rear sliding doors and took up residence on an Adirondack chair in the cool evening air. As soon as he sat, he decided a sweater was necessary, so his pipe-smoking reverie became delayed briefly while he went back inside to put on something appropriate. Once reseated, he pulled out his tobacco pouch and began carefully filling the Castello bent billiard he cradled in his left hand. As he took a pinch of tobacco, he thought to himself, this looks like it will be at least three-pipe problem. And then he said under his breath, "I've watched too much Jeremy Brett." Jack settled into his chair, struck a match against the side of its box, and began carefully lighting the tobacco while puffing to get the pipe going. The ashes stood up and danced as they burned, and he used the pipe tool to tamp them down, after which he relit the pipe. It was a large pipe, so Jack expected at least forty minutes of blissful contemplation from the first bowl. He ejected a blue-grey stream of smoke from his mouth and his eyes settled on the stem of the pipe, out of which swirls of smoke gently rippled, wrapping themselves around the bit and then dissolving into nothingness. A well-packed pipe, he thought, will virtually smoke itself. It wasn't a novel idea, in fact having come to his mind almost every time he lit up over the past forty years.

The paisley curls of smoke normally calmed his mind and allowed him to think more clearly about whatever ethnographic problem he was trying to sort out. Human cultures are so diverse and complex, he thought, and the goal of the cultural anthropologist is to unpack the underlying logic that motivates individual behavior. As his eyes focused on the smoke, he realized he had seen several things that the inspector seemed to have missed. Was it willful lack of careful observation, as Taitsu maybe was implying? Was Matsumoto a sloppy detective? Why would he be so quick to automatically assume that Takahashi's death was a suicide when the context seemed to display unexpected evidence? He drew in a mouthful of smoke from the pipe and blew it vertically into the air while looking at the stars above that rain clouds no longer obscured. A full thirty minutes passed as Jack puffed on his pipe and pondered the day's events. The shoes bothered him, but what was most troubling—and what he couldn't believe the inspector seemed to have ignored—was the candle. Why on earth would someone hold a burning candle in his hand while hanging himself? And equally perplexing was the question of why someone would use an *onbuhimo* as a noose when a rope would be easy to find and more reliable in terms of strength. None of it added up.

At about 21:00 hours—most Japanese used the 24-hour system of telling time due to the extensive rail system—Jack's phone vibrated, dislodging him from his contemplation of smoke-shrouded stars. It was Taitsu. He pressed the answer button on the screen.

"Hi Taitsu-san."

"Jack, I just wanted to check in to make sure you're ok. It was quite an afternoon."

"Yes, it was. I'm sitting on the porch, smoking a pipe, and thinking about all of it."

"Jack," admonished Taitsu, "you really need to stop smoking that filthy thing. It's not good for you."

"I know, but it helps me think."

"Can't you think in a healthy way?"

"Not really, most of my thoughts are unhealthy..."

They laughed and then Taitsu started to explain a conversation he had with Inspector Matsumoto after Jack left. Although Matsumoto had seemed completely resistant to the idea that anything was going on other than a standard elder suicide, Taitsu concluded that he might be more receptive than it seemed. After Jack left, he noticed Matsumoto looking around the grounds of the temple carefully and asking a few questions about locked doors. Taitsu didn't think there was going to be an autopsy, but he also told Jack he felt Matsumoto might suspect more was going on than seemed apparent from the scene they all had observed.

"That's good to hear, Taitsu-san. But I can't help thinking that something else is going on with Matsumoto-san. Maybe it's just because I'm foreign, but he seemed resistant to even thinking about the idea that it could be anything other than suicide." Jack let out a large puff of smoke to punctuate his comment.

"I agree. And nothing he said would make me assume differently. I was just interested that he started poking around after taking such a strong stance against it being anything other than suicide."

"I'm still stuck on the candle and *onbuhimo*. If we assume for a moment that this was not a suicide, but was a murder, then both objects should have some sort of meaning—in other words, they weren't accidental. The question is, what do they mean?"

The phone was silent for a few seconds and then Taitsu raised a thought. "The *onbuhimo* is used for strapping an infant to a woman's back. It could be that if there were a message being sent, it has something to do with childhood…"

"Or maybe it has something to do with motherhood…" interjected Jack.

"Or maybe it was just handy and doesn't mean anything," mused Taitsu, dryly.

"Right. Let's keep thinking about this, Taitsu-san. Tomorrow, I'll head over to the library. I want to do a little research on candles…and hangings."

"We should leave this to the police, Jack," and then before Jack could reply, "but I know neither of us will be able to do that…"

"Two of a kind, eh, Taitsu-san?"

"Indeed."

The next morning, Jack awoke at seven o'clock to sunshine and the sounds of Saori sweeping the back porch. He stretched, pulled himself off the floor where his futon had provided a firm, deep sleep, and folded it over in thirds, after which he picked up the bundle of futon and blankets and put it in the closet that formed one wall of the room. Traditional Japanese rooms were multi-purpose, functioning as sleeping quarters at night and sitting rooms during the day. Japanese efficiency.

Coffee perfumed the air in the rest of Jack's house as he departed the bedroom and turned toward the kitchen. Saori was coming inside as he arrived.

"I've already eaten. Got up early today."

"Today? You always get up early. When do you ever sleep past five?"

"Was up at three."

"Oh, sorry. Was I snoring?"

"No, just couldn't sleep."

Jack pulled a yogurt cup out of the refrigerator and a spoon from the drawer. He sat at the table eating his yogurt and reading over the front page of the morning newspaper while Saori poured coffee—hers black, his with cream. Saori perched at the breakfast counter and took a sip from her mug. "What are your plans for today?"

Without looking up from the paper, Jack replied, "Going to the library. Want to do a little research."

"Really? On what?"

"Hanging."

"Jack! Leave it alone!" She came close to shouting at him.

"It's okay," he replied calmly. "I'm just curious. I also want to see if I can do some looking into the issue with the candle in Takahashi-san's left hand. That's really bothering me. I feel like it might be related to something I studied a long time ago, but I can't seem to recall what it was. Maybe looking around at the books will help bring it back. Who knows…" his voice trailed off. At that moment, Saori's phone started to ring.

"It's Irene on Facetime."

"Cool."

"Hi Irene," they said in unison.

"Hi Mom and Dad. How's the new house?"

"Good. We're still settling in. What's up?" asked Saori, thinking that Irene didn't usually call unless there was something important to discuss or she needed money.

"Well, I actually have some time over the next month. School ends tomorrow. So, I was thinking of flying over to see you." Irene was a student at Yale majoring in astrophysics with a minor in voice. Smart and pretty with long black hair with natural auburn highlights that sparkled in the sunlight, she had been fortunate in the gene lottery to get her mother's good looks. Her features were almost entirely Japanese, with dark, full eyebrows and brown eyes, which she complained about because she thought had she inherited her father's blue eyes, she would look more striking. Her smile was bright and warm, the charm of which was added to by the fact that she had a dimple only on her right cheek. One thing that she didn't inherit from her mother's side was her height. At five feet, six inches, Irene towered over Saori.

Irene was always a challenge. Her middle school years had been an ongoing nightmare of stress and anxiety, mostly over grades, but also as a result of the social vicissitudes of early teen life. In high school, she relaxed somewhat from a social standpoint, but became even more focused on studying. Somehow in Irene's mind, the grading curve had a very narrow range: 100=A, 98=B, 95=C, 92=D, 90=F. Jack often thought that should Irene ever become a professor her students would be in for a very rough ride. However, her driven nature had served her well for college acceptance and she was performing at a high level at Yale, with anticipation of following in the steps of her parents and earning a Ph.D., most likely in astrophysics. For years, she had joked that her goal was to take the Lucasian Chair at Cambridge, held in the past by the likes of Isaac Newton and Stephen Hawking. It often seemed that Irene's focus and intensity would allow her to achieve even such a lofty aim. And as good as she was at math and physics, she was also blessed with an operatic singing voice which she had developed to a high level through years of private lessons and practice. In high school, she won several international voice competitions.

"Who's paying for the ticket?" said Jack.

"Daaaad…" Irene knew her father was teasing. Throughout her youth it had never stopped. She deadpanned into the camera and replied, "I was planning on swimming, actually."

"Good. It will give you quiet time to think. It should be a pacific experience." Irene ignored him, but in the back of her mind was trying to think of another pun she might fire back using the word pacific. Growing up, the Riddleys had routinely dined amidst pun wars that went on sometimes for well over thirty minutes after they had finished eating. For a long time Saori had quietly tolerated the puns, but over the years even she started to chime in with the occasional groaner. The punning could become quite complex, because the entire family was multi-lingual and the puns came in both English and Japanese varieties, with Irene throwing in an occasional Latin entry and Jack using German at times. It was a fond memory that the entire family shared and if George were on the line, he would no doubt be tossing out his own salvos. Saori intervened before an endless string of puns could explode.

"Put the ticket on your credit card, Irene. When can we expect you?"

"Thanks, Mom. I plan to leave at the end of next week. I was actually able to get a good price on a flight. Is it okay if I stay for a month?"

"Hmm. That's kind of long…" said Jack with a frown.

Saori interrupted, "Of course, Irene. Stay as long as you want. Ignore your father."

"I usually do, Mom. I'll email or text you with the details and when you can expect me at Kanezawa station. I might spend a couple of days in Tokyo before heading north."

"Sounds good. We look forward to having you home!" They ended the Facetime call with the usual good-byes and see-you-soons. Jack abruptly stood up from the table.

"I'm going to take a shower, then head to the library."

"Have fun," replied Saori absently, who then turned to some work she wanted to complete on her laptop before the morning was over.

Jack took a quick shower, shaved, and put on a short-sleeved shirt and blue jeans, his typical daily fieldwork uniform. As he exited the house, he called out, "*ittekimasu*," literally "I will return having left." It was a beautiful day. Grass glistened in the sunlight from the previous night's rain and water droplets intensified the blue flowers of morning glory, whose vines were beginning to stretch across the trellis on the side of their house. The air was comparatively dry and pleasant, if a little on the cool side. A perfect morning for a bike ride, thought Jack. Because they still only had one car, the options for transport were limited. Uber did not exist in this part of Japan and taxi rides were expensive. It would probably cost him 2,000 yen or about twenty dollars to get to the library only a few kilometers away. And it was an easy ride.

Jack pedaled in the direction of the main street in Nakadomari Town, where the village of Tanohata was located. Everywhere he looked, he could see the effects of depopulation. Most store fronts were boarded up, and it looked like many houses were empty. The tell-tale sign was that no laundry hung in front of the houses and the curtains had been drawn. Years of out-migration of young adults for college, work, and adventure, combined with decades of low fertility, had left the area largely devoid of young people. Jack noticed as he rode along the main street that there were no mothers taking infants for a stroll and virtually all of the wrinkled faces he passed looked over the age of sixty. Tiny elderly women pushed rolling carts with built-in seats around narrow roads as they embarked on their daily errands. Usually, these women were bent at the waist at almost a ninety-degree angle, unable to stand erect due to severe osteoporosis that was common among older Japanese women, a result of the calcium deficient diet most had experienced earlier in life.

Concerns within the government about population aging and depopulation were long-standing and considered among the most serious social problems Japan faced. It was hard to imagine how a country would manage a population crash from 125 million to forty-five million over the course of less than a century, although there were numerous innovative ideas being implemented in areas like Tanohata. As the empty structures rushed past, Jack recalled driving Irene and

George to the local elementary school during summer research trips when they were little; there were sixty total children attending a school designed for about 200 by the time Irene had enrolled. And as Jack embarked on his new life as a retiree, forty-five percent of the local population was over the age of sixty-five. Jack was on the young side at sixty-four. The future did not bode well for the region unless creative solutions to the loss of population continued to be developed. As more elderly people died off, the economy would continue to shrink and the streets would increasingly come to look like some empty post-apocalyptic landscape. Stopping at the only traffic light on the main street, Jack thought about a place not too far away in the mountains that had become a ghost town, where *kamoshika*—an animal that looked like a cross between a deer and goat—wandered the streets while black bears took up residence in abandoned buildings.

He turned left at the traffic light, pedaled across an arch-shaped bridge, and then headed right onto the bypass route that took traffic away from the narrow streets of the town center and had also displaced most of its businesses when a small strip mall was built, anchored by a grocery store and pharmacy, both of which were regional chains. The other storefronts in the mall were empty, but the grocery store, known as Big House, was usually crowded because it was the only place to shop within several kilometers. Jack glided past Big House as large trucks rumbled next to him, reminding him to be cautious because he was now riding on the left, rather than the right, side of the road. He turned left onto a narrow road that quickly dissolved into rice fields. About a kilometer later, he arrived at his destination, the local public library. A modern design, constructed in the 1990s, the town library had been a useful resource for Jack over his years of research. The librarian and other staff all knew him by name.

He threw one leg over the seat and glided to a stop near the bicycle rack and placed the bike on the rack, not bothering to lock it, since nobody would be likely to steal it. And the small locks that came on bicycles were so flimsy that anyone who wanted could easily break it open.

5
THE LIBRARY

The doors automatically slid open, and he walked in, keeping his shoes on as was now customary in public buildings. When he first arrived in the region, people removed their shoes and donned green or red slippers placed on racks at the entryway. One could always hear the slippered schfff, schfff, schfff of male feet shuffling or slap, slap, slap of female feet jogging through the hallways of any public building. That was a sound of life in Japan, Jack thought, that had faded into the past. He walked toward the circulation desk and saw Chiba Tomoko, who was in practice the head of the library, although the title belonged to a retired government worker in her sixties who was given the position for a few years as a perk to make some money before her pension kicked in, as was customary in the area.

"Jack-sensei!" Tomoko's face lit up with a broad smile, framed by the sensible Japanese-style bob with bangs in which she had always worn her piano-black hair. Jack had long ago abandoned the customary use of his family name, preferring Jack-sensei, or even better Jack-san, over Riddley-sensei, because Riddley was quite difficult for Japanese to pronounce due to the combination of Ls and Rs, sounds that the Japanese language does not differentiate. "I heard that you have now moved into your new house," she said.

News travels fast around here, he thought. "Yes, we are still getting settled in. It's been a while since we saw each other, Tomoko-san. Are you well?"

"Yes, I'm doing great. And you?"

"Just fine."

And then in a more hushed tone Tomoko said, "I heard about what happened at Taiyō-ji yesterday. I can't believe it. How sad. And what a terrible thing to do to poor Priest Murakami," the implication of the last comment being that one of the negatives to suicide was that it was rather selfish, because the living were left behind to clean up the mess, both physical and emotional, made by the person who killed him or herself. This was a common attitude among people in the area. "And you were with Murakami-san when he found the body, right?"

"Yes, I was."

"*Taihen desu nee!*" How terrible. Jack acknowledged her comment with a nod and quickly changed the subject.

"Tomoko-san," when Jack had asked her several years earlier to use his given name, she had happily reciprocated, "I'm doing some research and am wondering if you have anything on local rituals in the library."

"Of course. You know where the section on local history is—it hasn't changed. There are several books that deal with religion in Tōhoku. You can search on the computer, or it may just be easier to walk over there and browse the stacks. It's not that big a collection."

"Thanks, Tomoko-san," he said, followed by, "*osewa ni narimashita*" to assure her that he appreciated her help. As he walked in the direction Tomoko pointed, he pulled his pocket electronic kanji dictionary out. Jack was fluent both speaking and reading Japanese, but there were always characters, particularly when it came to specialized terminologies such as those in religious texts, that required looking up or careful investigation to absorb the entire meaning. He started to scan the shelves. Virtually every book related to local religion was a tourist guide describing the various historical Shinto shrines and Buddhist temples in the area. There were a few in-depth works written by local authors that discussed the histories of important temples and shrines, but these books were notorious for having inaccuracies. A friend and scholar at a university in Morika had explained to him that while the authors were well-meaning, they also were not usually trained archaeologists or historians. Jack noticed a book on the life of Goto Juan, the early seventeenth century Christian lord of Fukuwara in the western part of Kanezawa who had encouraged Christian missionaries to proselytize the local farmers and iron-workers in the area. When Christianity was outlawed by the Tokugawa Shogunate in 1623, Goto eluded arrest for maintaining his faith by working as a surveyor. He developed the system of irrigation canals still in use that allowed for growing rice in the region. Many of his converts went into hiding in the Kanezawa area, practicing their religion secretly to avoid condemnation and execution at the hands of the Tokugawa authorities, and a few of their descendants still lived in the area.

Hidden Christians, thought Jack and then he started to think about other secretive groups that had existed in the region over the years. As his eyes scanned the stacks, they settled on a small, brown paperback with no distinguishing features. On the spine, there were only the characters 隠し念仏. He pulled the book from the shelf and turned it over in his hands. There was no author and no indication of where and by whom the book had been written and published. In his head, Jack repeated the title, *kakushi nembutsu*, a couple of times and then translated it: secret *nembutsu*, *nembutsu* being a word that referenced chanting the name Amida Nyorai, the celestial Buddha of the Pure Land Sect who had accumulated virtually infinite merit over many lives. As Jack thumbed through the book, he started to feel uncomfortable, as though someone was watching him. He looked up and saw the shaven head of a Buddhist priest quickly turning away. The priest was adorned in a black robe and as he walked off Jack noticed a slight limp in his slow gait. Although Jack had not clearly seen his face, given the squat structure of his body and hunched shoulders, he thought the priest must be old. He didn't think much more about the encounter. Although foreigners were now common in the area, when Jack first started visiting Tanohata, people often stared at him and children sometimes would point and call out, *"gaijin da."* It's a foreigner! Elderly people wouldn't usually say anything, but he had more than one experience in which a person would halt and look at him with a surprised face. It rarely happened now, but once in a while, an older person might still be shocked at or curious about his presence.

Jack returned to the book cradled in his hand. Finding an open table, he sat down and started to leaf through the pages. Some of the characters were difficult and parts of the book appeared to be reproductions of classical Japanese, which Jack could not read without a special dictionary, because the characters were quite different from the modern form. He decided to borrow it so that he had time to go through its contents carefully at home. Setting the book aside and then pulling his laptop from his briefcase, Jack started to explore the other project on his mind—research on hanging. This he could pursue on the Internet in English, so he didn't need to stay at the library. But he enjoyed the atmosphere of the reading room and the Wi-Fi connection was good.

As he learned about hanging, some interesting points arose that he had never imagined might be important. As Jack read, he concluded that there was a Goldilocks aspect to hanging deaths. If the drop was too short, death tended to be the result of slow strangulation. The victim could remain alive for anywhere from ten to thirty minutes, depending on factors such as the weight of the body. If the drop was too long, the head of the victim tended to be pulled off when the rope reached its full length. And if the drop was just right, the victim's neck broke, causing a quick death. As he read a few journal articles devoted to the effects of hanging on the human body, one fact caught his attention. Suicides by hanging virtually never resulted in a broken neck or the head popping off, because the length of rope, and thus the drop, was typically too short. The only time a suicide typically led to an outcome other than slow strangulation was if the victim was unusually heavy. And one thing was for sure: Takahashi Eizo was not heavy enough to have caused a broken neck. If the police ordered an autopsy and found the neck broken, it would be strong evidence in favor of murder. And the fact that Takahashi was still holding the candle in his hand suggested he did not struggle, so it was probably a quick death. Jack needed to talk with Taitsu.

6
TAIYŌ-JI

Jack retraced his path on the bicycle, diverting in the direction of Taiyō-ji rather than his house, as he entered the village. He parked the bike at the bottom of the stairs, again not bothering to lock it since no-one in the village would even think of theft. Racing up the stone steps by twos he found Taitsu weeding the garden in front of the temple.

"Taitsu-san," called Jack.

"*Konnichiwa*," replied Taitsu in a low monotone, not looking up from his weeding.

"Taitsu-san, I learned something interesting."

"What's that?"

"I went to the library..." and he paused to catch his breath.

Taitsu interrupted as he stood up, "Good, Jack, I encourage foreigners to learn about Japan."

Ignoring the mild insult, Jack continued, "Did you know that hanging by suicide rarely results in a broken neck?"

"Uh, no, I'm sorry to say that I've never spent much time thinking about that."

"It's another reason for an autopsy. If Takahashi-san had a broken neck, it would strongly suggest he didn't kill himself."

Taitsu sighed. "Actually, that's pretty interesting," letting out another breath as he stood from his squatting position and brushed off his hands. "Unfortunately, it isn't going to help much. The body has already been released to the family, who decided to forego having it rest in the house for three days, as is customary. They are going to have the funeral quickly. Preparations were made for the ceremony here at the temple following cremation in the morning."

"Why the hurry?"

"I'm not sure. It could be that they just want to get everything over with following the ugliness of Takahashi-san's death. His daughter was pretty broken up over the whole thing."

"Doesn't it seem strange to hurry given the problematic aspects of his death?"

Taitsu frowned. "The police don't think there is anything problematic. It was a suicide."

Jack changed the subject and asked Taitsu, "What do you know about *kakushi nembutsu?*"

"Not much. Why do you ask?"

"I'm not sure. I found this book in the library." Jack pulled the volume out of his satchel and handed it to Taitsu. "It's probably nothing, but something clicked in my head when I saw this on the shelf. When I was doing my dissertation research, I talked about the ritual a few times with people, but never really pursued it."

Taitsu pulled the book from Jack's hand and thumbed through it with an occasional "hmm." As he handed it back, he commented that it looked interesting, but couldn't see how it was connected to Takahashi's death.

Swatting in the air as a mosquito started to circle, Taitsu shifted the topic slightly, "Jack, I'm leading the ceremony for Takahashi-san's funeral tomorrow. I'd like you to be at the cremation and temple ceremony. Maybe you'll notice something. The more I think about this, the more I am convinced that there *may* be something suspicious going on." He paused as if in thought for a moment and continued, "Anyway, I asked Takahashi-san's widow if you could join because you are interested in funerals as an anthropologist studying religion in Japan and she said it was okay. You'll need a black suit, white shirt, and black tie."

"Right. I'm going to have to go shopping this afternoon, then."

"I can lend you a suit…" Their eyes met and both broke out laughing. There wasn't much chance that Taitsu's clothes would fit Jack. "Maybe I can wear one of your robes," quipped Jack.

"I'll pick you up at nine o'clock tomorrow morning."

"Thanks. That way Saori will have the car. Much appreciated."

Jack bowed slightly and turned for the temple gate, "See you tomorrow, Taitsu-san."

"*Mata ashita.*" Again tomorrow, replied Taitsu.

Jack descended the stone steps, hopped on his bike, and headed straight home.

"*Tadaima!*" Jack called out as he entered their *genkan*, which basically meant "I'm home!"

"*Okairinasai!*" came the standard reply from Saori who was still perched at the kitchen table working on her laptop.

"You haven't moved," said Jack.

"I have. And I ate lunch, which you missed."

"I did? What time is it?"

"Fifteen hundred."

"Shit, that's later than I thought. Is it okay if I take the car for a few hours? I need to buy a black suit."

"Takahashi-san's funeral?"

"Yup."

"Sure, mind if I come along? I have some shopping to do. We can go to Aeon Department Store up by Kitakami. They have a whole section devoted to funeral clothes."

"Perfect." Saori hit save, rose from her chair, and said, "*ikō ka?*" Shall we go? "We can pick up a couple of *onigiri* from Lawson's on the way that you can eat for lunch."

"Sounds like a plan. Maybe we can get dinner while we are out. I can skip the *onigiri*."

"Okay. Any ideas where you want to go?"

"I'm feeling like ramen. There are a couple of good ramen shops up that way."

"Great!" She smiled. As Jack looked at his wife, he thought about how much more at ease she seemed now that they were permanently in Japan. With the shift in politics, America had become such an unpleasant place to live for people from other countries. Saori had commented frequently that she never knew who hated her just because she was foreign, but with 40% of the population supporting a far-right, racist President with delusions of dictatorship, her guess was that it was a lot of them. Jack couldn't disagree and found Japan to be a much more congenial and free place to live than the States. She had given up much to live with him when they married and Jack was glad that now he could reciprocate by living in Japan. And seeing her happy and relaxed brought him satisfaction.

7
OFFICER SUZUKI

It certainly didn't fit like one of Martel's finely tailored Brooks Brothers suits, but it was adequate for the purpose. He probably wouldn't wear the outfit more than a few times for the rest of his life. And Jack didn't care much about sartorial elegance. While at Aeon, Saori purchased several small boxes of Japanese cakes. That evening, she intended for the two of them to knock on the doors of their neighbors and introduce themselves, offering the cakes as a small gift to say, "thank you for letting us live here"—not that anyone had any control over that—and establish a relationship as new residents of the village. It was a Japanese custom that worked opposite the Welcome Wagon in the States. Since most of the neighbors already knew Jack and Saori, it wasn't all that important to do other than for the purpose of being polite and following protocol, but the small ritual made for a pleasant walk in the clear evening air. And it was enjoyable to say hello to their new neighbors, all of whom welcomed them with large smiles and comments about how happy they were to have new people in the village. Jack wondered when the last time was that someone had moved into the village. It had probably been several years prior, when five new houses were built on an open plot of land sold by the stepmother of one of the residents after his father passed on, sending the son into a long bout with depression and alcoholism due to the loss of his inheritance.

When they returned from their shopping trip, Jack noticed that the front door was open. "Saori, did you close the front door?" he asked, knowing that she had a propensity for never closing either doors or jars. He once grabbed a plastic bottle of laundry detergent on which Saori had simply set the cap, rather than screwing it down. When he squeezed the bottle to pick it up, the cap flew off and detergent shot out making a tremendous mess on the floor. Liquid soap is surprisingly difficult to clean up, Jack learned.

"I think I did...Why?"

"It's open."

"Yes, I see that now. Maybe I didn't get it shut or maybe it bounced open. I'm sure I didn't lock it."

"Just in case, look around and make sure nothing's missing," he said, doubting that anything would be.

"Really? No one steals things here."

"I know, but just make sure. Okay?" They moved around the house and found nothing missing, but after the search, they both commented that some things had been knocked over. It was subtle, although the kitchen seemed to be more disheveled, with the contents of a sugar jar spilled on one of the counters.

"I don't like this, Jack," said Saori with a slightly worried look on her face.

"Yeah, clearly someone was in here while we were out. Maybe we should call the police?"

"Let's ask the neighbors if they saw anyone around our house," said Saori.

"Good idea, but it's too late to bother anyone now and the police aren't going to be able to do much at night. Let's do that in the morning."

After a fitful night, the doorbell rang at six o'clock the next day, shocking Saori from her shallow sleep. She staggered out to the *genkan* and rather than stepping down into shoes, leaned across the open space with a foot on top of one of Jack's shoes and slid open the front door. On the other side of the threshold stood an older man holding a bag.

"*Ohayō gozaimasu!*" he said as Saori opened the door, still in her pajamas, covered by a flannel robe.

"*Ohayō gozaimsu*," she replied sleepily. People in Tanohata usually awoke around four o'clock, so six was the middle of the morning and didn't seem too early to be knocking on doors. However, it was definitely too early for Saori and Jack. The man was their neighbor, Suzuki Tamotsu, one of the people they had visited the previous evening. He was in his late seventies and had a somewhat blank look on his face. When walking he tended to shuffle and his left hand often shook mildly, which Jack thought was likely the result of Parkinson's Disease.

"I brought you some of my wife's homemade pickles. We remembered how much Jack enjoyed them the last time he was at our house a few years ago."

"*Arigatō!*" responded Saori with a polite smile. "You didn't need to do that."

"It's nothing, really." And then Suzuki's tone changed slightly. "Also, after you left our place last night, I thought I saw something moving around the front of your house. I didn't get a good look at it. Maybe it was an animal. Just wanted to let you know." Neighbors in Tanohata typically were attuned to the activities of those around them and paid attention to what happened at the houses in their immediate vicinity. Years earlier, Jack had one of his regular pollen-induced sneezing fits in the morning; later that day as he passed his neighbor along one of the village streets she asked if he had caught a cold, having heard his sneezes from next door. Saori thanked Suzuki as he handed her the pickles while bowing. She then slowly began to slide the front door shut, having stepped down into shoes while they were talking about the pickles and possible intruder. Slipping out of the shoes, she stepped back up into the house. Jack had gotten up and was now scratching his head and yawning in the middle of the kitchen.

"Coffee?" said Jack.

"I haven't made it yet."

"Who was that?" he asked as he started grinding the beans.

"Next door. Suzuki-san. He brought some pickles."

"Ah. Yes, I did show quite a bit of enthusiasm for his wife's pickles the last time I visited his house."

"And there's something else," her voice grew slightly darker. "Suzuki-san said that he caught a glimpse of something moving around the front of our house last night after we left his place. He didn't get a good look and thought it might have been an animal."

"Fat chance. Someone was in here last night."

"I agree. It's kind of scary. I'm going to call the police now."

"Yes, I think it might make sense."

"I'll be around here for a while looking over some of my old fieldnotes on the computer before Taitsu-san arrives. Let's make sure we both remember to lock up when we go out."

"Yes. What are you looking for?"

"The book I brought home last night on *kakushi nembutsu* is bothering me. I think I've talked to a couple of people briefly about this in the past. If I have, it will be in my fieldnotes. Something about the candle, I think."

"Jack. Don't cause trouble. We just moved here and don't need to have difficulties with the neighbors."

"I know, but the fact that someone broke into our house last night tells me that something strange and potentially dangerous is going on here. I need to know what it is, not only to satisfy my curiosity, but also because the police don't seem to be terribly concerned about investigating Takahashi-san's death. I'm sure it wasn't a suicide, but Inspector Matsumoto has no interest in anything other than wrapping up the case. If someone really did enter our house last night, then we need to have enough evidence to show Matsumoto-san he needs to take this seriously—for our own protection."

And then with a worried look she said, "Please be careful. This isn't New Haven and this isn't the States. Things work differently here, particularly since we are in the countryside."

"I know that things are different here. I'm an anthropologist, remember?" Jack shot back curtly and then felt immediately sorry for his tone. "Sorry, Saori. I didn't mean to sound like that. I think this has put me a little on edge and I'm annoyed that Inspector Matsumoto isn't taking this seriously."

"Are you bothered that he isn't taking this seriously or that he isn't taking you seriously..."

Jack took a moment to answer. "Probably both. Maybe more the latter. But the fact is there's something going on and if our home is at risk, I need to see if I can dig around enough to get Matsumoto to pay attention." Jack spoke quickly with an intense look on this face that Saori had come to recognize when something was deeply important to him. And she agreed that this was potentially dangerous. The idea that someone was poking around and entered their house was frightening—that sort of thing just didn't happen around Tanohata.

Saori was accustomed to Jack's stubborn nature and decided not to push any further. She had made her point and knew it would eventually enter Jack's brain. She just hoped that it didn't sink in after he got into trouble. While Jack retreated to his study to read the book he borrowed from the library, Saori made some tea and looked up the number of the local police station. The officer on duty said that he would come around shortly to look over the house and ask a few questions; they should stay at home until he arrived. Twenty minutes later, the black and white police car pulled into their driveway and Officer Suzuki, who was their neighbor Suzuki Tamotsu's eldest son, stepped out and started looking around. He walked up to the front door and slid it open, leaning in slightly while calling out, "*gomen kudasai*," a phrase that had no equivalent in English, but functioned as a polite way to let the occupants of a home know that someone was at their front door seeking an audience. Saori headed to the genkan while calling to Jack that the police had arrived.

"*Ohayō gozaimasu!*" she said with a smile when she got to the door. "*Dōzo, ohairi kudasai.*" Good morning; please come in. As Officer Suzuki removed his shoes and stepped into the house, he replied "*ojyama shimasu*," a mild apology for the intrusion meaning "I'm in the way", customarily said upon entering someone's house. They headed for the kitchen and sat around the table. Saori offered the officer tea and put some tangerines on the table, encouraging Suzuki to take one. Jack arrived after a few minutes and in Japanese apologized for the delay, indicating he was trying to figure out the meaning of a difficult kanji character.

Officer Suzuki took a sip of his tea and looking at Saori asked, "So what happened last night?"

Saori smiled gently, "We went around to the neighbor's houses to thank them for letting us move into the neighborhood. When we got back, the front door was open and both of us felt like there were subtle differences in the locations of objects in the house as well as a few things knocked over. But we didn't notice anything missing. When your father dropped by this morning to bring us some of your mom's homemade pickles, he also told us that he thought he saw movement in front of our house while we were out last night. This got us more worried."

"Thank you, Riddley-san," and then he turned to Jack, "Jack-san did you notice anything else?" Suzuki and Jack had known each other for many years and Suzuki was well aware that Jack's Japanese was fluent enough for normal conversation, so he didn't hold anything back and didn't try to talk through Saori as the inspector had done with Taitsu.

"No, I don't think so. But yesterday I did have a peculiar experience at the library. While I was looking over some books on the shelves, I felt like someone was watching me. I turned and saw the back of a Buddhist priest who seemed to be quickly turning away from me just as I looked in his direction. I didn't think much of it at the time..."

"What did he look like?"

"I'm not sure. I didn't see his face, but he had hunched shoulders and walked with a limp."

"That could describe a lot of people around here," said Suzuki. Jack nodded, and then the officer added, "I'll walk around the outside of the house. It was wet last night, so there could be a footprint. I'm not sure what to think..." As he finished his thought, the doorbell rang and they heard the door slide open.

"*Gomen kudasai!*" It was Taitsu's basso profondo echoing into the living room.

"Crap," said Jack in English as he rose quickly and then called out in Japanese, "Taitsu-san, I'm running a little late, come in and have tea while I put on my suit."

"*Hai,*" he replied as he slipped out of his shoes. When Taitsu entered the kitchen, he saw Officer Suzuki and his eyebrows rose subtly in surprise.

"*Ohayō gozaimasu*," said Taitsu.

"*Ohayō gozaimasu*," replied Officer Suzuki. Saori looked at Taitsu and explained that they had an intruder last night and Officer Suzuki was there to investigate. She took out a teacup and filled it with green tea for Taitsu, who picked up the cup with an "*itadakimasu*" and took a sip. The three of them chatted about the unusually cool weather of the past few days and then Jack entered the room in his new black suit.

"You look good!" said Taitsu, "I'm not sure I've ever seen you dressed so formally. You even combed your hair for the occasion." Always calm, Taitsu's delivery was so expressionless that sometimes it was difficult to tell that he was joking. "I think we need to go, Jack-san."

"Yes, we don't want to be late for the cremation."

"Oh, are you going to Takahashi-san's funeral?" asked Suzuki looking at Jack.

"Yes," Taitsu quickly interjected, "Jack wants to observe the funeral process for his research."

"Ah, I see," replied Suzuki, with a wisp of suspicion in his voice.

Taitsu thanked Saori for the tea and the duo headed for the *genkan* as Jack called "*ittekimasu*."

"*Itterasshai*," replied Saori, who then looked back at Officer Suzuki. "I find this a little scary, Officer Suzuki," she said with a worried look in her eyes.

"Yes, indeed, but I don't really think there is anything to worry about. Let me go outside and look around. Maybe I will find a footprint or something else that will give us a clue as to what happened." He thanked Saori for the tea, stood, and turned for the *genkan*. Saori dutifully followed him to their front door and thanked him for coming over so quickly, which was to be expected since there was usually very little for police to do around Tanohata. Twenty minutes had, in truth, been a bit long, given that the police station wasn't far away. Suzuki slid skillfully into his loafers and headed outside. Saori decided to follow him, putting on a jacket over her robe and slipping into a pair of flip flops.

Suzuki carefully looked over the entryway door and then started hunting around on the ground directly in front of the entrance. The ground was somewhat squishy under their feet as they walked around the house, a remnant from the previous evening's rain. As they carefully proceeded to the back of the house, something caught Suzuki's eye and he stepped in the direction of the hill that led down from the village to the expanse of rice fields below. He squatted down and carefully looked at the ground, stood up, and then walked over to the edge of the hill.

"Riddley-san, could you come over here?"

Saori started in his direction as he told her to go around the spot where he was squatting.

"What is it Suzuki-san?"

"I think I know what happened. Do you see that bush at the top of the hill there?" She nodded. "Notice anything?"

"The branches are broken on one side." As Saori said it, she felt her stomach jump with tension from the idea that someone had been moving around their yard and in their house.

"And please follow me over here, Riddley-san," he said politely. "There is a footprint." Suzuki seemed to be enjoying the role of sleuth and was milking the drama for all he could. They stood around the footprint and Saori sighed.

"I see," she said, and then started to laugh slightly.

"Yes, Riddley-san, you did have an intruder last night. It was a bear. We've been having more and more problems with this due to the depopulation of the area. A variety of wildlife have become aggressive in looking for food or just rummaging around in people's houses. Bear sightings are becoming common. Did you lock the front door?"

"No, I didn't."

"Well, you should. Everyone assumes that there's nothing to worry about around here when it comes to theft, which is probably right. But there are other dangers. Bears are among them."

"Yes, officer, I understand. I'll be more careful in the future," she replied somewhat sheepishly. "Still, it's frightening to think a bear was in our house last night."

"He wouldn't likely have done anything. In fact, if he heard you or something else around the house, that may be why he wasn't inside when you got back. He probably took off as soon as he heard the sounds of people outside or maybe a car going past. The bears around here are not particularly aggressive. They're not like the brown bears up in Hokkaido, that's for sure."

"Well, it's still scary. I'll lock the doors from now on."

"That is a good idea."

Saori smiled and politely invited Suzuki in for more tea, knowing he would decline, which he did, indicating that there was work to do back at the station. He opened the door to his patrol car and sat behind the wheel as Saori stood next to the car, arms folded in front her as she tried to keep warm, waiting for him to depart. She bowed as he carefully started the motor and bowed his head slightly in response. Through the open car window, he looked at her and said, "Please be careful," and started to back out as Saori replied, "Yes, I will. Thank you! You were very helpful." And then she bowed again.

8
THE FUNERAL

A few minutes past nine o'clock that morning, Taitsu's Prius pulled up in front of Takahashi's house, where a somber group of relatives and neighbors gathered. Everyone was dressed in black, the men in suits and the women in conservative, one- or two-piece outfits, sometimes accompanied by a string of pearls. As mourners arrived, they entered the house and knelt before the casket and the Buddhist family altar known as a *butsudan* to pay their respects. They then moved to another spot where everyone knelt on the floor, with their rear-ends resting on the backs of their legs. Taitsu, adorned in his black robe and freshly shaven head, settled before the *butsudan* and chanted something inaudible. He then stood, approached the casket, which had been placed in the center of the room, and after a few minutes rang a bell to signal the start of a brief ritual held around the casket that involved chanting and continued ringing of a bell. After Taitsu completed his work, the room was silent as the funeral director removed the cover of the pine coffin while one of his assistants brought out a box of white chrysanthemums accompanied by yellow and purple flowers, none of which had stems. Takahashi's wife, followed by other family members, and then neighbors in the village, carefully placed one flower each around the head of the deceased, entirely filling the space between his temples and the walls of the coffin.

Following this, an older male family member collected money from everyone, which was placed into a pouch along with two rice cakes. Years earlier at another funeral, Jack learned that this symbolically represented travelling money and food for the journey of the deceased. Symbols everywhere, Jack thought. And as his mind wandered, the anthropologist Clifford Geertz's thoughts on religion as a system of inherited ideas expressed in symbolic forms that people use to communicate and perpetuate understandings and attitudes about life kept rolling around in his head. Murder, he thought, is no less of a symbolic system than religion. Where there are humans, there is meaning expressed in symbolic form. Everything in that temple hall where they found the body—the candle, the ligature, and even the chair must have some meaning—but what is it?

As Jack's attention veered from Takahashi's departure ritual, the pouch was gently placed on the dead man's chest and the mortician returned the coffin lid to its place covering the body. The group looked on as the mortician employed a gold-colored hammer to pound six golden nails about half-way into the lid, one at each corner and two in the middle. The tap of the hammer brought Jack back from his thoughts about the murder. Takahashi's wife was handed a black stone, one side of which was flat, that she used to tap each nail a single time. After she finished, the stone was passed to other family members and then the rest of the villagers who proceeded to tap each nail once. Both Taitsu and Jack were included in the nailing rite. As the attendees finished, the mortician began hammering the nails completely into the coffin. Jack heard sniffles and a few deep breaths as the final metallic smites of death echoed through the room.

Most of the group promptly filed out of the house and stood quietly in the refreshing morning air. Shortly thereafter, six of the men carried the coffin through the sliding doors of the house. Jack didn't know any of them. They delicately placed the coffin in the hearse, which surprised Jack because it was a Cadillac, just like what is found in the States, as opposed to the ornate hearses decorated with golden dragons more common in the area. The group boarded the small bus parked along the street that would carry the grievers to the crematorium, a trip made largely in silence. The hearse arrived at the crematorium first, which allowed funeral workers to place the casket on a rolling contraption similar to a gurney in front of the doors to the furnace before everyone filed out of the bus. Surrounding the casket, each guest was handed a single stick of burning incense that they held while Taitsu and another priest Jack didn't know chanted. After a few minutes, the funeral director rolled the coffin into the cremation chamber, closed the doors, and placed a portable altar, on which had been set flowers and a picture of the deceased, in front of the furnace. Each person stood his or her burning incense stick in the ash pot situated directly in front of the picture and then departed from the furnace area, gathering outside at tables that had been set up with food, beer, and juice. Some people started to chat over the thunder as the furnace fired up disgorging huge billows of grey smoke from the smokestack overhead, signaling that Takahashi's body was on its last journey.

As the corpse and its coffin burned, mourners sat or stood around the tables. They chatted, drank beer, and one older man seemed to be getting mildly intoxicated. There were gentle, sympathetic smiles and a few tears as everyone waited. Some of the mourners decided to sit in the tatami-mat waiting room inside of the crematorium. Snacks of *dango*, compressed rice balls covered in various sweet sauces, were passed around, after which the leftovers were placed on the altar in front of the cremation doors as an offering to Takahashi's departed spirit.

Eventually the man who ran the crematorium came outside wearing a white lab coat and informed everyone that the process was complete. The cremains were rolled out from the furnace on a large stone slab and although most of it was bone dust, many clearly identifiable bones, including the pelvis, remained. Having finished his part in the ritual, Taitsu returned to the Prius and waited for Jack, who continued to watch the unfolding event. Jack wondered what had happened to the other priest who was briefly involved in the ritual; he hadn't noticed him departing.

Large wooden chopsticks were handed to the family members and Takahashi's wife used them to remove three bones from the cremains and placed them into a wooden box held by another family member. The remaining relatives followed suit and eventually all in attendance participated, including Jack, who was asked by one of the men to join the line for the bone picking.

"Jack, why are you standing over there?"

"Well, I'm not part of the family."

"You've been a member of this village for a long time and, basically, we are all related. You should join, as well."

Jack hesitated and then moved over to the end of the line, thanking the older man for inviting him to participate. With the completion of the bone-picking, a few taxi cabs appeared, and a minibus also arrived to take anyone needing transport back to the village. Jack thanked the people around him for allowing his participation and then started walking in the direction of Taitsu's Prius. As he turned, he caught a glimpse of the black-clad mourners boarding the microbus. And then he stopped. Boarding the bus was a hunched man with a limp. Jack wasn't sure if the limp involved the same leg as the individual from the library, but the overall dimensions of both men seemed about the same. For a moment, Jack thought about walking over and confronting him, but then realized that there was nothing to confront him about— there is no wrong in getting on a microbus, and Jack could not even be sure it was the same man he had seen at the library. As Officer Suzuki had noted dryly, an older man with a limp and hunch could describe many of the area's residents.

Jack opened the car door and sat next to Taitsu.

"Did you see him?" asked Jack.

"Who?"

"The guy with the limp. I saw him getting on the microbus while I was leaving. I think he might have been the guy I saw in the library."

"Really? How can you be sure?"

"I'm not. It's just a hunch."

Taitsu turned right out of the parking lot and headed for Tanohata and Jack's house. They remained largely silent throughout the drive, both immersed in thought about the events of the past few days and the mysterious presence of the limping man. They arrived at Jack's house and Taitsu told him that the temple portion of the ceremony would be held at 15:00.

"I think I'm going to pass on that, Taitsu-san. I've got some research to do."

"Sure. And the *nembutsu* will be held tonight at 20:00 in Takahashi-san's living room. I won't be at that since the priest isn't invited."

"I think I'll go to that, if it's okay."

"I don't see why not, Jack. You're a resident of the village and every household normally sends one representative."

Jack leaned back into the window of the car and reached over, putting his hand on Taitsu's shoulder. "Thanks, Taitsu-san. I really appreciate your letting me participate in this."

"No problem, Jack-san. I'll call you later or tomorrow."

"Great."

Jack stepped away from the car as Taitsu backed out of the driveway and bowed. Jack turned and headed toward the empty house, finding the front door locked. "Shit!" came the loud English response to the situation. He didn't have his key. "God dammit…" followed with a slight rise of intonation. Jack checked his pockets once more but knew where his keys were—sitting on the shoe rack in the *genkan*, which wouldn't do him much good. He stared at the front door, as if he were trying to will it open with his mind, but the door stubbornly refused to respond to his attempt at telekinesis. After a few minutes, he started tossing around how he might get into the house in his head. The back door could be unlocked, he thought, so he wandered around back only to find it in the same condition as the front. "Figures. She never locks anything and on the one day I decide to forget my keys, she carefully shuts up the house completely." As he plodded to the front of his house, the sound of a car approaching caught his attention. He turned and saw Saori pulling into the driveway, no more than the crunch of tires alerting him to the arrival of her ever-silent Tesla.

She stepped out of the car and looked at Jack, "Forget your keys?"

"How did you know…" replied Jack darkly, brows shifted downward in annoyance.

"How long have we been married?"

"Right. Can you let me in?"

"Yes, but you can get the groceries from the back of the car." Jack quietly pressed the button on the automatic trunk lid and grabbed the grocery bags. As he entered the kitchen, Saori smiled and said, "I have some news."

"News?"

"Yes, about last night."

"Oh, really. Let me guess, that great sleuth Suzuki-san arrested the intruder," responded Jack with a sarcastic tone.

"Not exactly. But he did solve the case."

"Really?" came the disbelieving reply, "I didn't know he was competent."

"Jack! Yes, really. There *was* an intruder and we know who it was." Jack's eyebrows raised and he tilted his head to the right in consideration of her attempt to drag out the explanation for dramatic effect. After a pregnant pause, Saori blurted it out: "It was a bear."

"Shit! I thought they lived up in the mountains. Are you kidding?"

"No, it was really a bear. He found a paw print behind the house. He also said that bear visits are getting more common so we should be careful to lock our doors."

"And remember our keys…"

"That, too."

"Well, I guess that's good news, although I'm not thrilled about the idea of bears waltzing around the village at night."

"Suzuki-san said that the bears are not aggressive and will normally just take off if they hear humans, which is probably why we didn't find him in the house last night when we got home. He either heard us or something going on at a neighbor's house that spooked him and he took off, not bothering to close the front door as he left…"

Jack smiled and drolly responded, "One would expect Japanese bears to be more considerate."

9
THE BLOOD OF GUTOKU

The groceries put away, Jack retired to the peace of his study. He opened the library book and continued where he left off. *Kakushi nembutsu*, he read, had a long history in the area and represented a ritual that initiated children into the community through the "blood of Shinran," one of the most revered Japanese monks and founder of the Jōdo Shinshū sect of Buddhism. As Jack read the introduction of the book, he was reminded that Shinran lived from 1173 until 1263 and his ideas profoundly influenced the development of Buddhism in Japan. Frustrated in his failures as a monk and inability to achieve enlightenment, he retreated to a temple in Kyoto where he pursued intense meditation and experienced a vision directing him to seek out another disillusioned monk named Hōnen, becoming his disciple in 1201. Supposedly, at age twenty-nine, Shinran attained enlightenment through his vow to Amida Nyorai, the Buddha of infinite light, who was usually shown sitting on a lotus pedestal with her hands together in the meditation mudra, forming a triangle above her crossed legs. Hōnen entrusted Shinran with a copy of his secret work, the *Senchakushū*, that explained the importance and method of reciting the name of Amida as a means to achieving salvation and entrance into the Buddhist Pure Land.

Shinran was a radical egalitarian. Among his more problematic notions was that Buddhist priests in Japan should not be forbidden to marry and have children, nor should they be prohibited from eating meat. He also believed that salvation through commitment to Amida should not be limited to monks and priests, but should be available for all people, regardless of social status. Enlightenment was, according to Shinran, achieved through sincere chanting of the *nembutsu* or the name of Amida, which didn't sit well with the Buddhist establishment in Kyoto, who managed to convince the military to ban the practice in

1207 when two of Hōnen's more prominent followers were accused of using *nembutsu* practice as a cover-up for sexual liaisons. The accused monks were executed while Hōnen and Shinran were exiled, with Shinran being defrocked and banished to the area of northern Japan known as Niigata.

Having lost his status as a monk, Jack read, Shinran took a new name, Gutoku, which meant "foolish, bald-headed one" and came to present himself as neither monk nor layperson. He had been required by the military government to take up farming as way to humiliate him, but Shinran instead used the opportunity to spread his ideas about enlightenment through commitment to Amida among lower social classes and his teachings spread widely, eventually forming the Jōdo Shinshū or True Pure Land sect of Buddhism, which grew into the largest sect in Japan—not exactly what the military government had in mind. However, in the region where Jack was living, Sōtō Zen Buddhism had historically been dominant and for centuries, practice of the *nembutsu* had been prohibited by the Zen priests. This led to the formation of secretive cults, usually consisting of farmers early on, but eventually even involving members of the samurai class, that practiced rituals related to the *nembutsu* despite the local ban. The remains of these cults could still be found in the *nembutsu* chanting groups that met on the night of a funeral in the house of the deceased, although these were no longer secret—in fact the *nembutsu* ritual for Takahashi was announced at the funeral in the Sōtō Zen temple so that all in the village would know what time chanting would begin.

Jack continued to read through the book, stopping often to look up difficult kanji that appeared on the pages. As the title promised, the book discussed the covert ritual that had been practiced for centuries in the area. On the pages was a fair amount of local history about the locations in which the ritual was performed, but little detail about the actual practice—most likely because it was secret. Jack dwelled for a moment on the irony of a book written about a secret ritual and smiled. The lack of detail was unfortunate, because it was this ritual that kept nagging at Jack's mind. He felt he had heard something about the practice many years in the past. Setting down the book, he opened his laptop and began a search on *nembutsu* in the database where his fieldnotes resided. There were a few entries related to the practice, but details were limited. He found one entry that discussed the involvement of children and candles and realized that was the connection he had remembered. But his notes lacked much in the way of detail of the ritual itself, instead referencing anecdotes from a few people with whom he had talked about other topics early in his fieldwork. However, his notes did point to someone who might be able to help—Abe Setsuko—a woman who was now in her late 80s and lived only a few houses away.

Jack didn't want to visit Abe that afternoon, because he needed plenty of time to have a detailed conversation; but he might see her at the *nembutsu* in the evening, he thought, and could ask then if he might visit her house the following day. So much had been going on over the past couple of days that he needed to clear his head, in any case. He grabbed his pipe, leather Dunhill tobacco pouch, matches, and a tamp, and strode out the back door to the porch that overlooked the rice fields below. Saori was coming in from hanging some laundry and admonished Jack to put outdoor flip flops on rather than walking around the deck in his stocking feet, to which he absently obliged. Jack sat in his favorite chair, filled the bowl of his Caminetto bent bulldog, and lit up. Billows of grey smoke curled from his mouth as Jack puffed. The tobacco emerged into incandescent being while thoughts of Heidegger briefly drifted through his brain. The atmosphere was hushed, with only the occasional whisper of wind. No machines whined in the distance; no voices drifted from neighboring houses. Just blissful silence. In his left hand, Jack cradled the warm briar as he gazed through the cedar trees framing the mantis-colored fields of rice in the distance. Forgetting about the smoldering tobacco, his eyes started to grow heavy as the glowing red ember extinguished itself, lacking the draw of human breath to keep it alive. He fell asleep.

After about forty minutes, the whine of a small engine startled him awake. Jack's nostrils picked up the scent of Saori's cooking—must be close to dinner time, he thought. Setting his pipe on a table, he wandered into the house where Saori was busy in the kitchen. She enjoyed cooking and thus spent quite a bit of time crafting various Japanese and Western meals for the couple; Jack enjoyed cooking, as well, but his abilities were pitifully limited compared to Saori's.

"Soba?" asked Jack as he entered the kitchen.

"Yup."

"Smells good."

"We'll be eating in about twenty minutes, could you set the table?"

"Sure. Saori—?"

"Yes."

"Do you know anything about *kakushi nembutsu*?"

"Not really. I think my mom did it when she was a child, but by the time I was growing up, no-one around our area was doing it. Why?"

"I took out a book from the library on the ritual, but it doesn't have much detail on what actually happened in the ritual itself. It's mostly just historical information on where it was performed. But I did find something interesting in my fieldnotes. A couple of people commented that the practice involved children and the use of candles."

"That's my understanding. We heard about it once in a while growing up, but I didn't pay attention. The old people around the village will certainly know. I would guess that most of them did the ritual when they were kids."

"That's what I was thinking. I'm going to try to talk to a few people over the next few days."

"I don't see why you are interested in this. Is it just curiosity?" Saori's voice rose and her left eye widened as she spoke, indicating that she suspected there was more to Jack's interest than pursuing some obscure research topic.

"No, it's Takahashi-san's death. I keep thinking about the *onbuhimo* and the candle."

"Jack—," and as Saori was about to admonish him to mind his own business, she suddenly closed her mouth and looked at him. "Hmm. That's interesting. You might be onto something."

"You see what I mean, right?"

"Yes, but I still think you should mind your own business. However, knowing that you won't, I also think you've found something worth exploring. Are you going to tell Inspector Matsumoto?"

"Not yet. I don't think he'd pay attention to me, anyway."

"You're probably right about that!"

As they were talking, Saori finished preparing their soba noodles and the couple began eating. Conversation drifted to Saori's activities for the day, which had mostly been focused on solving a complex statistical problem for a client. She had a very logical mind and was good at careful, stepwise reasoning, which was different from Jack who, although highly observant and able to focus on details, also heavily relied on intuition to arrive at solutions to the problems he encountered in his fieldwork. An exchange of ideas with Saori always had a way of pulling Jack away from leaping to conclusions about whatever he was studying.

"That was delicious, as always," Jack said as he started to clear the dishes.

"Thanks. I'll clean up. You need to get over to Takahashi-san's house for the *nembutsu* this evening, right?"

Jack looked at his watch. "Oh, it's later than I thought. I've got to go." He stood and rushed to the bedroom to throw on his new black suit and then headed out the door, calling out *ittekimasu* as he slid into his loafers. Jack had long ago learned that in Japan, shoes requiring the tying of laces were the mortal enemy of a smooth departure.

It only took about five minutes to walk to Takahashi's house. Jack encountered one of his neighbors along the way and they strode together, commenting on how sad and unexpected Takahashi's suicide had been. Jack decided not to raise the issue of murder. The sun was setting, creating an orange glow over their approach to the house along with other mourners dressed in black walking to the same destination, with a few ahead of them already entering the building. Everyone removed his or her shoes upon entrance into the *genkan*, stepped up into the house, and found a spot at which to kneel in the large tatami-mat room where a temporary altar had been set-up for the funeral, adorned with flowers and a picture of the deceased. Two of the older men were opening an old, wooden box as Jack entered the room. From it they pulled a large string of prayer beads carefully covered in a mulberry-colored silk cloth—the beads were long enough to encircle the entire room. Each bead was about the size of a fist and there were two larger beads equidistant from each other on the narrow rope that held the entire string of beads together. From his previous fieldwork, Jack knew that they had been used in the village for at least 300 years, maybe more. The age was obvious—each dark brown bead had been worn smooth over centuries of being handled during the *nembutsu* ritual. At one time, Jack counted the beads and found that there were 849 altogether, and was told that some had gone missing over the years. Most likely, the leader of the *nembutsu* group told him, there had been 1008 at one time, "It's an auspicious number in Buddhism," he explained, "but I really don't know why that's the case."

Jack helped the men spread the beads out around the room as people knelt to form a circle at the room's walls. By the time proceedings were ready to start, there were about thirty people present—one representative from many of the households in the village—all of whom were over sixty and about equally men and women. Jack could overhear a few people chatting about the households that didn't have representatives in the group and commenting that it was rude not to send someone.

After a few minutes, Satō Hitoshi knelt in front of the altar, slid around on his knees, and told everyone that they were about to begin. The tannish-green of the tatami mats generated a soft glow to the room, which was lit only by a few candles at the altar and the dim overhead lamp that dangled from the ceiling. The black clothes of all in attendance gave the room a somber feeling, but the light chatting and smiles among the group softened the pallor. Another man next to Satō, who was also named Satō, lit the two candles on the altar and removed a rod of incense from a box, lit it, and placed it in the ash dish directly in front of Satō-the-Leader. Gentle wisps of smoke arose from the altar as the spiced scents of incense began to permeate the room. Satō rang the bell next to him and started chanting in a way that was almost like singing. Dulcet tones of "*naamu aamidaaa buuutsu*," rang from the leader's voice that were then echoed by the group, all keeping time to Satō's tintinnabular ringing of the bell. As the chanting continued, members of the prayer group began circulating the beads through their upturned hands around the entire room, creating a chatter of clicking as the beads struck each other, that lasted throughout the entire twenty-minute ritual performance. When the chanting was complete, Satō turned again to the supplicants, bowed deeply, and thanked them for their participation. At that, everyone began to stand, and the sound of knees popping caused some light laughter among the group.

Jack saw Abe in the corner of the room and walked toward her as she stood. She smiled and said, "Jack-san. *Hisashiburi desu nee!*" It's been a while! Jack replied in kind and they exchanged small talk, after which Jack asked if she were free the following morning. Abe replied that nothing was going on and they agreed that he would drop by around ten o'clock. Abe smiled and bowed, as did Jack, and he started to leave the room as she turned to another of their neighbors to chat. As Jack walked home, he was accompanied by three men headed in the same direction. He decided that it would be a good opportunity to ask a few questions he had in mind following the ritual.

"I was wondering..." he paused briefly, "why were some of the houses not represented?"

"Yes, that is a problem," replied one of the men. "Every household is supposed to send one representative. It's pretty rude if you don't do that."

Another man, who looked like he was in his eighties, but still walked briskly, interjected, "True, but some households also are not permitted to join. You have to be part of the *nembutsu-kō* to participate in the ritual and not all of the households are included in that group."

"Really?" said Jack.

"Yes, you actually have to pay dues as part of the group, but not everyone wants to join."

"Not everyone *can* join in," commented the last one in the group as they walked in the dark. "You have to be initiated into the cult to participate."

"But I'm not initiated," replied Jack.

"Well, you're different. We know you are interested in this for research, and no-one is really all that strict about it anymore. I don't think anyone would stop representatives from households outside of the cult from joining in for the *nembutsu*. Other more private meetings would require membership, but we are kind of loose about this ritual."

"How is one initiated?" asked Jack.

The oldest man in the group stopped and they all followed suit. "Well, that's complicated. Children are initiated into the cult when they are about five, but the ceremony for that isn't done in this area anymore. Everyone here tonight went through the ceremony, other than you, but there are few under the age of fifty who have done so. It has largely died out, although I hear that in some of the villages out in the rice-growing areas they still do it."

Jack was silent for a moment as he thought about what he was hearing. He then asked, "What is that ceremony called?"

"*Kakure nembutsu*," replied two of the men simultaneously.

"Oh, not *kakushi nembutsu*?" said Jack.

"That's the same thing. There are just two different words for the ceremony. Children would be initiated into the cult and become one in the blood of Shinran with everyone in the village, and basically with everyone else who had gone through the ceremony. I don't think they do this in other parts of Japan."

Jack noted a tone of local pride as the older gentleman spoke about the ceremony. Clearly it no longer had the secretive qualities it once held, but it also was not something people seemed to talk much about. They started to walk again and were soon at Jack's house. He thanked them, bowed, and said goodnight as he moved to his front door, which, thankfully, was locked. He rang the bell, and Saori soon slid open the door and welcomed him home with a broad smile, followed by "*otsukaresama deshita*." You must be tired.

10
INITIATION

The following morning, Jack awoke early to spend more time reading his library book and then headed for Abe's house as planned. She and her daughter-in-law, Makiko, were waiting for Jack, happily welcoming him into their house where they sat on chairs in the living room. Makiko brought out tea and an assortment of Japanese cookies. After a few minutes of catching up, Jack indicated he had something specific he wanted to ask about. Jack had been to their house many times while conducting research in the village, so both women knew that he probably had something on his mind that he wanted to learn about—and they were always happy to oblige. It was interesting seeing their village through the eyes of an outsider with his unusual questions.

"I was wondering," asked Jack, "if either of you know anything about *kakushi nembutsu*."

There was a short pause and then almost in unison they replied, "Oh yes."

The older woman said, "I'm surprised you know about that. Nobody really talks about it nowadays. But when I was a kid, we all did it. My daughter-in-law also went through the ceremony."

"Yes, I did. I remember it well—it was scary!"

Abe began to recall her experiences, which she said were a little dim, given that it was so long ago, but she still remembered much of what happened in the ceremony, particularly with the regular confirmation of Makiko.

"I think the whole thing lasted around a week, with a big ceremony on the last day. You know this area of Japan was all Sōtō Zen temples a long time ago, which is why the ceremony was kept secret—it's connected to a different sect of Buddhism and the priesthood wouldn't have liked the idea of lay people doing the *nembutsu* ritual in the old days. At least that's what I've been told. Anyway, it was done around here up through the end of the war and continued in some areas like Tanohata for several years afterward. But no-one has done the ceremony in our village for a long time."

Makiko nodded in agreement and said, "I was in one of the last cohorts do it, I think."

"Yes, that's right," added her mother-in-law.

Jack was writing notes down carefully on his three-by-five cards as he listened to their recollections of the ritual. "Could you tell me what happened? How was the ritual performed?"

"That's secret!" laughed Abe. "But, of course, no-one cares anymore. That was a long time ago. I can tell you what I remember, at least. Maybe my daughter-in-law will remember more than I do." Makiko smiled and poured more tea as her mother-in-law continued.

"The ritual is for people who believe in Shinran. Or you can think of them as disciples of Shinran. The way I remember it is that on the day prior to the ceremony, there were practice runs that circulated around the village, occurring at a different house each day for a week prior to the actual event." Makiko nodded in agreement and both recalled that on the day of the ceremony, the street was blocked off and there were gate keepers all around the house to keep people who were believers of another religion from entering.

"That's interesting," commented Jack, "since Japanese religions don't usually require exclusive commitment in the way that Western religions do."

"I suppose it is. Never really thought about that. But the *nembutsu* was different. We were indoctrinated as children as believers bound together by the blood of Shinran. It was like a club," she paused, "… or…a cult. But it was what everyone around here did, so we didn't think much about it."

"*Okaa-san…*" Mother… came the voice of Makiko as she smiled gently in her mother-in-law's direction, "what I've been told is that the process really began long before the actual ceremony. When a child was born, they were introduced to the highest status person in the village. This was considered the beginning of entrance into the *nembutsu* cult. The parents would take the child to say "*yoroshiku onegai shimasu*" which was a request for good graces of the village leader. Not much happened after that until sometime between the ages of three and five at which time the formal ceremony my mother-in-law was talking about was performed."

"That's right. I had forgotten about the first meeting. The big ceremony was a test, really, to see if you had the merit to become one of Shinran's followers. If you didn't pass the test, you couldn't become a disciple and could not gain a blood relationship with Shinran and enter the Buddhist Pure Land."

"Oh, so if you failed, you couldn't enter Heaven?

"Yes, that's right."

"How was the test done?"

Abe paused and closed her eyes as she recalled the ritual. "The test was done in a room so dark that not even the person next to you could see your face. Black curtains were drawn and there was no light in the room. Everyone looked toward the Buddhist altar and prayed, chanting *tasuke tamae...tasuke tamae...tasuke tamae*. Save me... save me...save me. The children chanted this for what seemed like a very long time. But they had to do it without opening their eyes and without crying. That was important. All of this was led by a Master, who was from a different village along with a side person who helped. The parents and grandparents were also in the room to support the children."

"How many kids were involved?"

"I don't remember exactly, but probably ten or fifteen. I've heard that in the village where this is still done, they only get two or three children and they are rarely able to do the ceremony, due to the lack of children being born these days."

Abe's daughter-in-law added, "And the parents don't like the ritual, either. Very few parents would allow their kids to go through the whole thing nowadays. It was really, really frightening."

"Because it was dark?"

Abe perked up a bit, "Oh no! ...that was only part of it. The darkness and the chanting were scary, but the worst part was that as you chanted, the leader came around to each child and knelt on the floor in front of him or her. He would take a candle and move it very close to the face of each child to see if their eyes were remaining closed and there was no crying. He put the candle right in front of my face! I could feel the heat."

Makiko added, "And many years ago there was an accident. It seems that someone dropped the candle and it started a fire. Several of the kids were injured. I don't know much about it, but I think it contributed to brining the ritual to an end in most communities."

"Wow, that does sound frightening. Do either of you remember how long the ritual took to complete?"

"I can't remember how long the chanting lasted, but it seemed like forever," answered Abe. "I was so scared, but I kept my eyes closed and didn't cry."

Makiko interjected, "I think altogether it took at least three hours, depending on how many children were involved. It certainly felt like it was that long."

"What happened then?"

"Well, when the ceremony ended, if the leader judged the children had made it through acceptably, there was a big party with lots of sweets held in the next room."

"What about those who didn't make it?"

"They were told they failed and would have to try again the following year. If you failed at the ceremony when you were seven years-old, then you could not be part of the *nembutsu* cult and you became sort of isolated in the village."

"An outcast?"

"No, I wouldn't say that, exactly. But you couldn't participate in some of the important rituals, mostly those related to care for the dead. There were a few other things, too, that they were excluded from. And I don't think people who had been excluded ever became leaders in the community as adults. I never really thought about it, but the kids who failed probably did feel marginalized from the village."

"I would think so," said Jack nodding.

"Oh, there's one more thing you might find interesting. It wasn't just children who were initiated into the discipleship of Shinran. Wives and husbands who came into the village from other villages that did not do the ritual as children also were expected to go through the ceremony, although they could decline if they chose not to be part of the *nembutsu* cult."

"Hmm…it sounds like the ceremony functioned as a way for people to be initiated into not only the cult, but the village, too." Jack was thinking aloud, not really addressing his comments to either of them.

"That may well be," commented the younger woman, "I do remember if someone wanted to enter the house where the ritual was going on, they would be stopped. Even if it were raining or snowing, the gatekeepers would stand guard at the corners of the property to prevent anyone from entering. They looked very powerful standing straight in their *hakama*…you know, the black and white formal kimono for men." She wanted to be sure Jack knew the meaning of the word. "Even people who were born in the village but had moved away were unwelcome, as were the adults who had failed the test as children. After the ceremony, there was definitely a feeling that the children who were successful had truly become part of the community. I guess in a way, from that point onward, they were fully recognized as people. It created a feeling that the connections among the community members were even stronger than those among family. People don't feel that way about their villages now."

"Was this ritual done the same way in every village?"

Abe thought about it for a minute and then replied, "I don't think so. I seem to remember being told that in another village they did the part with the candle, but they were told that if they failed they would be thrown into the lake. We weren't told that, but…as I recall…the children who failed were taken to the barn with cows and horses and told scary stories about what would happen to them if they continued to fail. I think the adults might have even pushed or hit some of the kids. And they were told that if they failed, life would be very difficult for them as adults. It was the same for boys and girls. Sometimes, they would run the ceremony a second time on the same day for those who couldn't get through it. I think they wanted all of us to pass."

"I'm curious. Do you know who the person running the ceremony was?"

"No—. As I mentioned, the *Ue-sama*, as we called him, was always from outside the village. His identity was secret and he wore a hood and a special black kimono that was different from everyone else. All of the people were wearing their best clothes, usually dark-colored kimonos, including the children. We were told it was taboo to say his name. And no-one was allowed to even speak to him when he came for the ceremony. He was always in a separate room, other than when the actual ritual was going on. There was no contact because he was viewed as a living *hotoke*."

"That's interesting," said Jack. "So, he was viewed as enlightened, a living enlightened spirit. Fascinating."

"Yes, everyone knew that he was enlightened, but we were not allowed to talk about it. I did hear that he had undergone ascetic training far up in the mountains and that's how he became a living *hotoke*. As I understand it, in his home village he just appeared to be a normal person, but when he did the ritual, his identity changed. He was supposed to be pure, so no-one could urinate, defecate, or spit at any time while he was there for the ceremony, because it was viewed as dirty. You just had to hold it!"

"Are the people who participated in *kakushi nembutsu* the same as those who participate in the *nembutsu* that's done after the funeral like last night?"

"Oh yes... You can't be in the *nembutsu* group without having done the ritual as a child."

"But *Okaa-san*, that's changed, I think. I'd be willing to guess that no-one checks that anymore."

"Yes, you are right, Makiko. But there is the other ceremony and that one is only done by those initiated into the cult."

"Other ceremony?" said Jack.

"Yes, even before the temple priest knows about the death of a parishioner, members of the cult are informed and gather as soon as possible to chant and help the deceased on the way to the Pure Land. It happens in secret, so I probably shouldn't have told you about it."

"It's okay, I won't tell anyone," Jack smiled and assured her.

"And there's one more thing you should probably know, Jack."

"Yes?"

"If a woman who is a member of the cult marries a Buddhist priest, she was forced to quit the cult. I only know this because there was talk when I was young about my marrying the head priest at Taiyō-ji. That never was arranged, but my parents told me that if it happened, I would have to leave the group. And even now, most of the people in the group do not eat fish or meat on the twenty-eighth day of each month, which is the death day of Shinran, I think."

"Thank you both for this information. It's very interesting." Their conversation drifted away from *kakushi nembutsu* to the unusually cold weather for June. They sipped more tea and enjoyed some rice crackers that Makiko had brought into the room. It had warmed up outside quite a bit and Makiko opened the sliding doors to bring some of the fresh air into the cool, unheated living room in which they were sitting. After another thirty minutes, Jack looked at his watch and said, "*soro soro*" indicating that it was time he depart for home. Mother and daughter-in-law thanked him with warm smiles and all bowed as Jack backed out of the genkan.

"*Mata asobi ni kite kudasai!*" Please visit again!"

"Thank you, I will come by again soon."

Jack turned and started to walk in the direction of his house. After only a few meters, he felt his cell phone vibrating and pulled it out of his pocket. It was Taitsu.

Jack pressed answer, "Hi Taitsu-san."

"Jack. Are you at home?"

"No, but I'm walking in that direction. What's up?"

"I'll be over in a few minutes. There's been another death..."

11
MURDER

Taitsu arrived at Jack and Saori's house only a few minutes after Jack. He looked somewhat frazzled and seemed to lack the usual serenity that was part of his general aura. Saori, Jack, and Taitsu sat around the table—Jack had already told Saori that Taitsu was coming over and there had been another death. Jack set out teacups while Saori prepared tea for the trio. Taitsu seemed much more worried now—he was even fidgety with his leg bouncing up and down—than he had been after the first incident. Jack looked at his friend and realized Taitsu had no thoughts that suicide was the motive behind this particular death, and probably not the other one, either.

"So, what happened, Taitsu-san?"

"As I said on the phone, there was another death. This time at the temple near the crematorium—Houn-ji. It's another Sōtō Zen temple and the head priest is a relative of mine. He called me this morning to let me know."

Saori had a concerned look on her face. She could see that Taitsu was struggling emotionally with the situation and was worried about her friend. "Does Etsuko-san know about this? I would imagine she would be very worried."

"Yes, I told her shortly after I found out about it. And, yes, she is very frightened."

"So... What happened, Taitsu-san? Do you have the details?" interjected Jack.

"I have some of them. It was similar to what happened the other day. They found an older man dead right in front of the altar of the main hall of the temple."

"Candle?"

"Yes, the man had a candle in his left hand, just like the Takahashi-san. It had been lit and burned down to his hand, as well. And there's something else…" Taitsu's voice grew increasingly ominous as he explained the murder at Houn-ji.

"Let me guess. He was hanged with an *onbuhimo*."

"I'm not sure about the weapon," and Taitsu's voice grew quieter, "but this time, it wasn't a hanging. And he *was* strangled. It is clearly a murder—no question of suicide on this one."

"Well, it is obvious that what happened at Taiyō-ji was not a suicide," added Jack. "And I don't see any way the two murders are not linked together. Have you talked with Matsumoto-san?"

"Right after I told Etsuko, he called me. He wants to meet with both of us in about thirty minutes at Houn-ji."

"Okay, let's go."

"Mind if I tag along?" said Saori, which surprised Jack mildly.

"Of course not," the two men responded together. They left the house, being sure to lock the front door behind them, and piled into Taitsu's Prius. The ride to Houn-ji only took about ten minutes and was travelled in silence as each of them thought about the events of the past few days and what might lie ahead when they met with Inspector Matsumoto. As their vehicle approached the temple, Jack could see the police cars in the parking lot at the bottom of the hill from which Houn-ji peered over the green rice fields stretched out below. In the parking lot, Jack noticed Matsumoto standing near one of the patrol cars, wearing a dark blue suit and conservative striped tie. It was the standard businessman outfit common throughout Japan and it seemed appropriate in its lack of originality; it correlated with Jack's opinion of the inspector's intellect. Taitsu steered the Prius into the parking lot, where a uniformed police officer waved his white-gloved hands to direct them to a parking space. They exited the Prius and walked in the direction of Matsumoto, who made no effort to meet them part-way and didn't actually even acknowledge that they were heading in his direction.

Taitsu was the first to speak. "Inspector Matsumoto!" he called out. The inspector looked up and trained his gaze on the three of them as they hurried in his direction.

"Murakami-san, thank you for coming so quickly. And, Liddley-san, thank you." Jack was rather surprised at how polite the inspector suddenly seemed. Maybe this wasn't going to be as unpleasant as he imagined.

"Who is this?" came the suddenly gruff query as Matsumoto looked in the direction of Saori. He had returned to his former blunt, or as Jack thought, rude pattern of speech.

Saori smiled and responded politely with her name, indicating that she was the wife of Jack and had decided to come along as well.

"Hmm," replied Matsumoto, seeming slightly offended that they did not follow his directions precisely. "And you are from this area?"

"Yes, I grew up just a few kilometers to the west of this temple."

"I see. Let's walk to the temple," and he abruptly began to walk toward the uneven stone steps leading to the main temple hall. They proceeded in silence, following the inspector as he worked his way through police cars and an ambulance that sat between them and the steps. The atmosphere became much quieter as they ascended above the activity in the parking lot and arrived at the green formal garden just outside of the main hall of the temple, at which Matsumoto stopped and turned toward the three visitors.

"Murakami-san, you know what happened, right?"

"Yes."

"And I assume you have told them about it?"

"Yes, I have."

"Good. Liddrey-san..." Jack, noting the struggle the inspector was having with the L's and R's in his name, interrupted letting him know that "Jack" was just fine and he didn't need to be so formal.

"Ah," said the inspector, "thanks—your name is a bit of a challenge." For the first time, Jack noted a mild hint of humor in the inspector's persona, which left him thinking that perhaps Matsumoto wasn't quite as stupid and wooden as he had initially thought.

"First, Jack-san... I owe you an apology," the inspector's body stiffened and he bowed slightly.

Jack's eyebrows lifted as he was completely taken aback by the comment.

"Uhh…" responded Jack, with something less than his usual level of articulation.

"You were clearly right. The hanging at Taiyō-ji the other day was not a suicide. It was a murder, much like the murder that happened here last night. I am sorry that I ignored your ideas. In fact, that mistake was costly, because—as you noted—we should have done an autopsy. I take full responsibility."

"I…uh…"

Matusmoto bowed deeply and said in a curt and somewhat louder voice, "*Sumimasen-deshita!*" I am deeply sorry! "*Yurushite kudasai!*" Please forgive me! The inspector offered his sincere apology in full bow with the bald spot at the top of his head facing Jack.

Still both tongue-tied and in a state of disbelief, Jack stammered a bit and then finally managed to blurt out, "*Mochiron desu. Zenzen mondai nai…*" Of course, it's absolutely no problem. He went on to assure the inspector that there were no hard feelings of any kind and that he was happy to be of any help possible. Looking on, Saori suppressed a mild chuckle as she watched her husband try to figure how to respond to the intense apology of the inspector. It was a rare occurrence to see Jack at a loss for words. In her experience, Sam had been the only person who ever managed to put Jack in such a position.

With the apology expressed and accepted, they quickly returned to a less formal approach to their conversation and both Jack and Taitsu noticed that the inspector's demeanor had completely changed. He seemed much less stiff and formal and much more conversational.

"I'd like to take you to see the body. Saori-san, perhaps you would prefer to wait outside?" said the inspector rather gently, "it is rather gruesome."

"No, I'll be fine. But thank you for thinking of me."

"Okay, then let's walk into the main hall." They removed their shoes in the genkan and stepped up into the main hall, where Jack noticed the same odor he had at Taiyō-ji. Saori's face twisted in response to the growing stench. Jack looked over at Taitsu, who had walked toward

the body and then turned back to face the group. His face was ashen—
it looked as though he was going to faint. They rushed in his direction,
but the priest remained upright.

"Taitsu-san, are you okay?" said Saori. And then Jack realized why
Taitsu looked so shocked. Jack peered at the body and knelt down
beside the twisted corpse. Just as Taitsu had indicated, the man had
been strangled. That was bad enough, but Jack quickly realized that it
was the murder weapon that had shocked Taitsu.

"Oh my god!" gasped Saori in English as she looked in the direction
of Jack.

"I would not believe this if I weren't looking at it," replied Jack in
a shaky voice, also using English in something of a monotone. The
inspector calmly asked them to return to Japanese.

"*Gomennasai,*" I'm sorry, came Jack's somber reply with a slight
bow. The four looked at the corpse lying in front of them. The man's
legs were wrenched in opposite directions. There clearly had been a
struggle. He was lying face-up and displayed purple bruising around
the neck and cheeks. And the look on his face was one of terror. His
right hand was clasped around the murder weapon at his neck, as it
must have been when the murderer dropped the lifeless body where it
rested. Jack leaned a little closer to the body to look at something that
caught his attention.

"Please don't touch anything, Jack-san," said the inspector politely.
Jack nodded. He then stood and met eyes with Inspector Matsumoto,
who was standing close to Taitsu in silence. Saori had turned away
from the scene and Jack could hear her taking a couple of deep breaths.

"I really don't know what to say." There was a long pause as Jack
gathered his thoughts. "Is the murder weapon what I think it is?"

"Yes," said Taitsu, "it's exactly what you think it is. There is no
mistake. He was strangled with a string of prayer beads just like the
one used at the *nembutsu* ceremony for Takahashi-san last night. It
looks like the same set of beads…" Taitsu choked his words and Jack
could see tears welling up in his eyes. Saori had returned and put
her arm around their friend, who was shaking. Buddhism, thought

Jack, is a religion of peace and caring, and in Japan, mostly caring for the dead. How horrible Taitsu must feel seeing this ghastly murder committed with a ritual object intended to help people feel calm in the face of lost loved ones.

"What was his name?" asked Jack quietly.

"Satō Makoto."

PART II

FIELDWORK IS MURDER

12
THE GHOST

O n a late August day in 1995, Fujita Fumie was enjoying a quiet afternoon reading in the large, leather chair that took up quite a bit of space in the compact living room she and her husband usually reserved for entertaining guests. Glass sliding doors opened out to look over a green formal garden with its carefully manicured bushes and trees, beyond which was a large vegetable patch planted with red onions, asparagus, and blueberries. The Fujitas were among the samurai descendants of Tanohata and, as a result, lived in one of the expansive and elegant homes that clustered together in a few parts of the village. Theirs was not among the centuries-old buildings with dark, hand-hewn beams and open rooms floored in tatami-mats. Like many of their neighbors, they had demolished the historic family residence during the post-war rush to create the future and forget the past. Besides, as Fumie had told Jack on one occasion, the ancient house was drafty and cold in the winters—not a good place in which to grow old.

Fumie turned the pages of her book as she enjoyed the warmth of the early afternoon sun that glowed across the gardens and into her living room. A gentle breeze billowed the thin lace curtains, softening the golden rays of light as they entered through the open sliding doors. Quite suddenly, the breeze turned strangely cold and Fumie set her book down, thinking that perhaps they were in for a quick rain shower. But that didn't make sense—there wasn't a cloud in the sky. A door slammed inside the house and then a strong breeze pushed through the room, sending a chill through Fumie's compact body. She stood and walked into the kitchen, where she thought she heard the door slam, and found all the cabinet doors open. More intrigued than frightened, she sat on a kitchen chair and wondered at the oddness of the situation. As soon as the event had started, she already had in her mind an idea of what might be going on.

Fumie's husband, Fujita Tsuyoshi, had long been one of the leaders of the village. Theirs was one of the most prominent households and although he had not been born into her household, his role was that of eldest son because he had been adopted into Fumie's family as an adult male to take over the responsibilities of first son. Fumie's older brother, who would have taken on that role, was killed during the war, leaving only daughters as descendants of their long family line. Due to the importance of the Fujita household in the village, Tsuyoshi had taken on many community leadership roles over the years, including heading-up the reconstruction of the cemetery, a project that had been completed only a few months earlier. It was a complex endeavor that involved removing every gravestone, one for each family associated with the temple, and their underlying human remains. The old stones were then replaced with new ones, after which they re-interred the village ancestors under new graves. It was a long and expensive process.

Fumie thought about her husband's role in the reconstruction and then about the upheaval to the graves that the project had caused. As she recalled, when the remains of the ancestors were exhumed, she frequently heard things like footsteps in the house and doors opening and closing. It often seemed as though somebody was in the house even when she knew she was entirely alone. At the time, she imagined there would have been many small pieces of bone, such as fingers, that no-one knew to whom they belonged as they reorganized and rebuilt the many graves in the cemetery. This might have, as Fumie thought about it, caused the creation of *muenbotoke*, Japan's wandering, unattached spirits of the dead for whom no-one conducted the customary ancestor memorials and who, as a result, were lonely and lost in the world of the living.

Fumie stood and looked around the kitchen, carefully eyeing every corner of the room. She then called out in a loud voice, "*Ikimashyō ka?*" Shall we go?

With that, Fumie purposefully started out of the house, slipping into her shoes at the *genkan* and calling once more with a softer voice and in a more informal style to reassure the spirit, "*Ikō-ka?*" Shall we go?

She walked past the formal garden, down the gravel driveway and turned in the direction of Taiyō-ji. As she approached the house of Kobayashi, another of the samurai descendants and one of the largest estates in the village, she started feeling a heavy weight on her body and finally couldn't continue. She decided to rest and sat down on the curb in front of what was left of the Kobayashi estate. Years earlier, the land had been occupied by one of the more opulent and expansive houses in the village. The Kobayashis were important— centuries in the past, their ancestors had been the highest ranked vassals who served the Lord of the castle that once was the center of village life. They were highly respected and successful in anything they endeavored to achieve. But all of that had been lost about twenty years earlier, when Kobayashi's father remarried after his first wife and mother of his children passed away from cancer. Upon the death of Kobayashi's father, the second wife managed to gain control of the estate—something that never could have happened before the end of the war—and sold off all of the property. The grand house was torn down and the land was divided into six plots on which five new, prefabricated houses for young families were built. These were the newest residents of the village.

Kobayashi sued his step-mother and managed to gain control of one of the six plots of land, on which he built a tiny, two-room shack with the small inheritance he also acquired from the lawsuit. The entire event had sent the once proud Kobayashi Tetsura, the eldest son and successor to the family line and its estate, into despair. As locals told the successor Kobayashi's story, he was often found passed out on the streets of the village, or in a drunken stupor wandering around late at night or even sometimes early in the morning. According to other residents, he had spent many months in a mental hospital trying to deal with the depression that had followed the loss of his inheritance, his title, and in many respects his sense of honor as the head of a once proud and powerful household.

Fumie rested and tried to catch her breath. As she sat on the curb in front of Kobayashi's former property, a neighbor came by and noticed her sitting on the roadside.

"Fumie-san, are you ill?" asked the neighbor, "your face is very pale. Are you ok?"

"I'm fine. Just resting. Nothing to worry about. But thank you!" Fumie looked up at her neighbor and smiled. The neighbor slowly moved on, but was clearly concerned about her friend, who stood and began slowly making her way again in the direction of Taiyō-ji. As she reached the bottom of the stone steps, she wondered if there was any chance she might actually be able to climb to the top with the heavy weight she carried. *Gambatte*, she thought to herself. Do your best. Persevere. She started to lift her cumbrous legs one step at a time, being careful not to lose her balance on the uneven stones. It seemed to take an eternity to reach the top, but when she did, she paused and took a few deep breaths, after which she walked through the temple gate and into the cemetery. She stood in front of the red-bibbed and hatted statues of the Bodhisattva Jizō, put her hands together in prayer, bowed, and asked for their mercy. The burden lifted.

Fumie felt good. Her suddenly light body turned toward the gate almost without any mental direction and she walked buoyantly down the steps back onto the road. As she followed the path to her house, she thought about the spirit of the *muenbotoke* that had been haunting her house. How sad, she thought... so lonely not being with the other ancestors and not being able to find his way home. Fumie knew that spirits of the dead were real and often haunted the world of the living. Of that she had no doubts. She had experienced the heavy weight other times in her life, usually when a relative died. And there was also the time that something was running all around the house opening and closing doors and windows. On that day, three of her friends were there and saw the whole thing. Nothing to be scared about, she thought, just lonely spirits trying to find some care and consolation from the world of the living.

When she arrived at home, Fumie strode directly to the kitchen, where she took out some rice grains and placed them at the altar and prayed for the well-being of the *muenbotoke* she had walked back to the cemetery. It was a little ritual she would continue daily for the rest of her life.

13
INSPECTOR MATSUMOTO

Inspector Matsumoto motioned to Taitsu, Jack, and Saori to leave the main hall of the temple. They had all had enough of the grisly scene, even Inspector Matsumoto. They moved through the *genkan* and out into the green open space near the house in which Houn-ji's priest resided. There was a picnic table next to the flower garden where they decided to sit and take a few minutes to inhale some fresh air and clear their heads of the images of the victim. After some moments of quiet contemplation, Matsumoto spoke in a calm voice. Jack found that, quite contrary to his initial impressions, he was coming to actually like Matsumoto, particularly once the gruffness faded and he could see more of the real person that inhabited the body across the table.

"The reason I wanted to see you and Jack-san, was to ask for your help. As you know, crime isn't much of a problem here, and in my twenty years as a police officer, I have never experienced anything like this. We have many good people on the police force and will also get some help from the Morioka police, but this is unprecedented. At the moment, I don't have any idea who would do something like this."

Jack and Taitsu nodded, but remained silent. Taitsu still looked shaken from the scene in the temple and Saori gently rested her hand on his arm.

The inspector continued, "As I said, I need some help. Taitsu-san, you are close to people around town—you know everyone in the village of Tanohata and are well-connected to people throughout the entire town of Nakadomari. Do you have any ideas about who might do something like this?"

Taitsu sighed with a deep exhale as he furled his brow in thought. "Honestly, Inspector, I can't think of anyone who would do something like this. Could it be an outsider? Maybe someone drifting through town?"

"It could be. There are occasional drifters who move through this area, but they are uncommon. Besides, how would such a person get ahold of the prayer beads?"

"Of course," responded Taitsu, "that would be virtually impossible. They are kept in the house of one of the residents of Tanohata. You would have to know they exist let alone where to find them."

"Right," responded Matsumoto. "Are there any standing conflicts or feuds in the village or its neighboring areas that might be lurking?"

Taitsu thought about the inspector's question pensively. After a few moments of silence, he began to speak slowly and with precision. "Well, I want to be careful here. I don't want to throw suspicion on someone without evidence."

Matsumoto quickly interrupted, "Yes, I fully understand. I'm not asking for you to suggest suspects. I'm just trying to get a sense if there could be any motives among residents of the village."

"Understood," said Taitsu. "There is one long-standing issue, but I can't see how it might have led to this. One of the samurai descendants in the village has had many difficulties in his life. His step-mother basically absconded with his family property and sold it after his father died. After that, he experienced depression and years of alcoholism. He certainly has suffered in life."

"That's very interesting," replied Matsumoto with a thoughtful gaze in the direction of Taitsu.

"It is, but there is more to consider here. As I said, Kobayashi-san suffered greatly over many years, but he also found his way with the help of a small group of Christians who make use of one of the old samurai houses as a meeting hall."

"Christians?" interjected Jack. "What sect? I was completely unaware that they were in the village."

Taitsu looked in Jack's direction and smiled weakly with his head nodding slightly downward. "They moved in several years ago, long after you were living here for your fieldwork. I think they are from a sect called *Ehoba*, or something like that. I really don't know anything about them. They visit everyone's house, it seems like once a month, trying to convert us all to Christianity. It's actually quite distasteful, but I will admit that they helped Kobayashi-san find his way. He's been a different person since he joined with them."

"Jehovah's Witnesses," commented Jack.

"Yes, that's it."

"Do you know anything about them, Jack-san?" asked the inspector.

"Not a lot, but they are basically harmless, I think. They are an evangelical sect of Christianity that believe they are the restoration of the earliest form of the religion. Like other Christian sects, they believe that all humans are fundamentally sinful. They have some unusual ideas—they reject all blood transfusions, but I don't know why they do this. They will refuse blood transfusions even in situations that are life-threatening. This has often come up as a problem in America when a Jehovah's Witness child is in need of a transfusion."

"I thought you didn't know much about them…"

"I don't, but I did read a couple of articles about them at one time—that's really all I remember."

"Doesn't sound like a group that would be bent on murdering old men in rural Japan," added Matsumoto.

"No, I think not," responded Jack, "but one wonders about the psychological state of Kobayashi-san. I've met him a couple of times and will admit I have always found him rather strange."

"I agree," said Taitsu, "but being strange isn't a motive for murder."

"True enough." There were again a few moments of silence among the group, eventually broken up by Saori's peaceful voice.

"The choice of murder weapons for both deaths has to be meaningful. I think that suggests that it must be someone local and someone with a long history in the area—who else would know anything about the prayer beads? Or the candles?"

"The candles, right," said Matsumoto under his breath, and then much more directly, "We have a lot of questions and some interesting, but difficult, evidence to interpret. Right now, I don't know what any of this means. And that's what I'm hoping you can help me with. Murakami-san, I'd like to ask you to keep your eyes and ears open at the temple and around town." He said this intently looking the priest in the eye. "Think about who might have an issue with these two men or maybe with Sōtō Zen. I don't know what, but it could be anything at this point. Jack-san, I'd like you to actually poke around. I did some research on you last night. You seem to be an accomplished anthropologist. I majored in anthropology in college, so I have some idea about what you do for a living. Perhaps you can make use of your knowledge of ethnographic methods to subtly investigate what's going on around here," he put a strong emphasis on the word subtly.

Jack was quite surprised by the request, and show of confidence, by Matsumoto. He replied somewhat hesitantly, "I… I'd be delighted to help in any way I can."

Matsumoto turned to Saori and said, "Liddley-san, your help would also be appreciated. Maybe you can just talk with people in the village and learn about what they are thinking. Nothing like some good gossip to point to the truth. And I think your being a woman will give you some different access to people. I believe that this is going to be a difficult case and I truly appreciate all of your help." Jack was starting to actually like Matsumoto.

"Of course, I'll do what I can, but I'm leaving for Tokyo on business tomorrow, so won't be able to help much, unfortunately. I'm sorry," responded Saori. "And in Japan I actually go by my Japanese name, so you can feel free to call me Ogasawara if you wish. Or I'm happy with Saori, as well."

Matsumoto smiled and said with a slight nod of the head, "*Arigatō*. That is greatly appreciated, Ogasawara-san. And even if you don't have time to talk to anyone, just having your ideas will be very helpful, I'm sure." He then turned to Jack and said with a smile, "You have an incredibly annoying family name…" They all laughed, and some of the day's tension eased. In unison, the group rose from the table and bowed. Matsumoto thanked them again, and they all thanked him for asking for their assistance. It was a typical Japanese departure, with many shows of appreciation and several bows. Jack, Taitsu, and Saori walked down the steps, through the parked patrol cars, past the ambulance where the body of the victim was being loaded, and into the Prius. As they pulled out of the parking lot, Jack said, "Lunch?"

"Yeah, I'm hungry," replied Taitsu. "Where shall we go?" And all at once, they said, "Maru Matsu!" It was a favorite family restaurant that they often dined at together. "Why don't you call Etsuko-san and see if she can join us?" said Saori. Etsuko was, in fact, able to join and the two couples enjoyed a pleasant conversation over standard Japanese fare while catching up on life. They largely avoided discussion of the murders. After a couple of hours, Taitsu dropped Jack and Saori off at their house and returned to the temple.

"Doesn't look like any bears have been poking around our house while we were gone," said Jack.

"Nope, all clear."

Once in the kitchen, Jack said, "I need a drink," and poured himself a scotch on the rocks. Saori poured some white wine into a glass. Jack started a fire in the wood stove to take off a bit of a late afternoon chill that had rolled in and they sat in the living room sipping their drinks.

"What do you think about this, Saori?"

"I really don't know. It's unexpected for this area. I've never heard of even one murder, let alone two in less than a week. And the use of the prayer beads was horrid."

"Yes. Well, not much we can do about it now. I think I will finish my scotch and then do some more reading to see what I can learn about the *nembutsu*. Tomorrow, I'll begin a little fieldwork along the lines the inspector suggested. An interesting challenge, to be sure."

"Jack, be careful. There is real danger here. I know Matsumoto-san asked for your help, but I'm worried; I wouldn't want anything to happen to you." They embraced, and Saori held on a little longer than usual. Jack then downed what was left of his scotch and headed into his study, where he sat at the desk and gazed out the window. He thought about the events of the past few days and started to write fieldnotes on his computer. It was important to get everything down that he could, not only to record what had happened but to help him sort through the complex maze of events. He typed for several hours, not even responding when Saori called that dinner was ready. She knew what he was doing and decided not to call out a second time. At about nine o'clock, Jack walked out of his study and into the living room where he found Saori sitting on the sofa and looking out the window.

"Hey, are you okay?"

"I'm okay, Jack, just a bit shaken from today, now that I've had time to reflect on everything." Jack sat next to her and put his arm around her shoulder. As they felt the warmth of the wood stove, they silently looked out the window and contemplated the darkness that had descended over their garden and their lives.

14
KOBAYASHI

U sually a light sleeper, Jack had an oddly good night's rest. Saori, in contrast, had not slept well. A fitful night had resulted from worries about the morning and her planned trip back to Tokyo. Despite knowing that Jack could handle himself quite well, she didn't want to leave him alone. But there was work that needed to be completed in the city and she had little choice in the matter. Several meetings had been scheduled with clients that required her presence in person, rather than remotely. She rose at three in the morning and started packing what she would need while away. At around seven, Jack awoke, showered, and joined Saori for a light and quiet breakfast. After eating, they packed the Tesla and Jack drove to the station where Saori would catch the next bullet train bound for Tokyo. They waved good-bye at the entry gate to the tracks and Saori took the escalator to the platform. After she boarded the train, she looked out the window thinking about the past few days and hoping that Jack would be safe.

Jack walked slowly back to the Tesla and listened for the whoosh of the bullet train departing the station before driving off. He would miss Saori, but was also somewhat energized by having a "research" project before him. And the thought of Saori being safely in Tokyo made him feel more comfortable. As he headed down the road from the station, he spied the Lawson convenience store at the corner and stopped to pick up a parfait. When Irene arrives, we'll have to make another trip, he thought. "Maybe she and Saori can head north together when Saori is done with her work in Tokyo," he said to himself.

The drive back to Tanohata was uneventful. He spent most of it thinking about how he would begin his fieldwork assignment. He'd have to walk around the village and see who he could talk with. Maybe start with Fujita, who always was happy to chat about her ghost stories and the local gossip. And she would have the scoop on how Kobayashi was doing these days. I should probably stop and talk with Kobayashi, too, he thought, although he didn't really want to do that, because Kobayashi always struck him as uncannily eerie. No matter; it would have to be done—and probably a good idea to get it over with. He pulled into their driveway and parked the Tesla in the car port. Rather than heading straight out for fieldwork, however, he went inside and enjoyed his chocolate parfait.

Thirty minutes later, Jack emerged from his house and started walking in the direction of Kobayashi's shack. It was only a hundred meters or so from Jack's place. He approached the tiny abode with its brown metal siding and red tin roof. The building looked out of place next to the shining, modern and large two-story houses with ceramic siding that had been built on his former family land. The building was shabby, with weeds growing uncontrolled all around and dull shades that suggested an immediate need for fresh paint. Jack walked around to the side of the shack, where there was a sliding glass door representing the only entrance into the building. He hesitated to ring the bell, remembering the last time he had visited Kobayashi at home. After a moment, he touched the button and heard the chimes inside. Noises rustled from within and he heard the shuffle of feet moving toward the door, where he saw a dark shadow emerge into the genkan through the frosted glass. Jack remembered the building was so cheaply made that the genkan did not even have a step up into the house. It was merely a concrete area cut out of the vinyl flooring that covered the rest of the house's foundation slab. The door slowly slid open and Jack saw Kobayashi exactly as he had remembered him. It was frightening.

Kobayashi's eyes bulged from beneath his bald cranium, which Jack thought gave him the vague look of something out of the 1960s American television show *The Outer Limits*. He was short and slight of build and always seemed to be wearing the same tan work pants and matching jacket. It was when Kobayashi smiled that the full terror of his appearance had become evident in the past. The last time he visited, Kobayashi's wide mouth opened to reveal two rows of black stumps that had once been teeth. The image was accompanied by a faint whiff of bad breath. In all his years traveling, Jack had never encountered anything quite like it and had no desire to see it again. And smile Kobayashi did, but instead of stumps, thankfully, there were two rows of gleaming white teeth. Dentures. Kobayashi welcomed Jack and told him that he was happy to see him after so long. Jack reciprocated and asked if he might chat for a few minutes, as he was working on a new research project and Kobayashi had been quite helpful in the past teaching him about local life. This wasn't entirely true, but they had at least talked a few times and Jack had always found Kobayashi receptive to conversation with the foreign anthropologist.

Jack thought to himself it would be difficult to ask Kobayashi questions about his past. How do you ask someone about his life as a drunk? And the Japanese generally didn't like to talk about mental health issues, a fact that Jack had long understood from his research on suicide, so he didn't expect to get very far. He was wrong. After only a few minutes, Kobayashi started talking about his experiences with the Jehovah's Witnesses and how they had saved him from despair and endless suffering. He was happy for the first time in years. Kobayashi did not, however, talk about how he had come to be in the difficult situation he experienced earlier in life. There was no mention of his father, nor his step-mother, although he did note that he missed his biological mother greatly at one point. Jack decided to ask him if he had done the *kakushi nembutsu* as a child.

"What? Oh, *kakure nembutsu*. Yes, I did that. We all did."

"Can you tell me what it was like?" Kobayashi's face grew slightly ashen and he seemed hesitant to answer.

"I don't know. It was a long time ago. I'm over seventy now. It's hard to remember. But I do know that it was dark, and I was very scared. They almost burned my face with a candle. I hated it. I think I cried... Maybe. I'm not sure. But I passed. I think it might have been the second or third try. I really can't be sure."

"Did they threaten you or try to scare you when you failed the first time?"

Kobayashi looked very uncomfortable. He nodded, but didn't say anything. Rising abruptly, he apologized for not having served tea and told Jack that he needed to go to a doctor's appointment. Maybe they could talk again another day? It was clear that the conversation had ended, and Kobayashi didn't want to discuss his childhood experiences with *kakushi* or *kakure nembutsu*. Was he hiding something? Or maybe they were just bad memories he didn't want to dredge up. Interesting. As Jack walked home, he tried to recall the *nembutsu* ceremony for Takahashi and realized that Kobayashi had been missing. That was not normal. Kobayashi was the *only* representative of his household and, thus, was expected to be at the ceremony. Why had he skipped it? He would have to ask some other neighbors if they had any ideas about that one. As Jack mulled things over, he realized that he was walking very fast, at a speed close to a trot. He hadn't realized just how much he didn't want to spend time with Kobayashi.

Jack's smart phone buzzed in his pocket and he pulled it out to find George on the line.

"Hey George."

"Hey."

"What's up?"

"Not much. Just thought I'd check in and see how the retirement is going."

"Just great. There have been two murders in Nakadomari since I arrived, one of them in the main hall at Taiyō-ji."

"Haha. Very funny. No, how is it really going?"

"That's how it's really going."

"What? Are you kidding? In Nakadomari?"

"Yeah, rather gruesome murders, too. One a hanging and the other a strangulation. It's pretty weird. How are things with you?"

"A lot better than that. I've been installing seismic stations around a volcano in Hawaii. It's a tough job, but someone has to do it." They laughed and the conversation continued on the lighter side with updates on George's life and the new girlfriend who had entered it recently. Saori would be happy. She always worried about George, who often seemed more interested in his research than other aspects of life like marriage and having a family. When Jack arrived at home, he walked around back and settled on the porch to chat with George. The conversation turned to music, something father and son enjoyed both listening to and making. After they disconnected, he put the phone down and pulled out a pipe. Time for some thinking, he thought to himself. The Ashton Cumberland poker was robust in his hand with rippled texture from the sandblasted finish. Just what he needed to think for a while before doing further walking around the village. He went inside to grab his laptop, not bothering to take his shoes off— since Saori wasn't home—and settled down on the porch to write detailed fieldnotes about his conversation with Kobayashi as smoke billowed from the pipe. He was following his normal fieldwork pattern, one he had learned in graduate school. As soon as possible after an important conversation, record everything that was discussed and describe the location of the conversation in as much detail as possible. Years of experience combined with careful training in graduate school meant that Jack was astute at remembering and recording details. The exercise of writing fieldnotes also had an additional function of helping the anthropologist to think about what he had experienced. Perhaps in working through their exchange, Jack thought, more ideas would come to mind.

They didn't. As Jack carefully recounted his conversation with Kobayashi, very little seemed to emerge that would be helpful. The only interesting aspect of their interaction was Kobayashi's unwillingness to discuss the *kakushi nembutsu* in any detail and his abrupt termination of their meeting. It could be that he was telling the truth and had a doctor's appointment. But it was also possible that he was hiding something and didn't want to talk about the difficult experience from his childhood and the feelings of marginalization that may have followed during his life in the village, although he did say that he had eventually passed the ritual test. It was also strange that Kobayashi had not attended the *nembutsu* ceremony following Takahashi's funeral. Jack had suspicions, but nothing solid enough to make it worth bothering Matsumoto with. Everything was rather opaque.

As Jack pondered the greenery beyond his porch, he decided to return to his practice of reading over old fieldnotes each evening whenever he was collecting ethnographic data. He had started as a graduate student when working on his doctoral dissertation research and had continued it each evening while in the field. Write up the day's fieldnotes and then spend at least a few minutes reading and pondering over notes from prior days. This evening, he thought, it might be more profitable to look over fieldnotes from several years ago, rather than thinking about events of the past few days. Something about this whole thing seemed very old. He searched on the term *nembutsu* and started to flip through the entries that contained information on the topic. As he read his summaries of each entry in the database where he recorded fieldnotes, one stood out. It was from an interview he had held over two decades earlier in which a man from the village was telling him about *kakushi nembutsu*. The man had given Jack a copy of an ancient document that was read at the completion of the ceremony to the parents of the children who had passed their test and was again read by the *Ue-sama* to the initiates at a ceremony later in life when they joined the village as new adults. As he looked through the entry, Jack remembered how difficult it had been to translate. It was hand-written and the characters were classical Japanese, making it virtually impossible for Jack to read without getting some help from a native speaker. The old man had kindly devoted quite a bit of time to helping Jack work through the document.

Bunmei 3 (Gregorian Calendar Year 1471)

You are fortunate to have your desire achieved. I am now going to tell you, as my mission, about the oath that you must follow as long as you live. You need to listen to me very carefully.

As all of you know, it has been believed that people go to Hell when they die because of their vices and worldly desires. However, since you have prayed to Amida enthusiastically, your vices and worldly desires will be wiped out with the miraculous power of Amida Buddha. You will be placed in eighty-four thousand lights and be ranked with the Buddha. You are so fortunate because once you get to this stage you never fall into Hell, no matter the hard situations and difficulties you may have. When you breathe your last, you will become a lotus-shaped pedestal for a statue of Buddha in flowered Heaven and enjoy infinite happiness. To have this privilege, you must state the words of repentance that show how you will live the rest of your life in front of The Light of The Five Precepts of Buddhism: No killing, no theft, no sexual misconduct, no lying, and no intemperance. Your repentance must be based on your firm resolution that you will entirely give up old values that emphasize worldly behaviors and accomplishments and devote yourself to the teachings of the True Pure Land school of Buddhism. I will tell you about repentance.

It takes too long if I give you a full explanation of the words, so I will explain them briefly. Please pay careful attention so that you do not misunderstand the concepts. I told you to give up various worldly behaviors and excessive self-confidence and to devote yourself to asking Amida for help with our biggest concern – the rest of your life. First, if you pray for worldly benefits in the names of multiple spirits and Buddhist saints, it is just worldly behavior. And if you think the only thing you can do is to ask Amida and pray to her for worldly desires it is worldly accomplishment. If even a small portion of worldly behaviors and excessive self-confidence is included, it is not the devotion to the teachings of Jōdo Shinshū. If it is not the real devotion, you will not be saved. Since you gave up worldly behaviors, accomplishments, and excessive self-confidence when you prayed to Amida, you must not have them again. If you have them again your faith is invalid and going to Heaven after death will not be fulfilled.

You should not speak ill of your fellows or the Buddha. This means not mixing unrelated things. So, knowing that offering rice, incense, flowers, and the light to the only Amida Buddha is for showing gratitude. Moreover, it is wrong if you place other Buddhas and Buddhist saints together with Amida Nyorai and hold services. You may only chant the name of Amida Buddha and must not chant the names of other gods and Buddhas. You are to only pray for Amida and pursue only this discipline because you gave up all vices when you decided to trust Amida with yourself. But do not speak ill of other Buddhas although you do not need to believe in them.

Finally, you must be loyal to the Master and be good to your parents. You may go to wonderful Heaven since your parents have been here cherishing you. If you were thrown away after being given birth, you could not grow up nor have piety. You owe your parents a great deal. So, you have to be good to them and repay their support by cooperating, being compliant, and trying to get them relieved of any burden. If you stick to wrong thoughts and make your parents anxious, your behaviors are very thoughtless. If you behave in such a thoughtless way it might do them harm. That is why you have to respect and not neglect your parents.

Now that you have completed the ceremony, you are one in the Blood of Shinran.

15
WALKABOUT

By the time Jack finished writing his fieldnotes and reading over entries from past research, much of the afternoon had drifted away. It was five o'clock. Jack decided to take a walk around the village and, hopefully, bump into a few of his neighbors with whom he could carry on some casual conversation and maybe learn a few more things that might help in figuring out what was going on. He gathered up his laptop and headed inside, this time leaving his shoes on the deck before entering the house. Once inside, Jack put on a light jacket and started for the front door but stopped when he realized he hadn't locked the door to the back porch. With the house suitably protected from bears, he slipped into a pair of sneakers waiting in the *genkan* and commenced a casual stroll around the village. His long-term goal was to arrive at one of the few restaurants that remained in the center of town, where he would enjoy his dinner—*katsudon*. He thought about forgoing the stroll and charging straight for the restaurant, but it was too early for dinner and he needed to talk with people to keep the flow of his fieldwork going.

His own street was quiet but when he took a right at the intersection, he saw an old woman squatting in her garden. She was weeding. Jack slowly moved toward her and after a few steps she heard his approach and stood up. She was tiny and bent over at the waist, so standing didn't make much of a difference from squatting. When she noticed Jack, the woman smiled and waved. He waved and continued in her direction.

"Yamazaki-san," called out Jack, "*ohisashiburi des nee!*" It's been a long time! "*Ogenki desu ka?*" Are you well?

"*Oban de gasu! Hisashiburi des nee.*" Good evening! Long time, indeed, came the reply. Jack asked again how she was doing and after a moment she said wistfully, "*Anmari omukai ga konai...*" She said this with a light laugh as she tipped her head slightly to the right. Jack thought about the meaning of the sentence, "I have not yet been taken..." which basically was a way of saying, "I'm still alive and ticking" but always seemed slightly morbid to Jack. Yamazaki Yai was in her mid-80's and had the physique of a tightly woven ball of yarn. Like many other women her age, due to severe osteoporosis, she could not stand erect, which meant that she always seemed to be about the same height, regardless of whether she was sitting, squatting, or standing. She wore a dark paisley blouse of blues, purples and greys accompanied by dark grey pants. On her head was a white bonnet with a long brim in front that framed her wrinkled face and served the important purpose of shading her eyes and keeping bugs out of her hair. Yamazaki's hands were grizzled not only with age, but also with decades of manual labor she had toiled through in the family's rice paddies and the large garden in front of their house. She no longer participated in the rice cultivation—and most of that was mechanized anyway—but being useful and productive was important to Yamazaki, so she tried to do as much as she could around her house, despite the fact that her son and daughter-in-law were constantly telling her to relax and just enjoy her life. But like other women of her generation, she couldn't just sit around. She had to be useful. And gardening was something she could do without too much stress on her aging body.

"Ah... my back hurts!"

"From the weeding?"

"It always hurts but squatting like this can make it worse."

"Why don't you stop?"

"That's what my kids and grandkids are always saying. But that's no good. Can't let the garden go to pot, you know."

"Hmm. It seems to me," said Jack with a smile, "that you could let the garden go a little. You can get good produce from Big House and then you wouldn't need to squat weeding like this. Maybe that would help your back..."

"That would be nice, but it's not possible. I have to take care of the garden. This land was given to us by the Lord of the castle centuries ago. I can't ignore that. We have an obligation to take care of the land because it was given to us. Besides, if it turns to weeds, then the seeds will end up in the neighbors' yards and they will have weeds everywhere. That wouldn't be right. It would be very inconsiderate." Jack thought to himself about the looming presence of the ancestors in rural Japanese life.

"I see. Well maybe you could plant something that doesn't require quite so much work."

"I suppose, but the vegetables we produce taste a lot better than what you get at the grocery store."

"True enough." Jack laughed as did Yamazaki. She then turned and a more solemn look came over her face.

"It's awful what's been happening around here, isn't it?"

"Yes, it is. I never would have imagined such things in Nakadomari. It's always so peaceful."

"I know. What do you think, Jack-san?"

"I really don't know what to think. It's hard to believe anyone around here would be capable of committing a murder. Who would have it in for someone like Takahashi-san? Or, for that matter, the man who was killed out at Houn-ji—Saito-san? What would motivate that? Makes no sense."

"Maybe, but some people around here have had pretty tough lives and hold very long memories. You've only come here for brief periods of time and just moved in for good. But over the years, not surprisingly, there are always conflicts and disagreements. You know about Kobayashi-san, right?"

"Yes, I do. I've thought a lot about him and actually met with him for a little while earlier today."

"You should stay clear of him, Jack-san. He's scary. And he belongs to that weird religious group that meets in the old Ozawa house. They're scary, too—keep coming to the front door trying to get us to join. For a while, it was almost every week!"

"I agree, he's a bit scary, but I'm not entirely sure he could kill someone."

"Maybe not. But his life has been terrible, and he's spent time in mental hospitals. Who knows what's really going on in his head—he's not normal." She pointed to her head for emphasis as she said this. "Although I will say things seem to have been much better for him in the past few years. I don't see him out drunk anymore, that's for sure. He seems to have gotten his life put together."

"Is there anyone else around here who has had a tough time or had problems in the village?"

"Hmm. There was Kikuchi-san…"

"Kikuchi-san? I don't know him."

"He died. About ten years ago, I think. He was in his fifties and suddenly dropped dead in his house—heart attack. He actually lived in the old samurai house in the middle of the village." Yamazaki spoke with the clipped nasal tones common of the regional dialect that was often heard among the elderly. *Zūzū-ben*, as it was called throughout Japan because of the nasal and buzzing quality of many of its pronunciations, was so distinct from standard Japanese that it could be difficult even for native speakers from other parts of the country to understand. Fortunately, after his years of fieldwork in the area, Jack had come to be relatively fluent in the dialect and understood most of what Yamazaki said.

"You mean the one that they turned into a museum as part of the historical preservation project?"

"*Nda nda.*" Yes.

"Wow. I didn't know anyone had lived there recently."

"He was quiet. Kept to himself. Divorced, you know? His ex-wife and two daughters lived in Kanezawa. I don't know why she left him. But I do know he was struggling. The house he was living in had no indoor plumbing. He had to use an outhouse and there was a separate bathhouse. It was like he was living 150 years ago. And then someone came by and found him spread out on the floor. He had been there quite a while, but no-one noticed. It was sad."

"My goodness. I wonder why he lived in such a difficult house. Was he having financial problems?"

"*Naze de gasu bē nē…*" Why, indeed… She said this as she pondered the situation and squatted to pull out another offending weed she noticed. "He had a job working to install satellite dishes. I know that. So he had some income. Maybe it was related to his divorce. I don't know." As he listened, Jack thought to himself, no-one from Tokyo would understand what she just said.

"Do you think he had any conflicts with people here in the village?"

"Could be… His father never really got along with people all that well. He was something of a contrarian. Anytime we had a village meeting about fixing something like the playground or putting in new bathrooms in the park, he would argue against it. It got to the point where everyone just ignored him at those meetings. He'd start talking, and the head of the village would just talk over him and change the direction of the discussion. I felt bad for him when I went to those meetings, but he brought it on himself."

Jack was quiet for a moment as he recalled a village meeting he attended during an earlier fieldwork trip. He remembered a man doing exactly what Yamazaki described, but didn't recall who the man was. Probably Kikuchi's father. It would be something to look at in his fieldnotes.

Yamazaki continued, "His attitude actually got him into some trouble in the village. Living in a village like this involves a lot of cooperation among residents."

"Yes," said Jack, "there is a great deal of social solidarity in rural villages, at least."

"Well, there used to be a lot more than there is now. Everyone used to pitch in and help with work like building irrigation systems or paths, and of course, with rice farming. We had quotas in the old days and if a village didn't make its quota, it was embarrassing, but a fair amount of prestige could be gained by making the quota and turning it in early—it was supposed to be done by each household, but the village collected the crops and turned them in together. Everything was like that. Weddings, funerals, house building. We also voted as a group in elections; even though we voted individually, it was decided through village meetings who the entire village would support and then we would vote that way. That meeting still happens, but I suppose there was nothing to prevent anyone from voting for a different person. I think most of us followed the decision of the village. The key was to keep quiet if you were going to do something different, and Kikuchi-san didn't do that. It was probably fifty years ago, but I remember he objected in a village association meeting about the way we paid taxes. There was one person in the village who was the tax collector for everyone. He would then take all of the taxes for the village to city hall and submit them. Kikuchi-san didn't think it was right and believed that we should all submit our taxes as individual households, so he went to the police to complain. That was a big mistake."

"Mmm. I would think so…what happened?"

"Going to the police meant loss of face for the village and the village leadership, which did not sit well with people. The village did something called *mura hachibu.*"

"I'm not familiar with that," said Jack.

"It doesn't really happen now, but it is an old practice and continued for many years after the war. If you did something highly inconsiderate of others, like setting a fire through carelessness, or behaved in ways that led to a reputation of being unhelpful and disagreeable, or constantly objected to village decisions, then you were ostracized. Going to the police was particularly bad because it meant the village lost face."

"That's very interesting. What did they do to ostracize someone?"

"As you know, the word "*mura*" means village and "*hachibu*" refers to eight parts. People used to say there were ten things that involved community help or ceremonial cooperation in a village. It was things like wedding ceremonies and funerals, fire prevention, sickness, and so on. If you were submitted to *mura hachibu*, you had eight of those taken away. Usually, the ostracized family would only get help with fire prevention and funerals because fire is a risk to everyone and if the dead are not cared for properly, they can become dangerous to the living. Other than those two parts everyone in the household was ignored. People wouldn't greet them, it was impossible for adult children to marry within the village, the household could not send a representative to village association meetings, and they received no help with work like bringing in the rice crop or repairing damage from a storm. Even small children would be shunned at school."

"How long did the ostracism last?"

"There was no time limit. The offending household had to submit a formal letter to the village association requesting readmission, apologizing, and claiming responsibility for causing the situation."

"Did Kikuchi-san do that?"

"I think so, it was a significant inconvenience not only on the ostracized household but to everyone else who had to make it a point to avoid them. So, it was mutually beneficial to get the situation resolved. But once *mura hachibu* has happened, it's never entirely forgotten. In fact, when his son died he became very upset because quite a few people from the village didn't attend the *nembutsu* on the night of his funeral, even though the *mura hachibu* had ended years earlier. Maybe they were sending him a message that he was still difficult to deal with—I'm not sure. But I remember that he took it as disrespectful to his family and made a point of that at one of the village meetings. But the funny thing is that he didn't visit his son much—had he done so, he would have found the body a lot earlier than it was found. I still remember the *nembutsu* the evening of his funeral, with his ex-wife and daughters sitting on the tatami in the circle as we passed around the prayer beads. The younger daughter couldn't have been more than three and was smiling the whole time. The little girl had no idea what had happened, but she thought passing around the beads was a lot of fun. I guess she didn't really know her father..." She said this with a tinge of disapproval.

As Yamazaki trailed off thinking about that night, the sound of a younger woman's voice rang out across the garden, "*Obaa-san! Denwa-desu!*" Grandma, there's a telephone call for you! Jack smiled and bowed as Yamazaki apologized for the interruption and then turned in the direction of her house. As he watched her crossing the garden,

Jack was surprised at how quickly she moved despite her physical limitations. It was almost as though the ball of yarn was rolling rapidly across the garden. In the background, he saw Yamazaki's daughter-in-law, who waved at Jack and called out, "Ah—Jack-san!" with a broad and bright smile across her face. Jack smiled and waved back at her and then bowed and turned to continue his walk as Grandma Yamazaki reached the genkan.

He turned left at the next road and found it to be empty. No cars and no-one outside weeding, planting, or doing anything else. People tended to eat dinner early in the village, so most were probably inside preparing their meals or tending to other indoor chores. He cut through the large field in the center of the village, past the old house where Kikuchi had died and that had now been turned into a museum showing traditional architecture and lifestyles of the past. He then entered a dark dirt path that felt like a green tunnel under the trees arching across it that obscured the afternoon blue sky. The path emerged onto the main road that passed through Tanohata and connected the town of Nakadomari with the neighboring city of Kanezawa. After only a few meters, he turned down a narrow street that wound around the house in which he and Saori had resided—and the house that George first came home to—when he was conducting his dissertation fieldwork in the 1990s. Little had changed in the interim years, although it was clear that the houses of two of their former neighbors were now empty, with curtains drawn and no sign of recent activity. Jack had learned a year or so earlier that the woman who lived next door and was quite impoverished had passed on, as had the husband of the couple who lived on the other side of their house at the time. His wife moved to a nursing home.

Jack kept walking at a slow pace, carefully observing his surroundings and recording in his mind differences from the last time he was there. He stopped a few times, pulled out notecards from his shirt pocket, and wrote down a few jottings to help him remember what he had seen for when he generated detailed fieldnotes later in the evening. Almost every time he pulled out his notecards, he recalled his dissertation advisor, L. K. Greene, who was a brilliant ethnographer and had taught him many basic techniques like this which had become part of Jack's regular arsenal of research methods. After about 150 meters, he arrived at the Shinto shrine that served the needs of most people living in Tanohata and its surrounding neighborhoods. He walked through the *torii*, a gate that usually identified the presence of a Shinto shrine, and past two *komainu* lion-dog statues on either side of the path. The lion-dogs guarded the shrine. As was customary, one *komainu* had its mouth open while the other was closed in a pattern known as *ah-gyō* and *un-gyō*—the ah-shape and un-shape whose sounds represent the beginning and end of the Sanskrit alphabet and in Buddhism signify the beginning and end, birth and death. Despite their historical connections to Buddhism, many larger Shinto shrines had these statues on either side of the path as one approached the main shrine building. It was but one example of the cross-pollination that existed in Japan between Buddhism and Shinto, making it difficult at times to conceptually separate the two religions.

The shrine building was empty, as Jack expected. Shrines in Japan varied quite a bit, from the larger ones staffed daily by a priest and several assistants, to medium-sized shrines like this one, that were only opened for festivals and other special occasions. And then there were the much smaller shrines that were kept in people's yards or some corner of a village and might not have a Shinto priest connected directly to them. The priest who took care of Nakadomari Shrine, as the building he stood before was called, lived in a house only a few meters away. He was not usually home during the day because he worked as a high school teacher for his regular job and only handled shrine duties when requested or for festivals and the annual new year celebrations. Most Shinto priests in Japan couldn't make a sufficient income to survive if all they did was shrine work.

Jack stepped up to the door of the shrine and tried to open it. It was locked, which was expected. The ground surrounding the shrine was damp and there was a dark-emerald hue to the entire area on which a carpet of moss spread out, covered by the canopy of cedar trees. It seemed like one of those places in Japan that were perpetually wet, regardless of the weather or season and recalled in Jack's mind images from the Miyazaki movie *My Neighbor Totoro*. Jack's stomach grumbled. He had a decision to make. Should I continue to poke around, he thought? Or should I go and get the *katsudon*... Hmm. Red pill, blue pill. I'm an anthropologist, but I'm a retired anthropologist. I don't always have to be doing fieldwork, do I? He elected for dinner over continued fieldwork and picked up the pace, exiting through another *torii* while ignoring the house of the Shinto priest as his mind turned to thoughts of rice and Japanese beer. A few years earlier, he would have made it a point to stop, ring the bell of the priest's house, and ask a few questions about recent activities at the shrine. Retirement was different, he thought.

16
KATSUDON

The restaurant was not crowded when he arrived. In fact, Jack was the only customer. The proprietor, whom Jack had met a few times but did not know well, welcomed him in with a hearty, "*Irasshai!*" and motioned him to sit wherever he wanted. Jack chose one of the low tables on a raised area near the windows and sat on a pillow resting on the tatami mats. He took a couple of minutes to look over the menu, but already knew what he wanted. Looking in the direction of the counter, he called out, "*Sumimasen…*" The proprietor returned the call with, "*Hai*" and his wife materialized to take Jack's order.

"*Katsudon, onegai-shimasu.*"

"*Kashikomarimashita.*" Of course. She bowed slightly and called out *katsudon* to her husband.

"*Bīru mō ippon.*" A bottle of beer, too.

"*Hai.*" She departed and a few moments later returned with his beer. Jack filled his glass and lifted it to his lips. As the golden lager flowed across his palate, he savored the crisp, dry taste working its way into his gut. It was his first beer since getting back to Japan and he was going to make the most of it. Presently, the *katsudon* arrived, exhaling the sweet smell of the soy-sauce infused eggs as they blended with the onions and pork cutlet that rested on a glistening bed of white rice. *Gokuraku*, he thought. Heaven.

Jack sat cross-legged at the low table. He took another swig of beer and removed his chopsticks from their box—like many Japanese, he always brought his own chopsticks to restaurants to reduce the waste from the disposable type that restaurants provided to their customers. He dug under the pork cutlet with his chopsticks and lifted a load of rice and egg to his mouth, saving the pork until last, as it was his favorite part of the dish. The *katsudon* was perfect. Jack's legs began to cramp a little, so he extended them out under the low table. The restaurant was quiet. Occasionally, a sound from the kitchen, such as the clang of a pot, would break up the peace, but the atmosphere was ideal for thinking. It had been a long day and Jack was tired. But he decided to pull his laptop out of his satchel and spend a few minutes looking over his old fieldnotes. He opened his fieldnotes database and began running searches on various words to see what he could find that might help him remember this contrarian individual. Several attempts failed, but he finally hit pay dirt with "village meeting." Jack scrolled through the entry and focused on the last few paragraphs that described an afternoon meeting he attended during his earlier fieldwork:

18 November 2010
Written jottings, photographs, weather is clear and chilly
…I left the house at about 1:00pm because I wanted to attend the meeting for deciding who would be supported as representative from the district to the Town Assembly and planned to get there a little early to watch the preparations. This took place at the Tanohata meeting hall only a few meters away from where I was talking with Takano-san the other day. The meeting started at 1:30pm and lasted until about 3:00pm. The scene was typical. The group included most of the elder men from the village. Sakamoto, Suzuki, Satō, Ozawa, Torisawa, Itō, and others. There were about twenty men in attendance. I would guess the average age to be about seventy. There were also seven women present, who huddled in a group in the back, while the men sat towards the front. The women served tea; the men smoked. The women were as far back as possible, perhaps to make access to the kitchen easier. The men completely dominated the meeting, which was led by the head of the Jichikai, or village government, and by Takamatsu Hiroshi, who is a local piano teacher and functioned in the meeting as the moderator. Interestingly, someone would ask a question and he would repeat the question to the Jichikai-chō (head of the Jichikai), even though the Jichikai-chō could hear it. Only after it had been repeated/summarized, did the Jichikai-chō answer. The meeting was not particularly complex. The gist of the discussion was

related to Watanabe-san's election bid. After the usual opening speech (which was short), the Jichikai-chō, Itō, began asking if they would approve Watanabe as the representative. This was moving along with little discussion until one of the men in attendance complained that since Watanabe represents three villages, there should be consultation and an opportunity for others to run. The basic problem seemed to be that Watanabe's name had been written up on the blackboard at the front of the room and the entire beginning of the meeting went as though it had already been decided that he would be running unopposed. The man complained that it was like there was no room for anyone other than Watanabe to run. This irritated one of the other men in the room, and then another one picked up and talked over the man who was beginning to restate his complaint. Itō asked for any opinions from the members of the village women's club. This brought giggles from the women in the back. After the giggling, Itō asked what was funny and they said that it was because there were no women's club members in the group—they were all over the age of sixty and were in the old person's club. Then one of the women simply said that they approve of what is going on and that was it. Indeed, that was all that they contributed to the meeting. The meeting was a men's meeting. But neither the majority of men nor the women seemed to have much to say in this particular situation. If it were not for the one man who spoke up, I suspect that Watanabe would have been approved without debate or any opposition. It seemed as though the contrarian was not so much opposing Watanabe as he were opposing the way in which he was presented as virtually having already been selected as the candidate for Town Assembly. Eventually, a few other men in the group supported the idea that more discussion should be allowed before selecting a representative. There was also the comment that the Jichikai of Tanohata is not the proper venue for this sort of thing because there were two other villages that Watanabe—or whoever else it might be— would represent. Both of those villages are adjacent to Tanohata and represent the former merchant district of the town. These villages are not where the people of samurai descent live. There should be more debate and an opportunity for people from those districts to run for the office, said Hanabusa-san who lives in the merchant area, "this is an election after all." There was a general agreement that there would be another meeting and more time allowed for people to volunteer to run for office. The Jichikai-chō asked for a "vote" in which he put forth the proposal and asked all who agreed to clap their hands together. Everyone clapped. Then the man who had started the entire debate started to shout out complaints about the toilets that were going to be placed behind the village meeting hall. "Will it be hooked to the new public sewer system? Who pays for this?" One of the other men at the head table announced that City Hall would pay for twenty or thirty percent of the cost and the village would pay the rest. Then he said that they still had not agreed on whether to put in a Western-style toilet or a traditional Japanese trough toilet. The man with complaints started to ask again about why they were paying so much, but he was cut off by the Jichikai-chō. He repeated his question much louder, and several in attendance told him to calm down. At that, the Jichikai-chō adjourned the meeting.

As we filed out of the meeting hall, I walked alongside Sakamoto, who is from the merchant district, but his house is inside the Tanohata borders. We talked about the weather a little and then I asked him about the conflict in the meeting. He said that Kikuchi often does that in meetings and usually is just making trouble for everyone. "But this time he has a point. The samurai people in Tanohata think they are entitled to all leadership positions on the basis of their ancestry. This leaves out people like me, who live in the merchant district. You know this history, right Jack? In the old caste system, the samurai were at the top, the farmers below them, and the merchants below the farmers. Merchants were looked down upon by the samurai as being selfish—only interested in gaining money. There's still some of that today, over 200 years later.

Then Sakamoto said, "The samurai families look down on the merchant families and also the newcomers. [He used the word mikudasu 見下す which is interesting since the kanji characters mean literally to look down.] When it comes to newcomers, that way of thinking is still strong. Kikuchi-san is a newcomer. His family moved to the village about a hundred years ago. This is actually why I don't usually attend most of *the village meetings. I don't like interacting with the samurai people. All of the power is in their hands. Younger people like me [he looks like he is around fifty-five] have little or no power. I don't like Kikuchi-san very much. He's rather loud and obnoxious. But he also has a point."*

As Jack read over the text displayed on the computer screen, he was reminded how long the memories of people in this area could be retained. A hundred years, he thought, and still a "newcomer," which was another way to say outsider. And being an outsider meant having little access to local power and local decision-making. Governmental elected offices were different—everyone could vote. But when it came to village-level politics, "voting" was another story. Most of the important decisions were made through the practice of *nemawashi*, the informal process of laying the foundation for a decision through quiet, backroom conversation with those concerned as a way of getting feedback and support. Normally, when a village meeting like the one Jack was just reading about in his fieldnotes had been called, a course of action for the issue up for discussion had already been decided. The meeting was just a formality to approve the ready-made decision brought to the assemblage of household representatives. That's why they voted by clapping rather than a counted show of hands. It was also part of what made Kikuchi's complaint so problematic. He was disrupting the normal flow of decision-making in the village. And as Jack thought about it, since he was a newcomer and not of samurai descent, it was more than probable that Kikuchi had not been included in the process of *nemawashi* prior to that gathering. That moment at the village hall was likely his first opportunity to speak and he took advantage of it—blowing up the process as he raised the hackles of dissent. In the end, Jack recalled, Watanabe was still put forth as the only candidate for representative to the Assembly from the combined neighborhoods. But the process had been much more difficult and far more conflict-ridden than anyone had expected going into that village meeting. And then, thought Jack, Kikuchi's son had suddenly died. And it certainly was strange that Kikuchi himself apparently so rarely visited his son—who lived within a hundred meters—that someone else found the body after it had been laying in the old house for several days.

Jack was a little bewildered. He had been around the village long enough and done sufficient fieldwork to know that there was always conflict among the residents, regardless of how peaceful and cooperative everything seemed on the surface. If human beings are involved, then there is usually disagreement and conflict somewhere lurking covertly in the background. And even in peaceful Tanohata, conflict was not always hidden. Jack had seen it on the gateball court in the middle of the public park on several occasions. Gateball was a game played by older people that was like team croquet. Old folks liked it because they could get out and enjoy some exercise with friends along with congenial conversation. Some of the players were quite competitive and tried to push the village team to enter tournaments at the local and prefectural levels. They had once even entered the national tournament held in Osaka. Jack recalled one older man who tended to dominate the practices. He was loud and a bit obnoxious. Many of the women complained quietly to Jack that they didn't like him because he was so domineering and rude. His behavior maybe wasn't all that abnormal for a competitive older man who saw himself as powerful and important, but it never seemed right to most of the women and some of the men who played on the village gateball team. For most of those involved, the purpose of the game was social interaction rather than winning. Jack remembered one woman who told him how, if things got too competitive, tempers could get out of hand. Every year, she explained, there seemed to be at least one older person somewhere in Japan who was murdered with a gateball mallet after some petty disagreement ignited overly competitive players into screaming matches.

Jack drifted into thoughts of anthropological theory and how people take on, or embody, the cultural features of their social context. Expectations are imprinted on the person; they are structural aspects of the individual that contribute to who that person is. It may be, in a sense, that the entire self is comprised of expectations. The human identity is comprised of expectations about what one should do, who one should be, and who one wants to be. These are drawn from or based upon social and ideological structures that define the limits of how we think about individuals in a society on the basis of characteristics such as age, gender, nationality, race, profession, etc. And these characteristics are important components from which people derive and use power.

When expectations are expressed through actions, they have a kind of automatic quality to them. Expectations are so deeply ingrained that people often don't notice that they even have them. Expectations are built on embodied social and cultural structures that themselves structure the expectations we have. Culture is an endless feedback loop. Is it perhaps that expectation is the mechanism through which we embody cultural values? Is it through doing what is expected that one takes on and habituates the social structures and values of a society? By doing what you are expected to do, you begin, yourself, to expect a specific type of behavior and treat certain behaviors as unambiguously natural and normal. If such expectations are developed early in life, then they will be so deeply engrained that they become indistinguishable from cultural patterns observable within a group of people. Culture resides in the expectations of individuals. Maybe culture is just the pattern of expectations operating in a given society that people use to navigate their interactions with others. Expectations are constantly being negotiated and improvised upon and sometimes the process of negotiation and improvisation can cause root changes in one's expectational patterns. Culture, Jack thought, is the pattern of expectations imprinted on individual bodies or in individual minds as people interact with each other from the moment of birth until the moment of death. When behaviors of others fall outside of the patterns of expectations, then one is forced to react in order to organize those observed behaviors into a way that fits into the range of acceptable expectations operating in a given cultural context. This response, a kind of improvisation, may include adjustment of one's own expectations or interpersonal conflict as one attempts to modify the expectations and behaviors of others. Conflict, of course, may take a wide variety of forms from simple verbal disagreement to the violence of murder or war. Anthropologist Mary Douglas, Jack recalled, was quite right in her notion that some things fall outside of the realm of the socially "clean" and become matter out of place. Put more precisely, they fall outside the realm of what is expected. Kikuchi had done what was not expected by pushing against the prevailing approach to decision-making and thus challenging the tacit power structures that operated in the village. And in so doing, he had irritated quite a few people. Could it be that his son ultimately paid the price for his father's insolence?

17
A CALL

Jack was completely immersed in thought when he noticed the vibration of his smart phone in his pocket. He pulled it out and saw that Sam's name was displayed on the screen. Rather than answer within the restaurant, which would be rude, he rejected the call and texted Sam that he'd call him back shortly. Swinging his legs out from under the table, Jack stood and promptly almost fell over. His left leg had gone to sleep and he could feel nothing below his knee. Good way to break an ankle, he thought. After looking like an idiot as he tried to dance his tingling leg back to consciousness, he called out "*Sumimasen!*" to indicate he wanted to pay. Jack stepped down into his shoes and walked toward the cash register where the man who had cooked his delicious *katsudon* rang up the bill and then pointed to the electronic display so that Jack would know what amount to pay. This was a common occurrence among those who didn't know Jack could speak Japanese, and, of course, there was no good reason to think that he could if you didn't know him personally. Most of the foreigners in the area had limited or no Japanese language skills. Jack slid a 5,000 yen note from his wallet and placed it in the tray for money on the counter. The proprietor efficiently returned 3,500 yen. Not much money for such a great meal, thought Jack.

"*Gochisō-sama deshita!*" smiled Jack. Thank you for the feast!

"*Arigatō*," replied the chef, "*mata kitte kunansei.*" Thanks, please come again, was the response, with a bit of local dialect thrown in for flavor. I need to know this guy better, thought Jack as he left the restaurant. And now that he was living in Tanohata, that would be possible. As he exited through the sliding glass doors, ducking the curtain that hung outside, indicating the restaurant was open for business, Jack decided to wait to return Sam's call until he arrived at home. Walking and talking on the phone in Japan was viewed as weird and somewhat impolite. And in any case, it was early in the morning in New Haven, so Sam could wait a few minutes until Jack wandered back to his house, where he could sit on his deck and smoke a pipe. It would be a short stroll as long as he didn't run into anyone along the way who wanted to chat.

He didn't. In fact, the streets were largely empty with only a few cars driving by as he moved in the direction of home. The evening air was getting a little warmer than it had been since Jack arrived in Nakadomari and the humidity was beginning to show inklings of its summer potency. Jack noticed he was sweating—time to take off the jacket. It only took about fifteen minutes to arrive at his front door, even with the relaxed pace of the stroll. Once inside, he went straight to his study where he stood in front of his pipe rack contemplating which briar would be the best choice for this evening. He looked over a few Dunhills, picked up and returned an Ashton bent bulldog, and then struggled to decide between the Ben Wade freehand with its rugged, natural shape and the beautifully sophisticated straight grain Charatan bulldog from the 1960s that he had picked up used in London during a conference trip. Jack settled on the Charatan. He loved the feeling of a smooth finish with the bulldog shape's sharp ridge toward the middle of the bowl that made it fit comfortably in his hand. The professor grabbed his leather Dunhill tobacco pouch filled with Presbyterian blend, a couple of pipe cleaners, and a tamp and strolled to his favorite outside chair, picking up his phone along the way.

Once settled in, Jack filled the pipe and ignited the tobacco, causing smooth billows of smoke to stream from his mouth. He punched in Sam's number.

"Hey, Jack! How the hell's it going?"

"Well— it certainly has been interesting. How about you? What's up?"

"Nothing much really. Everything is the same. You'll get a kick out of this. Harwick has spent the past week being a complete asshole. He and his wife have been on a hiring committee for a joint position between religious studies and philosophy and they've been trying to create a voting block to make sure they get what they want for the hire. Harwick's been really arrogant and nasty."

"You mean he's been his usual self…"

"Exactly. But I think the hire is going to fail. The philosophy department is pissed at them and seems to have formed our own voting bloc. We have enough votes to prevent a hire, which isn't really what anyone wants, but the list of people his committee is suggesting we invite for campus interviews is stupid. It just replicates people in Harwick's area but doesn't actually add areas we need in either department. It's all a power-play."

"Sounds like Harwick. That's for sure." Jack sighed and thought to himself how much he didn't miss university politics.

"So, what's been going on with you and Saori?"

"Well, not much. I'm all settled into the house. Everything is pretty much unpacked. Saori is back in Tokyo for a couple of weeks cleaning up work stuff. Two neighbors have been murdered since I got here. Just the usual."

"Okay, sounds like— What the fuck? Two neighbors have been murdered? That's not funny. Well, it is… but it shouldn't be."

"I'm not joking. Both murders have taken place in Zen temples. One of them here in Tanohata and another in a different part of Nakadomari. They seem to be linked. Do you remember Taitsu-san?"

"Sure, the tall priest with the big feet."

"Yeah. He and I have been helping out a local police inspector trying to figure this out. It's pretty weird stuff. Both murders involved unusual religious objects and both victims were holding a candle that had burned in their left hands. Taitsu and I were the ones who found the first victim. He'd been hanged in front of the altar at Taitsu's temple."

"Holy shit. I didn't think there was any crime at all around there, let alone violent shit like that. The place was so dull and peaceful when I visited. I can't believe it. Why does the police dude want your help? Are they short of detectives? What do you know about crime?"

"Almost nothing. But he thought Taitsu and I could be eyes and ears on the ground, basically, and he thought I could poke around using my fieldwork as something of a smokescreen. I might find out some tidbit that could be useful to him."

"How's it going?"

"I really don't know. I've had a few conversations that raised ideas in my head about tensions in the village, but I'm not sure any of these would be sufficient to kill someone. What I am learning is that there are a few deep-seated conflicts in the village that have simmered for decades. Who knows, it could be related to one of those. And there seems to be a connection, at least in my mind, to a ritual called *kakushi nembutsu*."

"What's that?"

"Basically, it's a secretive initiation ritual that used to be done with kids when they were around five. It transitioned them from their little liminal selves to full members of the local community, as well as making them disciples united in the blood of Shinran. They used candles during the rituals. The candles were held close to the faces of the kids in pitch black rooms and if the kids showed emotion or fear, they would fail. Three strikes and you were out, as it were. And not making it through the ritual the third time meant that as an adult you couldn't participate in a variety of village activities. One became something of an outcast, although not quite that severe. I've been thinking that this could be a motive. Maybe some person who failed at this as a kid is out to get the people who passed judgment on him. Both victims were old men and men of their generation led the ritual when it was still being performed. It has largely died out."

"Seems like a long time to hold a grudge."

"Maybe, but I'm having a hard time finding any other sort of motive. And the candles are not the only connections. The guy who was hanged was strung up with an *onbuhimo*."

"Uh, a mombomombo? What the hell is that?"

"*Onbuhimo*. Right. You wouldn't know. It's a long, cloth rope-like thing that was used to tie a baby to a mother's back so that she could work. Seems like it could be symbolic for childhood. And then the other murder was done with a set of Buddhist prayer beads—the really long ones I showed you pictures of a while back."

"Yeah, I remember those. Super old, right?"

"Yup." A few moments of silence passed as both men contemplated the situation. Jack broke the hush with a blast of smoke from his mouth, but neither said a word. Finally, Sam brought them both back to the conversation.

"Jack?"

"Yeah."

"How do you know that the objects you are focusing on are symbolic of something related to the murder?"

"What do you mean? It seems obvious that there's a connection."

"Yeah, too obvious. Maybe the candles, the *ombobubu* or whatever it is, and the beads are not intended to send you clues, but to throw those investigating the murders off the trail. Maybe they are planted clues intended to confuse the police. There'd be no logic in providing the police with such clear pointers to the motive unless one actually wanted to get caught."

"Shit, Sam... you're too smart."

"I know. I often tell people that. Philosophers are generally smarter than everyone, and much smarter than anthropologists, who are naturally dumb."

"Up yours..." They laughed and then Jack thought to himself that Sam's logical mind always helped in changing Jack's perspective. Sam was right. The "clues" might well not be clues at all. They might be intentional false leads planted to throw investigators off the path.

"This messes up my thinking, Sam. Thanks. It's very helpful. Now I'm totally confused, but I think you may well have hit an important possibility."

"Anything to make you more confused. I enjoy that." Sam started to light up a cigar.

"Kind of early for that, isn't it Sam?"

"Emily isn't home."

"Oh, okay."

"Jack, I should probably move on. I've got some work to do on an article this morning. Deadline is looming."

"Sure thing, Sam. Take care of yourself, okay?"

"Yeah, you too my friend. Don't get yourself into any trouble poking around."

"Everyone keeps telling me that."

"That's because they're right."

"I know. Thanks."

The friends disconnected and Jack sat staring at the stars glistening in the night sky. His pipe had gone out, so he took out a match and reignited the embers in the bowl. Smoke again wafted from his mouth, slightly obscuring the glimmers of light above, and he relished the woody taste of the tobacco on his tongue. He kept thinking about Sam's observation and decided that it was time to talk with Matsumoto again. Maybe the inspector had already thought of this, but it was an important point that should be brought to his attention. Jack decided he would call first thing in the morning.

18
A STRANGE, RAINY MORNING

"*Hai. Matsumoto desu.*"

"*Moshi, moshi*, Jack desu."

"Ah, Jack-san, I'm glad you called. I was going to call you to see if we could meet sometime today."

"Have you made any progress?"

"Not really, but I have a few ideas. What about you?"

"Same."

"Are you free at 13:00?"

"Yes, that would work well for me. Where do you want to meet?"

"How about Maru Matsu, up near the shopping mall. We can get lunch. I'll call Murakami-san and see if he can join us."

"Sounds good. I will see you there. *Yoroshiku onegai shimasu.*" They ended the call and Jack thought to himself that there just isn't a good translation for that frequently used phrase. The literal meaning, "please treat me favorably" just doesn't work in English.

Jack decided to organize his thoughts before the meeting. Based on what he had learned poking around, there were two people—at least—in the village who might have a motive for murder. There was Kikuchi, who might be holding a grudge about the death of his son and the time his family had been ostracized from the village. *Mura hachibu*, he thought. Could it be that Kobayashi had had the same experience at some point? Or perhaps there was lingering resentment for his experiences with the *kakushi nembutsu* ritual. Neither of these seemed likely to be sufficient to lead to murder, particularly the gruesome and well-planned murders that had occurred. But other tensions seemed to be potentially lurking in the background, such as the status differential between those of samurai and merchant class descent. And then, of course, only one of the murders had happened in Tanohata. The second murder was in another part of town. There was no good reason to think someone in Tanohata had been responsible for either of them. Maybe Matsumoto will have some ideas that might help.

Jack looked at his watch. It was nine o'clock in the morning, so he had plenty of time before meeting with Matsumoto. Should he go out and collect more data or stay at home and continue to plow through old fieldnotes? It was raining, so he decided to stay inside and work at his desk. But instead of looking at fieldnotes, he thought it might be useful to spend some time trying to map out the symbolic possibilities of the objects he had found associated with the murders. First were the candles. They were the kind of white candles used in rituals performed at one's Buddhist altar when memorializing ancestors. Could they symbolize Buddhism? Death? Does the white color mean something? And then there is the possible connection to the *kakushi nembutsu* ritual. What about the prayer beads used to strangle the second victim? Maybe there's a binary opposition there—the beads and the *onbuhimo*—plus and minus, polar opposition between life and death. No, that's just too Lévi-Straussian. Humans are much more complex and the symbolic content of these is tied to how they might be interpreted if they were being employed to send some sort of message. But if the use of the two objects as weapons was intended to send a message, why such a simple one? And Sam's probably right. Why would a murderer telegraph clues that might help implicate him?

"But the prayer beads cannot have been an accident," Jack said aloud. Use of them as a weapon required prior knowledge of both their existence and location. The murderer must be someone with at least a connection to Tanohata. So that's mild conclusion number one, he thought. It also would seem that the murderer has some sort of problem with Buddhism. Could it be with Zen? Someone committed to Jōdo Shinshū who has issues with Zen? No, he thought, that's just not how Japanese think about their own religious behavior—that would be a very unlikely connection, because Japanese generally don't view religious affiliation as exclusive. It's normal to be both Buddhist and Shinto at the same time and most Japanese I've met don't really grasp why Abrahamic religions like Christianity, Judaism, and Islam have problems with each other, particularly since they all have the same god. But there should be a reason for committing both murders in the middle of Buddhist temples.

Jack pulled out a mechanical pencil and decided to write down a list of key points and problems to the case. As he set pencil to paper, the doorbell rang. "Shit, who could that be?" he murmured, and then in a loud voice called out, "*hai!*" to let the person at the door know he was on his way. He stepped down into the *genkan*, unlocked the door, and slid it open. Standing in the rain with her clear, plastic umbrella open was a woman who looked like she was in her forties. Jack invited her into the *genkan*, "*Dōzo, ohairi kudasai.*" Please come in. As they exchanged some small talk about the rain, Jack observed the woman standing in his entryway. She was unusually tall for a Japanese woman of her generation, standing a little under two meters in height. And her bone structure was also on the large side, although she was slender. The woman had conventional black hair cut in a simple bob accented by dull wire-framed glasses. She wore a blue business suit with a white blouse and black flat-soled shoes. From her left arm hung a black canvas bag that clearly had something heavy inside.

"My name is Kondo Reiko. You are new to the neighborhood, right?" As she said this, she started to reach into the black bag.

"Yes, that's right." Jack already had an inkling of why this woman was standing in his entryway, which proved to be an accurate assessment.

"I'm with the *Ehoba* group that meets here in the village. We saw that you moved in and since you are from a Christian country, thought you would be interested in the group." She pulled a hardcover book out of her bag. It was dark red, with a cross on the front and a few kanji characters that he could not see very well, as they were obscured by her hand. But he knew it was likely a Bible or an informational book about the Jehovah's Witnesses. Jack found himself conflicted. On the one hand, he had a rather strong distaste for Christianity in general and a particular dislike for evangelicals like this one, who went door-to-door selling their religion. On the other hand, the anthropologist in him wanted to learn what the woman was about, so he had some interest in having a conversation with her. The anthropologist side won out, as it usually did in Japan. In the States, he would already have ushered the woman out and closed the door. Instead, he motioned for her to sit down with him on the edge of the floor from which one stepped down into the *genkan*, a common practice in the area when someone visited briefly and didn't want to impose by removing their shoes and entering the house. Sitting at the edge of the genkan signaled that this would be a relatively brief visit.

She handed him the book, which he accepted with a nod of his head while saying "*Arigatō gozaimasu.*" As he looked at the woman next to him, he thought everything about her screamed plain, even her somewhat vacant smile. Once sitting in close proximity, Jack noticed a faint odor that seemed to recall the distant past—moth balls. There was a slightly awkward pause which Jack thought to be probably a result of the fact that Kondo didn't really know how well Jack could speak Japanese. This was immediately confirmed when she asked, "Are you able to read Japanese? I can come back with an English copy if you prefer. It's a Bible."

"Thank you, but I can read Japanese, so this should be fine. I will look it over."

"We hope that you will join our group for Bible study."

"I see. I will think about that." Jack was intentionally guarded in his responses. While he wanted to know more about the group, he also was not particularly interested in getting dragged into a Christian organization of any kind. This was not an unusual problem for ethnographers, who sometimes found themselves torn between a desire to learn about a context and a dislike for what they were learning. In the case of Christian groups in Japan, Jack had long since decided to avoid them not only because he disliked Christianity, but also because he knew that his general distaste for the religion biased his ideas about what he might observe. Jack was about to stand up as a way of suggesting that it was time for her to leave when she interrupted his plans.

"We have a very energetic group here in Tanohata. Everyone is committed fully."

"I see. So how long have you been involved?"

"I joined when the group formed, about ten years ago."

"That's a long time. Is it just you or is your family also involved?"

"It was just me, but about a year ago, my brother joined, too. I'm very happy about that. He needed to find a new path."

For a moment Jack thought she might be referring to Kobayashi, but then realized the timing was wrong. This must be another person with social, emotional, or psychological issues who needed help. Interesting, he thought to himself. And then Jack was somewhat surprised when Kondo brought up the man he was thinking about.

"I heard that you visited with Kobayashi-san yesterday."

"Yes, I wanted to ask him some questions related to my research."

"He is a very kind man. We are fortunate to have him as part of our group. He's such a nice man."

"I don't know him very well, but he does indeed seem nice. How long has he been with the *Ehoba* group in the village?"

"He came to us about three years ago," she smiled and some of the dullness of her persona lifted briefly. That's interesting, thought Jack, it's as though she lights up a little when she says Kobayashi's name. And then suddenly her face darkened and very softly she said, "He suffered so much before coming to us. We all felt so bad for him. His life in this village has been so difficult..." Her voice trailed off as she realized maybe she was saying more than she should to this foreign stranger who had just moved in.

"I heard from someone that he had struggled with depression." Jack carefully worded his comment to avoid both the problems with alcohol and mention of his stints in a mental hospital. But he also knew that the word for depression—*utsubyō*—could be problematic. He quite intentionally used the term as part of a probing question to see how Kondo might respond. And the response what not what Jack had expected. Kondo's face paled slightly and took on a loathsome pall as she looked down toward the stone-tiled floor.

"Yes, the people around here would say that sort of thing about

Kobayashi-san..." Her voice was measured, dark and close to a whisper. As soon as the sentence ended, she abruptly stood and in a much higher pitched voice, apologized for taking up Jack's time when he must be so busy with moving in. She spoke hurriedly as an artificial smile punctuated her desire to leave. Backing away from Jack and bowing several times, she reached behind her for the sliding door and upon finding the handle, opened it and backed out into the rain, apologizing for the intrusion and thanking Jack for accepting the book. She turned and headed straight for the small, white van parked at the end of Jack's driveway. Jack realized her umbrella was leaning against the house just outside of the front door and called out, "Kondo-san, you forgot your umbrella," as he slipped into his shoes and grabbed the umbrella on the way out of the house to bring it to the suddenly hurried woman. She turned back just before reaching the van and met Jack half-way to retrieve the umbrella, by which time both of them were soaked amidst the downpour. Bowing and apologizing profusely in the rain, Kondo managed to get herself into the van, which she started quickly. The vehicle backed out of the driveway with a high-pitched whine as the tiny K-car engine struggled to get van and woman quickly moving.

When Jack returned to his *genkan*, he mumbled to himself, "What a strange encounter." Over the years, Jack had experienced several odd moments with Christian missionaries and evangelicals in Japan, but this one was different. Usually, the oddness came as a result of the uncharacteristically pushy approach that some Japanese Christians took to spreading their beliefs. The Japanese generally keep to themselves and are disinclined to go door-to-door trying to get others to join in their religious activities. There is no evangelizing among Japanese Buddhists nor anything like that associated with Shinto. In fact, this aspect of Christianity bothered many of Jack's friends, who at times commented that although they knew Christianity was a major world religion, in Japan it seemed more like a cult, in the worst sense of the word. Jack remembered one friend in Tokyo commenting that Christians who came door-to-door reminded him of the Aum cult that had gassed the Tokyo subway system in 1995. He didn't really think that Christians were dangerous like Aum, but he did feel as though their strategies had the same overly aggressive and impolite qualities. And he didn't like either group.

Jack stood in the *genkan* dripping. He would have to change his clothes. Rather than dripping on their shiny new wood floors, he undressed in the *genkan* and headed to the bedroom stark naked. Saori would have given him a lot of grief, had she been at home, which is why he wouldn't have done it if she had been at home. He decided to take a quick shower to warm up and then dressed himself in a pair of green corduroy pants and a blue oxford-cloth shirt, which he thought would be appropriate for his meeting with Matsumoto and Taitsu later in the day. As he put on his watch, he saw that it was already 10:30. The morning was passing quickly and he was not getting anything done in terms of thinking about the murders. He headed back to the genkan where he picked up his damp clothes and put them in a basket to carry to the laundry room without getting the floors wet.

Back at his desk, Jack grabbed a pencil and tried to pick up where he left off in his contemplation of the murders. But Kondo's visit kept creeping into his thoughts. Clearly this wasn't going to get anywhere—time to do something else. Groceries. It would be about a twenty-minute ride to Maru Matsu, given the heavy traffic likely to be on National Route Six at this time of day, which would leave some time to do groceries at Aeon before meeting with Matsumoto. The diversion might also help his brain work in the background as he wandered through the store. He headed for the Tesla, unplugged it from its charging station, and started his drive northward. It was turning into a nice day; the rain having stopped and the sky beginning to clear. The viridescence of the Japanese countryside in June was beginning to glow with the emerging sunlight. It would be a pleasant afternoon away from the village.

Jack arrived at the Aeon store and wandered through the aisles, grabbing some produce and several packaged foods, such as ready-make *karaage* chicken nuggets. The shopping took his mind off the murders and he had a couple of conversations with people he knew from town who happened to be at Aeon, as well. Aeon was the Walmart of northern Japan—it had everything from groceries to clothing. One could pick up apples, a new suit, and a television all on the same trip if so desired. Jack started feeling a bit nostalgic as he remembered how much both of his kids loved the store when they were little. And Irene continued to have a deep attachment; it would be one of her first stops when she arrived in town in a couple of weeks along with the 100 Yen Shop across the street that had an amazing variety of products at dirt-cheap prices. The 100 Yen Shop was George's favorite, too, because he could buy excellent kitchen utensils for little money.

With his basket full, Jack headed to the check-out. The cashier smiled and showed Jack the amount due on the screen, after which she asked Jack if he needed bags. He didn't, so she placed the groceries back in the basket, Jack paid with his credit card, and then he carried everything over to a table where customers bagged their groceries. The mindlessness of shopping had been good. Jack felt refreshed and was now looking forward to his meeting with Matsumoto and Taitsu. He arrived at Maru Matsu a few minutes early and decided to sit in his car, gathering his thoughts prior to their meeting. Somehow Kobayashi kept coming to mind as he thought about who might have a motive to kill someone in a Buddhist temple. At the same time, Kobayashi didn't really seem like the killing type. He was weird, to be sure, but he didn't come across as violent. Jack reminded himself that he was not a psychologist nor a detective, so that sort of analysis didn't add much value; it wasn't based on observation. Just on a feeling—and feelings didn't usually provide very good analysis of data. Jack looked in his rearview mirror just as Taitsu's Prius pulled into the Maru Matsu parking lot. Time to get lunch.

Inspector Matsumoto was already inside when Taitsu and Jack walked in. He had taken up residence at a booth and signaled for them to join him. The three men looked over the menu and Matsumoto asked if they were ready to order, to which they both nodded in affirmation. He pressed the button on the table and a young woman promptly arrived to take their orders: soba noodles with tempura for Jack, a beef bowl for Taitsu, and Salisbury steak for Matsumoto. Matsumoto didn't waste any time as they waited for their food to arrive.

"So, what have you guys found out? Anything that might be helpful?"

Taitsu quickly interjected, "Not really. I've been asking around subtly to see if anyone knows of a reason why someone around here might be troubled with Zen or Buddhism in general, and I've gotten nowhere. I asked a couple of people about *kakushi nembutsu*, given Jack's interest in this, and got the standard answer—it was scary. I feel like I've hit a dead end on this."

"Hmm." Matsumoto's brow furled and he took in a deep breath through his teeth, which made a mild hissing sound. "Too bad. I was hoping you might find something helpful. Thank you, it is greatly appreciated. Jack?"

"I'm not sure, but maybe I'm onto something…"

"Good, because I have not been getting anywhere, either…"

"Okay, so I decided to visit a few people to ask about *kakushi nembutsu*, because the candles and some of the other objects seem to me, at least, to have symbolic meaning that might be connected to Buddhist ritual and childhood. I'm convinced that the prayer beads and *onbuhimo* are not accidental but have some sort of intentional meaning—I just don't know what that meaning is. I talked to a few of the older residents of the village and got the same thing Taitsu-san got—it was scary and kind of nasty. I think most people are happy it's a thing of the past." Taitsu nodded and added an "hmmm" in confirmation.

"I then dropped by at Kobayashi-san's house because I knew he has had quite a few difficulties over the course of his life and is not very well liked in the community. I've been told by several people to avoid him, so I figured that was a good bet as a place where I might get some information."

"And?"

"Nothing concrete from Kobayashi-san, but he did have an odd response. I started to ask him about the *kakushi nembutsu* ritual. He answered vaguely about having not passed initially. When I asked him how he felt about that he stood, abruptly indicated he had a doctor's appointment, and ended our meeting. I felt like I hit a nerve; I just don't have any idea which nerve I hit or what it means."

"That's very good, Jack. This may be quite helpful. Maybe you should join the force and become a detective..." They all laughed.

"I'm retired, Matsumoto-san. I don't want to work."

"Doesn't seem like it to me—you look like you are quite engaged in doing your detective fieldwork."

"Point taken. You can hire me when the next murder happens..." A few more smiles and laughs rang out as the three men seemed to be increasingly enjoying each other's company.

Jack's face turned more serious. "There was another odd thing that added to my suspicions about Kobayashi-san." Matsumoto's eyebrows perked up while Taitsu took a sip of his beer. "This morning I had an odd encounter with a member of the *Ehoba* group that meets in the village. A woman came by to give me a copy of a book about their religion and to try to convince me to join."

"They do that all the time, Jack-san," interjected Taitsu.

"Yeah, but this was not a normal visit. In the past, I would have just smiled and told her I was not interested, but because Kobayashi-san is a member of that group, I decided to invite her into the *genkan* and ask a few questions. After we chatted for a few minutes, she mentioned that she heard I'd visited with Kobayashi-san yesterday and then talked about what a kind man he is. "*Yasashii, nee*," she said at least twice. Suddenly her face darkened and she mentioned some of the difficulties he had experienced, to which I noted that a couple of people in the village had mentioned he had struggled with depression throughout much of his adult life. At that, she murmured something about that being an expected comment from people in the village, stood abruptly, and with a curt 'thank you' dashed out the door, forgetting her umbrella in the pouring rain."

There was a momentary pause as all three men thought about the encounter and then Taitsu broke the silence. "I know it's a leap, but maybe she knows something about the murders and you got a little too close when you started talking about Kobayashi-san's history of mental illness."

"I had a similar thought—"

"Perhaps," interrupted Matsumoto, "but I think you know that mental illness has been something of a taboo topic in Japan until recently. It may well have been that she didn't want to talk about a friend's struggles with depression and alcohol."

"Mmmm," came the sound from Taitsu.

"Actually," added Jack, "I'm a bit more interested in Kobayashi-san's experiences with the ritual as a child. If he were in some way ostracized as a result of his failures with that ritual, it might form the basis of a motive—albeit a pretty weak one based on what we know as of now. I also started wondering if his household had ever experienced *mura hachibu*. That sort of ostracization could make someone very bitter and angry."

"I haven't heard that term in a long time," said Taitsu. "I don't think *mura hachibu* is even legal now, but it certainly did happen until fairly recently. I can check into that and see if Kobayashi-san's household ever was ostracized."

There was another pause.

"There's something else that's been bothering me," said Jack. "In both murders, a body had to have been moved significantly. If it was Kobayashi-san doing that…well, he's pretty old. He seems to be in good shape, but it would be quite a challenge for an older man to move the bodies around like they were. Takahashi-san was very small, so maybe. But the second murder showed signs of a struggle."

"Ah, that brings up the one useful thing we've learned at my end," inserted Matsumoto. "The second victim was drugged. Chloroform. We took your advice, Jack, and an autopsy was done on the second victim. We think that he woke up during the murder attempt and struggled as he was being strangled."

"So… you are saying he was drugged and intentionally brought to the temple to be strangled there?"

"Yes."

"Wow," said Jack in English, and then switching back to Japanese, "that might answer the other question I had: how did Kobayashi-san get Takahashi-san in a position to hang him? If he were drugged, it *might* be doable. But I'm still not convinced Kobayashi-san has the strength to lift a man into that position. He'd have to somehow throw the ligature over the beam, tie it, and then balance Takahashi-san's drugged, and limp, body on the chair while he put his head in the noose. Seems like it would require a lot of strength and stamina."

"There's a ladder in the back *genkan* at the temple main hall. I keep it there. It's useful sometimes when I need to change a light bulb in the main hall. Maybe he used that."

"Was the back door unlocked?"

"Yes, Jack, we determined that after you left the other day. It has to be how they got into the temple," added the inspector.

"How would the murderer have known there was a ladder there?" asked Jack.

"Good point," responded Taitsu. "Kobayashi-san might know. Although he belongs to the *Ehoba* group, he has at times come to the temple for funerals and used to come to all the events at the temple when he was sober enough to do so. So, he might have noticed it—it's been there a long time."

"Maybe," said Jack, "but it doesn't add up. He'd need a strong memory and excellent observational skills to have noted something that insignificant. Do alcoholics usually have good memories? And how many of us would take a mental note of the ladder stored in the back door?"

"You would, Jack" said Taitsu.

"Yeah, but I'm weird, and as an anthropologist that's the sort of thing I do. Also, villagers don't usually come in through the back door, so I'm not sure why he would have ever gone back there anyway. No… that doesn't seem likely. There's only one possibility if we are right that the murderer is Kobayashi-san. He must have had an accomplice."

19
THINKING ABOUT DATA

At home, Jack headed for the back porch, pipe in hand. He had driven home with his brain on autopilot and thought himself lucky he hadn't rear-ended anyone. Thankfully, the traffic was light. Things were not adding up very well with the case, although Matsumoto's revelation that at least the second—and likely first—victim had been drugged was helpful in connecting some dots.

"Damn!" he exclaimed, realizing that he had forgotten to mention Sam's observation about the candles and other objects as possibly being intended to mislead investigators. There will be another chance, he thought.

At least it was now clear how someone would have been taken to either temple and it also at least raised the possibility that someone of Kobayashi's age and stature might be able to commit the murders. But not much else made sense. Was he fixating on Kobayashi as a suspect just because he's weird? A small amount of circumstantial evidence vaguely pointed in the direction of Kobayashi, but it wasn't enough to base any conclusions on. He had nothing but hunches at this point. Data, he needed more data. As Jack thought it over, he realized there was only one way to get it. He would have to employ the most basic tool of ethnographic research—participant observation. Chatting with people in the village wasn't going to be enough—he would have to join the *Ehoba* group.

As he puffed on his pipe, Jack let out an audible sigh and then said, "Ugh, I really don't want to do that." But he also knew it was going to happen, because this was part of doing good ethnographic fieldwork. Participant observation is the core strategy of data collection for ethnographers. It's not enough to just watch people doing what they do and living their lives; if you really want to understand something—or at least come close to understanding it—you need to do it. If you watch baseball, you can know the rules and understand the strategies and plays in the game in detail. But that is entirely different from being on the field and playing the game—the only way to experience baseball as a player is to play baseball. The same is true for culture, he thought. If you want to understand what it is to be a player in a cultural context, you need to live in that context and do the things that players do. And sometimes that means the ethnographer has to join a group or talk with someone that is unappealing or uncomfortable. It's the only way to get a reasonably full picture of the people and practices associated with a context; you have to be willing to shed a bit of ego and dive into the lives of the Other. But Jack also understood that even with participant observation, any real understanding is quite limited. You can do what others do, but you can never be who those others are as people and as cultural beings. Not being Japanese, Jack could never fully understand what it is to be Japanese, nor what it is to be a Japanese person living in the village of Tanohata, let alone a member of a religious group with origins in a foreign land that was perceived as a weird cult by local residents.

Whenever Jack thought about this, his mind wandered to dogs and humans. Regardless of how close they might be to each other emotionally, it really was impossible for humans to understand what dogs think and how they construct their worlds. It was just basic anatomy. Dogs and humans have different arrangements of their sense organs. The average human might have twenty million scent receptors in their nose, while the average hound dog might have 220 million. Our eyes perceive of color in different ways and dogs can hear frequencies not available to humans. All of this meant one simple thing—dogs and humans don't inhabit the same reality, even if they do inhabit the same physical space. It's no different for humans from different cultures, he thought. An American and a Japanese person share the same anatomy and the same sense experiences, but they do not share the single most powerful element in making humans what they are—culture. One's culture forms an environment through which we grow and are socialized as children.

There is a constant interaction between individual and world that leads to specific pathways in the brain forming—those pathways are different depending on the social environment one happens to grow up within. Language, of course, is central to this. And Japanese and English are very different languages. It's not just that they are represented differently in writing, Japanese grammar is conceptually unlike English and the language is used in ways quite different from English. Japanese rarely use personal pronouns, instead depending on context to identify who is taking an action, or using someone's name when it is absolutely necessary to be clear. English speakers are so dependent upon personal pronouns that they have a filler for instances when there is no personal pronoun to use—that filler is "it." Japanese people don't use plural and singular when counting things; instead, they identify the shape, size, or function of an object with counters added to the number. So, five dogs are "*go-hiki*" but five cars are "*go-dai*". The word "*go*" is the number five, but "*hiki*" indicates that what's being counted is small animals while "*dai*" indicates it's large machines. Counting in Japanese is something of a nightmare for native English speakers.

As he pondered counting, Jack reminded himself that the point of all these thoughts was that Japanese and Americans are simply wired differently, even if they share the same sensory anatomy. And that meant that they think in different ways and use different logical structures to arrive at motives for action. To be Japanese or to be American means to be a human in different, but equally valid, ways. Of course, there is plenty of overlap; virtually all humans experience pain, suffering, love, hunger, sexual desire, etc. But the way they interpret those experiences can be vastly different from one cultural context to another. He needed to keep this at the front of his mind as he tried to work through the problem that stood before him. And the only way to even begin to push into that other way of seeing—a rural-Japanese-elder male-Christian-*Ehoba* perspective with all the complex life history that Kobayashi and other members of the group brought with them—was to try to participate in their story rather than just watching it from a distance.

It would seem strange for him to just walk over to the *Ehoba* meeting hall and try to join, so he would have to wait until another representative came by and attempted to pull him in. He would enter gently, rather than enthusiastically, into the community, being careful in order to be both respectful and avoid raising suspicions by being overly interested in the chance that Kobayashi really were the murderer. The group might be intent upon pulling Jack in, but that didn't mean they would lack caution in how they went about doing that. And if he were right in his thinking that Kondo left abruptly because Jack had gotten a little too close to the truth about Kobayashi, then he may have already blown any chance of joining the group. If his past experiences were right, he would know in a day or two when one of the evangelists again rang his doorbell to talk with him about their god.

In the meantime, he would have to busy himself learning as much as possible about Jehovah's Witness groups and continuing to gather other data that might help him understand and explain the murders. Time to open the laptop and do some surfing. Jack went inside and sat at his desk. He thought to himself, Saori won't be home for several days, so one pipe-full inside isn't going to stink up the entire house sufficiently that she will know I was smoking inside. He lit up.

It didn't take much effort to find information about the Jehovah's Witness religion on Google. His first stop was Wikipedia, which, despite what high school teachers had told his kids, Jack found to be an excellent starting point for many research projects. The entries in Wikipedia had a way of nicely laying out main points about a group, individual, or idea that helped him come up with ideas to guide his research into more scholarly areas of writing. It was a useful tool. Most of what Jack read he already knew, but there was one point that caught his attention. The Watchtower Bible and Tract Society of Pennsylvania, as the Jehovah's Witnesses were formally known, are viewed as the only apparent channel through which God communicates with humans on Earth. It is part of God's theocratic organization, which based on what Jack read, appeared to be something of a dictatorship ruled from the top, meaning God, rather than a democracy run by rank and file members.

He decided to move on to the website of the group itself, thinking that would provide an excellent synopsis of their basic beliefs. What he learned was both surprising and interesting to Jack. One key point that he had not known was that Witnesses were not trinitarians. In fact, they rejected the idea of the Trinity and, although they saw Jesus as their savior, they did not seem him as a god. He also learned that Witnesses think of Heaven as a real place with a real government. There are other ways in which Witnesses are different from other Christian groups, he learned, perhaps most notable being that they regard the soul as mortal, so one's soul doesn't necessarily continue after death. Instead, death is thought of as a state of non-existence: according to Ecclesiastes 9:5, "as for the dead, they are conscious of nothing at all." The website made it very clear:

> *People who die pass out of existence. (Psalm 146:4; Ecclesiastes 9:5, 10) They do not suffer in a fiery hell of torment. God will bring billions back from death by means of a resurrection. (Acts 24:15) However, those who refuse to learn God's ways after being raised to life will be destroyed forever with no hope of a resurrection.— Revelation 20:14, 15.*

For Witnesses, Jack read, the only hope for an afterlife is resurrection at the hands of their god, who can provide the deceased with a new body. Hell, it seemed, was not the place of fire and brimstone, but an eternal non-existence for those members of humanity that fail to be resurrected by God. And then there was the interesting point that wicked angels or demons sometimes pretended to be spirits of the dead, a deception on their part that led humans to believe in ghosts. So, a *muenbotoke*, for a Japanese member of the Witnesses, would actually be a source of evil. Interesting, he thought.

Jack decided to look more specifically into the Japanese take on Jehovah's Witness belief and practice. He found an old article from the 1990s and not much else that had been written on the group's activities in Japan, but it was still useful. He read that like most other new religious movements in Japan, the majority of members were women and recruitment usually begins with women who then bring in their families. Members, he read, were not discouraged from seeking things like higher education, but were dissuaded from pursuing goals that focused on material and status acquisition. It was better, it seemed, to focus on one's ministry than to build a life centered on working in a corporate environment and achieving material gain. An ascetic lifestyle appeared to be the ideal.

Jack was aware of the popularity in the post-war era of various new religions in Japan, many of which drew on Buddhist and Shinto themes, in part due to their capacity to tap into traditional concerns related to ancestors, spirits, and sometimes even magical healing. The Witnesses, were different, according to the journal article he was reading. They forbade participation in indigenous religious activities, including community festivals and Buddhist funerals. But there was one thing that the Witnesses did share with other new religious movements in Japan. They were highly critical of the traditional religious establishment, such as the system of Buddhist temples, which was viewed as having lost touch with spiritual truth, followed corrupt doctrine, and focused on commercial gain through things like selling amulets to tourists. For Witnesses, this was the same criticism it levied at Christendom, but it seemed to have an even more powerful target in the form of Japanese religions that failed to recognize the love and authority of the Christian God.

And then Jack got to a section on blood transfusions. Not unexpectedly, the Witnesses had encountered problems with their beliefs against blood transfusion in Japan, particularly when it came to children. There had been an instance of a Witness child who was injured in 2005 in a bicycle accident that caught national attention in tabloids and on television when the parents refused a transfusion for their child. Not only did this seem to many Japanese a form of child abuse, but it made little or no sense since few Japanese understood Christian doctrine, let alone the peculiar ideology of a small Christian sect like The Watchtower Society. The group received immense negative publicity, but remained firm on the issue, showing a marked unwillingness to adjust its doctrines to widespread ideas in Japanese society. No doubt, most adult residents of the village would have followed this incident in the news, which may have contributed to the generally negative image of the Kingdom Hall that had been established in the village. From the perspective of villagers, members of the Witness group probably looked to be harsh and uncaring of life at best and outright monsters at worst.

Jack moved on to the Japanese website for The Watchtower organization and found they claimed about 212,000 members in roughly 3,000 congregations throughout Japan, which he thought was likely inflated. He learned that a great deal of their activities focused on publication of Watchtower tracts, magazines, and translated Bibles as well as the encouragement of door-to-door missionary activities aimed at growing the membership.

Jack yawned and looked at his watch as he stretched out his arms. Wow. Already eight o'clock, he thought. Forgot about dinner. He rose from his desk and moved to the kitchen to prepare some food, which involved microwaved rice, instant miso soup, and some of the *karaage* chicken nuggets he had purchased at Aeon. Not exactly high cuisine, but it would have to do. He grabbed the remote control and turned on the TV, which showed an NHK newscast. Having had enough Japanese for one day, he switched to Netflix and picked an old episode of Star Trek, which was sort of like comfort food for the mind in Jack's view. He'd seen every episode dozens of times but saw Kirk, Spock, and McCoy along with the other characters, like old friends who made life comfortable. Jack realized that he was very tired. He'd been so busy over the past few days that the usual jetlag had been delayed. He never had much jetlag when coming from the U.S. to Japan—it was always much worse in the other direction—but there were a few days in which his physical status was a bit off. Jack finished his meal, shut off the TV only about fifteen minutes into the episode, and headed for bed, leaving the dishes on the table. By half-past nine he was fast asleep, well ahead of his usual bedtime of eleven o'clock.

PART III

ANALYSIS

20
ONE STEP FORWARD

Jack awoke at noon. It had been a blissfully deep sleep and he felt more rested than he had in several days. The morning, actually the mid-day, was bright and it looked like it would be a pleasant afternoon. He checked his phone and saw that the temperature was 22°C, with a mild breeze, which encouraged him to bring in the fresh air by opening a few windows. Brunch would be eggs and toast, while sitting at the table on the back porch. Too nice a day to stay inside, he thought. He could hear an engine sputtering in the distance; probably someone cutting weeds, he thought. And there was the loud cawing of a crow that represented a regular auditory exclamation point to life in rural Japan, echoing from one of the trees behind his house. Locals didn't particularly care for the numerous crows that inhabited the area, but Jack found the sound calming.

It was two o'clock in the afternoon before Jack mustered enough enthusiasm to head back inside and take a shower. It had been a lovely day so far—more like he had imagined retirement—with plenty of sleep, no fieldwork, and most importantly, no murders. This was what retirement was supposed to look like. Jack decided to continue luxuriating and concluded that instead of taking a shower, he would head to an *onsen* or hot spring in the mountains, where he could soak in hot water and shed some of the events of the past few days. Before he managed to get his clothes packed in a canvas bag, the phone rang—it was Taitsu.

"*Moshi moshi.*"

"*Moshi moshi, Taitsu desu.*"

"Hi Taitsu-san, how are you doing?"

"I'm okay, but was wondering if you might have a few minutes to talk this afternoon. I can drive over to your place."

"Sure, but I need to take a shower—I got up at noon today."

"Taking this retirement thing pretty seriously, eh?"

"More like jetlag. It caught up with me last night and I passed out around 21:30. But I will say that so far, it's been a lovely day of retired life with a sleep-filled morning and a relaxing brunch on the porch. You're not going to ruin that, are you?"

"We'll see."

"Right. Give me thirty minutes. Any time after that I'll be dressed."

"Ok, I'll get there around 15:00."

"Sounds good. I'll probably be sitting outside, so just come around back when you get here."

They disconnected and Jack sauntered into the bathroom, disappointed that his plans for an *onsen* trip had been thwarted. Maybe tonight after dinner, he thought. I can drive over to Sengaishi Onsen, which isn't too far away. Ever punctual, Taitsu arrived at 15:00 on the dot and walked to the back of Jack's house, where he found Jack sitting at a table smoking. Jack looked up and immediately said, "Don't ask me when I'm going to stop smoking…" Taitsu laughed and pulled out a chair where he settled his tall, slender frame as Jack set down his pipe to let it go out. He didn't want to bother Taitsu with the smoke.

"So, what's happening? Have you learned something new?"

"Maybe. I've been doing a little digging into the backgrounds of both Takahashi-san and Saito-san. I think you are onto something with the *kakushi nembutsu* link."

"*Hontō ka…*" Is that so… Jack used the very casual form of Japanese reserved for relatives and close friends.

"*Ano—*" Umm. "I was asking some of the members of the temple parish if they knew either of the men. I wasn't getting anywhere, and then I decided to ask some of the people who live further away from Tanohata. I thought maybe they would be a little more interested in talking, since they are not really part of this community. It turns out that one person, who lives in another part of town, but whose family grave is at Taiyō-ji, had known Takahashi-san since childhood. They grew up together."

"What did he have to say about him?"

"It's a woman, and she didn't really tell me much about Takahashi-san himself. But she did indicate that his house was where they held the *kakushi nembutsu* when she was a child. She thinks his father was a leader of the ritual, but wasn't sure."

"The plot thickens," said Jack in English.

"What?"

He returned to Japanese. "Sorry, I was just thinking aloud. That certainly seems to support the idea that there is some connection with the ritual."

"I agree."

"What about Saito-san?"

"Well, he was Takahashi-san's relative on his father's side."

"Is that so..."

"Yes. He married out of his natal household and into his wife's, taking her name at the time."

"*Mukoyōshi?*"

"Exactly. He was adopted as an adult to take over the role of eldest male in his wife's family. They had two daughters, so there was no male to act as successor. Nowadays, of course, this wouldn't have been much of an issue and one of the daughters would have simply taken on that role. But at that time, it was an ideological necessity to have a male successor to the family lineage. It was his responsibility to take care of his parents and to ensure that the ancestors were properly cared for at the family altar and grave site. The successor also usually took over the family business. I'm not sure, but I suspect that Saito-san was, in fact, the *Ue-sama* for the ritual here in Tanohata until it died out. I know that the *Ue-sama* always came from another village."

"Which means that Saito-san wasn't just anybody. He was an enlightened being, at least when it came to his involvement in the ritual."

"Yes."

"So, if Saito-san were the *Ue-sama* when Kobayashi-san had his problems getting through the ritual, there could be a grudge."

"It would be an extremely long-term grudge, but it's at least possible."

"But Kobayashi-san has had a lot of other problems in the village. It's possible that Saito-san was just a symbolic aggregation of all of that history in one person...or maybe two people. How does Takahashi-san fit in?"

"I don't know. But because he and Saito-san are related and both tied to *kakushi nembutsu*, there's a good chance that's where the connection lies. I wouldn't be surprised if Takahashi-san did, in fact, have some sort of official position. It wouldn't have been as *Ue-sama*, despite what I was told, because the ritual took place in his house. But it's highly likely he was one of the gate-keepers or held a similar important role, during the ritual. If that's the case, then there's a clear connection."

"Maybe you should see if you can poke around a bit more on that end of things and I'll see what I can learn about Kobayashi-san from inside the *Ehoba* group."

"What?"

"I decided that when they come around again—and they will certainly come around again—I'll tell them that I'm interested and want to go to their meetings. That way, I might have a chance to learn more about Kobayashi-san, or at least to observe him as he interacts with other members of the group."

"I'm not sure that's a good idea, Jack. They are a very strange bunch of people."

"Agreed, but I don't think they are dangerous. Although, I'm beginning to think Kobayashi-san is potentially dangerous."

"What about that woman who came to your house? You thought that she might know something. If that's the case, then Kobayashi-san isn't the only one who might be dangerous."

"Good point. But I don't see any other way to get more on Kobayashi-san. And neither you nor Matsumoto-san can work their way into the group the way I can as both a foreigner and an anthropologist. They already assume that I'm a Christian, so they think I'm sympathetic to their religious ideas."

"If they only knew..."

"Yeah, well, let's not let on about that for now."

Taitsu looked at his phone. "I've got to run. I have a meeting with a carpenter about some work we are doing to the temple roof."

"Right. I'll let you know if anything happens with the *Ehoba* group. I might need you to come rescue me..."

"Let's hope not." Taitsu got up and strode with his long legs toward the Prius. Jack walked him out to the car and bowed as Taitsu backed into the street. They had talked for about an hour and Jack thought the day was largely shot. And then as he passed through the sliding door from the porch into his house, he heard the doorbell ring. Maybe it's Kondo, he thought. That would be a stroke of good luck. He called out, "*Hai*" and walked to the front of the house, stepping down into the *genkan* as he slipped into some shoes. He unlatched the door and slid it open, but it wasn't Kondo standing on the other side. Still, Jack's face lit up, because it had to be members of the *Ehoba* group. Just beyond the threshold, two men of medium height and build—both wearing white shirts, dark slacks, and striped ties—waited with large smiles and some books in their arms. The books were clearly in English. One of the men introduced himself in English and explained they were from the Morioka Kingdom Hall of The Watchtower Society and came at the request of the local group. "We heard that you met with Kondo-san yesterday. We wanted to make sure you had books you can read, so we brought you copies in English."

Jack decided it was time to show some interest, so he smiled and motioned for them to enter the *genkan*. He took a moment to decide which language to use, and settled on English, since that was how they had started. Sometimes people who had English skills very much wanted the opportunity to practice, and Jack also thought it might be interesting to see how they presented their ideas in English, rather than Japanese. He spoke carefully, "Thank you. I appreciate this and also appreciate you making the effort to drive all the way from Morioka—that's a long drive." The men smiled and nodded. "I'm quite interested in *Ehoba*. Do you think it would be possible to visit one of the meetings at the Hall here in Tanohata?"

One of the men sucked some air through his teeth and said, "Ah... that might be a little difficult. We are very happy that you are interested in the teachings of The Watchtower Society, but before you can come to our meetings, we prefer that you meet with one our members weekly for a while doing Bible study." Jack was quite impressed by the man's fluency in English and suspected he might have spent time in the States or Canada. "When we think you've progressed and your interest has grown, you are invited to join the Sunday meetings at the Kingdom Hall."

"That sounds good. How long does that take, usually?"

"It varies, but normally about a year." Jack's heart sank. A year would be far too long for him to get anywhere learning about Kobayashi and his connection to the murders. But he also didn't want to appear overly zealous, which might arouse suspicion if Kondo were also in some way involved. There was a narrow line to walk here. On the one hand, he was genuinely interested in the group in relation to what he might learn about the murders, but he didn't want to overdo it, because he also had absolutely no interest in actually becoming one of their members. He simply was curious about the meetings and wanted an opportunity to encounter a few more members of the group so that he could pursue his primary objective of learning more about Kobayashi.

"That's a long time, but I understand. When could I start meeting with someone?"

"We can ask one of the Witnesses here in Tanohata to come by tomorrow, if that's okay."

"That would be great. Anytime is fine. I should be around all day."

The men bowed and thanked him as they backed out of the open door. Jack thought it might work out well if he could talk to someone alone. If he could develop some rapport, he might learn something about Kobayashi. But that would likely take time. Without a solution to the murders, there remained a good chance that another would be forthcoming. Jack needed to work quickly, but the Witnesses were not going to make that easy.

21
EHOBA

At ten o'clock the next morning, Jack's doorbell rang and he knew it had to be one of the Witnesses from the village. Clearly, word passed quickly among members of the group. As usual, Jack called out while padding to the *genkan* and when he opened the door, he saw two middle-aged women, neither of whom was Kondo. Interesting, he thought. They both looked like smaller versions of Kondo—same haircut, same drab clothing, same flat shoes. It was like they were wearing a uniform. The woman on the right appeared to be somewhat older and spoke first.

"*Ohayō gozaimasu!*" she said with a pleasant smile. "My name is Hashimoto and this is Itō. We are from the *Ehoba* group here in the village." Speaking first indicated clearly that Hashimoto was of somewhat higher status than Itō. Jack asked them to enter and, rather than keeping them in the *genkan*, invited the women into the house. They removed their shoes and stepped up from the *genkan*, turning around and bending down to rearrange their shoes so that they neatly faced outward in preparation for their departure. The three walked into the kitchen and sat at the large wooden table, while Jack prepared some green tea for the group, which he brought out with some packaged Japanese cakes he had purchased at Aeon. He already had both the Japanese and English Bibles he was given on the table and had also placed a notepad and pencil next to them. Since it was unlikely that either of them could read English upside down, he thought he could openly take notes under the guise of writing down information related to the Bible study. As he sat down, he thanked them for visiting when they must be so busy—a common expression even when it was clear that one's guest was not busy at all.

They began by talking about the group and the older woman explained the basic beliefs of the Watchtower Society to Jack while he listened intently and wrote down notes. They read a few passages from the Bible and discussed the meaning, in this case focusing on the idea that Jesus was a human and that, therefore, the Trinity did not make sense. After enduring an hour of Bible study, Jack started gently moving the conversation to a more general theme as he asked the women about their involvement in the group.

"How long have you been in the *Ehoba* group?" Hashimoto responded that she had joined about five years earlier, while Itō said it had been three for her. He asked what had attracted them to the religion and both agreed that there was a sense of belonging they had struggled to find elsewhere. This was largely what Jack expected; their interest in *Ehoba*, at least initially, was motivated more by a desire to find a comfortable group to join rather than by ideological or theological zeal. The zeal came later. As they talked, Jack wanted to delicately steer the conversation in the direction of Kobayashi. Eventually, he decided to give it a shot and see if they might engage in a conversation that veered away from the Bible and the group.

"I'm curious about something."

"Yes?"

"I've spent many years learning about Japanese religions and I'm just wondering how you feel about Buddhism. It seems like most people are Buddhists."

There was a brief pause and then Hashimoto spoke softly. "The Watchtower Society believes that people should make their own choices about what to believe."

"Of course, of course. So, did you both grow up in households that practiced Buddhism?" Jack was confident that the answer was yes and both women nodded in confirmation.

"Then why switch to a different religion?"

There was another pause—a bit longer this time. Hashimoto took a breath and said, "You're not Japanese, Riddley-san, so maybe you wouldn't know about this, but there are a lot of problems with Buddhism in Japan. Many corrupt monks that are only in it for money. They don't care much about people." Jack nodded and thought to himself that he had succeeded in shifting their meeting over to an interview, which was what he had hoped would happen. "It's difficult to change from Buddhism, since almost everyone does some kind of Buddhist ritual for the dead, but it doesn't seem like Buddhism is there to help people with their lives."

"Mmm," replied Jack, "I can see how it would be difficult to convert to a religion like Christianity. It's very different from Japanese religions."

"Yes, I think so."

"How did your families feel when you converted?"

Itō entered the conversation with a gentle smile and said, "Oh that was difficult for me. My parents and other relatives were very unhappy. They felt that I was leaving the family because I could no longer participate in ancestor memorials and other rituals related to the dead. But that's not allowed in *Ehoba*. My father was very angry with me at first, but he sort of came around after a while." As Itō spoke, Hashimoto nodded in affirmation suggesting that she encountered similar resistance from family, a point that she confirmed after Itō finished speaking.

"It's hard on everyone who converts, I think," said Hashimoto. "So much of Buddhism is related to one's family and ancestors, that others feel like you're leaving the family if you join a group like this. I had a similar experience to what Itō-san described, but it was also with my husband." Jack had no idea that either woman might be married since most Japanese did not wear wedding rings.

"Really? He objected?"

"Yes, very strongly. He often shouted. He would say that it was my responsibility to take care of the ancestors and then one day he asked something that I could tell was at the root of his anger."

"What was that?"

"He asked how he should deal with my cremains if I were to die first. He didn't know what to do with them, because he knew that the rest of our family would want them interred in the family grave with the other ancestors, but my religious beliefs would prohibit that.

He asked me how our son would take care of his mother's ancestral spirit if I were not with the rest of the family. He accused me of being selfish."

"I see. That sounds like it was hard. What did you tell him?"

"I said I didn't know, but I couldn't have my cremains interred with the rest of his family. Something else would have to be worked out." As she said this, Jack could see that tears were forming in her eyes.

"I'm sorry. I didn't mean to pry. I'm sure it was very difficult."

"It's okay. You should understand what might happen if you join, but maybe not for you since you are already a Christian." Jack thought it interesting that she simply assumed he was Christian. "Do you have children?" Hashimoto had shifted the focus of conversation slightly.

"Yes, two."

"That's wonderful. I hope they can understand your feelings if you decide to join us."

"I think they will be okay. But what does your husband think of your belonging to the Witnesses now? Did he change his mind?"

There was a pause. "—I don't know. I never see him. We divorced a few years ago."

"I'm sorry. I didn't realize…"

"It's fine. Joining *Ehoba* has helped me get through a difficult time and I'm now happy with life. My son and I have been doing well since the divorce." Jack remembered from a conversation years earlier with another woman who had divorced that it is normal in Japan for mothers to retain custody of any children and for the father to be largely out of the picture. Usually, a woman and her children would move back to live with her parents, which was the case with Hashimoto, he learned, as she continued to describe her situation. Jack listened attentively, making sure to nod on occasion to alert Hashimoto that he was interested and paying attention—a standard practice from the ethnographic tool kit. She continued, talking about how much the Watchtower Society had helped her and her son, and when the opportunity arose, Jack decided to nudge the conversation in a different direction.

"I'm curious if you know Kobayashi-san. I met him many years ago when I was doing research in this village. I've had the feeling that he's been through hard times and that the Witnesses helped him greatly in getting his life together—in fact, another person in the village here mentioned that to me the other day."

"Oh, yes," replied Hashimoto, "it's my understanding that he had a very hard time when his step-mother stole his family fortune, but that was a little before I joined. However, we were lucky that he became a believer and he never misses a meeting. He is a very committed member of *Ehoba* and a kind person." Everyone within *Ehoba* seems to think the world of this dude, Jack thought to himself.

"Yes, that's what Kondo-san told me." The pleasant atmosphere in the room suddenly felt a touch cooler as both women became quiet and the smiles briefly departed from their faces. Was there some tension there? Jealously? No, that didn't make sense. They quickly perked up again as Jack returned to Kobayashi. "Is Kobayashi-san one of the leaders in the group?"

Itō quickly responded, "If you mean is he one of the Elders, no. But he has become one of our leaders through his good deeds and kindness toward others. Also, he has been a model of how to find peace through God's love. In Corinthians, it says, 'love is patient and kind. It bears all things, hopes all things, endures all things. Love never fails.' Kobayashi-san has committed himself to that idea and tries to show love in all of his interactions with others. He is polite and patient and truly caring."

Jack thought to himself that the description seemed a bit different from his own encounters, as well as the comments of others in the village when it came to Kobayashi. But there were also regular comments among villagers that he had changed in recent years. Itō's image of Kobayashi certainly didn't bear much resemblance to what one would expect of a murderer. Careful, thought Jack, don't let bias enter into your thoughts on this. Things rarely are as they appear on the surface. Regardless, the chat with the two women was proving to be quite helpful. Jack was gaining a clearer picture of both the *Ehoba* group in the village and a representation of Kobayashi that was quite different from what he had been told by most villagers. He decided to try his luck on another topic.

"I'm curious if either of you are familiar with *kakushi nembutsu*." There was contemplative silence as the women thought about it and both shook their heads, indicating a lack of awareness of the ritual. "It was a ritual to become a disciple of Shinran that used to take place around here. It was done when children were around five years old. Neither of you did this?"

They again shook their heads and then Itō exhaled slightly, "I didn't grow up in this area. I was born in Sendai and my parents moved up here when I was in high school. I don't know anything about local customs."

"I see. Well, it was part of the *nembutsu* cult around here. It was the way children were indoctrinated into the cult." Jack was trying to push a bit on the idea of cults to see how they might respond, given their involvement in what most of the people around them viewed as a cult in the negative sense of the word. "I know that they still do the *nembutsu* on the night of the funeral to help the dead move on to the afterlife."

"That's very different from our beliefs," interjected Hashimoto. "For us, the only way to have an afterlife is for God to grant it. Therefore, we don't do rituals like that. Our worship focuses only on praying to God and reading the Bible so that we can meditate on what we learn from God's Word. And, of course, we try to preach the good news of the Kingdom to others, like you, so we can help you find peace, love, and happiness." Jack's internal distaste for Christianity kicked in as he thought to himself, what makes you think I'm not happy just because I don't believe in your god? But he suppressed it and continued listening. "We don't do rituals like that, we try to help those in need, as it says in James 2:14. Members of *Ehoba* have helped prevent suicides, worked to clean up the environment, helped prisoners find a new path. They certainly helped me and I think Kobayashi-san, too. It's a wonderful organization full of kind people."

That made Jack wonder and he wanted to ask, "Even Kondo-san?" but thought better of the idea. That could easily end his connection to the group and he wasn't quite ready for that yet. But he needed to ask a few more probing questions to see if he could learn about Kondo. There was a moment of silence and Jack could see that Hashimoto looked at her watch, an indication that they were about to end the session. Think quickly...

"Do you know anything about Kondo-san's background? When did she join the group? She seemed very nice when she dropped by the other day."

"I think she joined a little before Kobayashi-san started coming to meetings," said Hashimoto. "Other than that, I really don't know much about her. She keeps to herself..."

Itō nodded and added, "...I know she was very helpful to Kobayashi-san. She was the one who met with him like we are meeting now. *Gambarimashita*! She put a lot of effort into helping him, which he needed because he was struggling so badly with life. I shouldn't really say this, but I did hear that he may have attempted suicide at one point. I think Kondo-san was always there to help him—she was very loving and selfless and still is when it comes to Kobayashi-san. I know she checks in on him regularly, even though he has been baptized and now continues to prove through his works that his faith is alive. I think in some ways, the two of them are very mutually supportive..." As she said this, Hashimoto put a hand on her arm and then looked at Jack.

"*Jyaa...oisogashii tokoro wo...soro soro...*" Well, I know how busy you are, I think we should move on. "Thank you for having us," Hashimoto rose from her chair, as did Itō, "I think you are off to a good start. Please study your Bible and we will meet again next week. Is the same time good for you?"

"Yes," Jack smiled and bowed slightly, "that would be fine. I have much enjoyed meeting you both. Thank you for coming." They all walked toward the *genkan* and the women stepped down directly into their neatly arranged shoes, aligned for a quick departure.

Jack remained on the raised area and bowed as they opened the door and headed for their white van, slowly sliding the door closed while bowing and thanking Jack. He retired to his study and began thinking about the meeting with Hashimoto and Itō. They had talked for about an hour and a half and the meeting was informative. Jack was becoming increasingly convinced that Kobayashi was at the center of the murders. But how?

His stomach roared tumultuously and Jack realized that it was close to lunch time. He set down the pipe he had been fingering in his left hand while thinking and moved to the kitchen for a quick bite. He had no idea what he wanted to eat, so just started opening cupboards to see what he could find. "Thank you, Saori!" A large smile crossed his face as he said this to no-one. "Peanut butter!" When he first started fieldwork in Tanohata, peanut butter was impossible to find. There was a disgustingly sweet paste called peanut cream, but it was nothing like real peanut butter. Over the course of thirty years, much had changed and virtually anything one might buy at an American grocery store could be found at one of the larger stores in the area or at Yamazaki Imports, which specialized in international alcohol and other goods, many of which came from the States. Jack could even find his favorite beer, Sam Adams, at Yamazaki sometimes. He lathered some peanut butter on a slice of *shokupan*, the thick white bread that was common in Japan and made with rice flour. Jelly, he thought, there must be jelly, too. Sure enough, he found grape jam in the fridge. It would be a perfect PB&J sandwich; *shokupan* made the best sandwiches, with its rich taste and fluffy texture. Since the weather was again pleasant, Jack grabbed a bottle of *mugicha*—roasted barley tea—and settled at the table on the back porch. Crows cawed as Jack slowly nibbled at his sandwich, which he followed with a quiet post-meal smoke. The Presbyterian blend tobacco complimented the woody flavor of his tea delightfully.

He missed Saori, and then started to wonder what she would think about his joining the Watchtower Society. Of course, she would know it wasn't in his nature to be religious and that his "membership" would be only for research purposes. But she would, no doubt, caution him about getting pulled into the cult—and she would most certainly see it as a cult. He'd give her a call in the evening and see how things were going in Tokyo.

22
NOTES AND QUERIES

Jack's smart phone began to vibrate.

"Sam! How's it going? You're up kind of late, aren't you? Or is it early…"

"Early, dude. I woke up at 3am."

"That's dumb. Why would you do that?"

"I have to represent our promotion cases to the College Tenure and Promotion Committee this morning and one of our cases is not very strong. I wanted to take time to go over his file so that I can put on a good defense if the committee attacks—which I'm sure they will."

"Why did you put up a sub-par candidate for tenure?"

"He's done good work. Excellent work, in fact. But he doesn't publish in the usual philosophy journals and that caused two members of the department to vote against tenure and promotion. It was petty. The guy is an excellent scholar—just different. You know the type, Jack…"

"Yeah, I do. That's what you get for being department Chair. But… that's why they pay you the big bucks…"

"Which bucks are those?"

"Okay, then, the little bucks…"

They laughed and then Sam said, "Jack, I want you to teach me how to smoke a pipe. I just ordered a new meerschaum and I want you to show me how to fuss with it so that I can actually enjoy it. I know keeping a pipe lit is a pain, but the pipe I bought is really cool. It has the head of a sultan or something like that carved into it."

"That's common with meerschaum pipes—I think they originate from Turkey, actually. I can teach you, just make sure you get a tamp, some good matches, and some pipe cleaners. You might want to start with a mild blend, like Presbyterian or Ashton Smooth Sailing. I like both of those. A strong latakia blend may not be enjoyable at first. When does the pipe arrive?"

"I should have it in a couple of days. Maybe we could have one of our on-nomis next weekend."

"Sounds good," and then Jack fell silent for a moment. "Sam, do you know anything about Jehovah's Witnesses?"

"Not much. I've used case studies related to their attitudes about blood transfusions in ethics classes, but that's about it. Why?"

"I joined one of their groups."

"Right. You don't really expect me to believe that…"

"No, but it's true. Sort of. I think the murderer is a member of a Jehovah's Witness Kingdom Hall that is located in the middle of Tanohata. I decided to get involved with the group to see if I can learn anything."

"Sounds a little dangerous, Jack. And why would a member of the Witnesses murder someone?"

"That's what I'm struggling with. Tell me more about the issue with transfusions."

"I'm not going to claim to be an expert on this, Jack, but it's a regular topic in biomedical ethics classes like the one I teach. As you know, Witnesses refuse to take blood transfusions and this has created problems in hospitals, particularly when children are involved. From their perspective, the Bible states that humans shouldn't ingest blood, so they reject any form of blood transfusion, including plasma, and they rely on various spots in the Bible to support that claim. I know one is in Genesis which states that God told Noah that we can't eat flesh with its soul, meaning its blood. And there's another line in Leviticus that says the same sort of thing; it says that you can't eat the blood of any flesh because God views the soul, by which they mean life, as being in blood, and the soul belongs to God. I look at it a couple of ways. One is that taking blood is sort of like cannibalism, but it's weird because they say you can't eat flesh with blood in it, so I guess they can't eat meat like steaks, but I don't have a sense that vegetarianism is common among them. The second sense is that since God gives us a soul, ingesting blood is an affront to that gift. Honestly, their position has always seemed rather weak to me, but it makes for good discussion in an ethics class. The students sometimes get pretty riled up as they debate whether or not transfusions should be given to the kids of Witnesses despite parental objections."

"That's helpful, Sam. I started thinking about the whole blood thing with Witnesses after I was reading an old text from the *kakushi nembutsu* ritual I mentioned the other day—the secret initiation ritual. I was told by the man who gave it to me that the text was read to initiates who had succeeded in getting through the ritual, later in life when they become adults, and tells them that they are now disciples united in the blood of Shinran."

"You're still fixating on the objects from the murders?"

"Sort of. I think you were right in the idea that they could just be meant to throw off suspicion. But it's still bugging me. I think the issue of blood could be meaningful."

"Maybe. But why would they have issues with people who aren't Witnesses having been indoctrinated into a blood-cult of Shinran?"

"You've got a point, as usual."

"I should get back to my work, Jack. Gotta deal with this tenure thing. I just wanted to check in and also see if we can do that *on-nomi*."

"I'm alone for a couple of weeks while Saori is in Tokyo, so really anytime, Sam. Just let me know when the pipe arrives."

"Got it. I'll email you in a couple of days—let's shoot for Saturday."

"Cool. Oh, and when you get some tobacco, open the tin and let the leaves dry out a little—maybe 30 minutes or so. It will make for a better smoke."

"Thanks, dude."

After they disconnected, Jack sat and stared into nothingness. There were a lot of pieces and they weren't coming together very well in his head. He had always prided himself on his ability to solve puzzles, but this one was proving to be daunting. Back at his desk, he started to look over the written notes from the case he had produced. Maybe something would come to mind as he reviewed all of these parts. He spread the notes out on his desk and started to carefully read through them, organizing them into groups with common themes. This had always worked when he tried to deal with a tricky ethnographic problem, so he figured it might help. Over the next several hours, he silently moved note cards around, wrote some new note cards as ideas popped into his head, and created piles of cards that seemed related to each other. He didn't think about his pipe, nor about much of anything else—it was a period of intense focus—so intense that he had no idea if anyone had called or visited during that time. He wouldn't have heard even if they did.

At about six o'clock, Jack stood from his chair and absently walked toward the kitchen, where he found his smart phone resting on the table. He picked it up and entered the number for Inspector Matsumoto.

"*Hai, Matsumoto desu.*"

"*Matsumoto-san, Jack desu.*" Jack waited a moment for a bit of dramatic flair, "I know who the murderer is. And I think I have a motive, as well."

"What? How? I've been wracking my brains and am not really getting anywhere. What did you find out?"

"A lot, but most of it is vague. I spent time this afternoon putting the pieces together and I think I have it figured out. The problem is, I don't have the evidence we need. Everything is largely circumstantial or based on my analysis of the data I've managed to collect. Do you have time to meet?"

"Absolutely. Why don't I come over to your house so that we don't have to worry about anyone overhearing anything we say at a restaurant. I think I can be there in about thirty minutes. And we might get some help on evidence. I've got a couple of people working on finding the source of the chloroform. If we know that, we can probably trace a path to the person who obtained it. We'll see."

"Excellent. I'll call Taitsu-san and see if he can make it, as well."

"See you soon." They disconnected.

Jack immediately called Taitsu who told Jack that he was busy for another thirty minutes but then would head over. When Jack went back to his study to collect his pipe, he looked for any missed calls or messages on his phone. He hoped Saori had not tried to call him because she might get worried if he didn't answer and was relieved to find no calls since he went into his mental isolation. He wanted to call Saori, but there wasn't enough time before Matsumoto and Taitsu arrived. At the moment, it was more pressing to get all of his thoughts in order. At a few minutes before seven o'clock, Jack heard the sound of tires on crushed stone and knew Matsumoto must have arrived. He opened the front door before the inspector rang the bell and invited him in. Matsumoto offered the usual pleasantries, removed his shoes, and stepped into the house.

"Nice place, Jack-san. I really like all of the wood, and it smells new— like fresh pine and cedar." The nose of an observer, Jack thought. Most people don't notice how smells vary from one building to another, but a careful observer will pick up scents and catalogue them for future reference. Jack had decided that Matsumoto was clearly good at his job.

"We had it built for us and just moved in." Jack didn't feel like sitting at the kitchen table, so he motioned Matsumoto to the living room, where they could relax on comfortable furniture. "Would you like a beer or something?"

"Ah…," he said slowly, "that would taste good, indeed. It was a very busy day. Thank you, Jack-san."

"I've got Sapporo or if you're willing to try something new, I also have Sam Adams, which is an American beer. It's not like Budweiser, however."

"That sounds good. I'll go with the Sam Adams." Jack poured a couple of bottles into glass beer mugs that he had pulled out of the freezer and brought them over to Matsumoto, who was sitting with his legs crossed in the plush leather chair near the window. Jack handed him his glass and sat on the matching leather couch. They raised their glasses and said, "*Kampai*" together and both took a healthy swig of their beer, which Matsumoto followed with a refreshed "Ahhhh."

"That's really good, Jack. Not what I expect of American beer."

"Actually, nowadays there are so many micro-brewers that there are some amazing beers in the States. It's not like the old days when you could only get Budweiser, Miller, and a few others, all of which tasted the same—bad."

"I like Budweiser, actually, but it's not as good as Japanese beer."

"On that, we entirely agree!" They smiled and chatted for a few more minutes while Jack heated up some *edamame* and brought the salted soybeans into the living room. Taitsu arrived a little earlier than expected and the three men sat around the *edamame* with beer in hand ready to discuss their findings. Each of them had new observations and thoughts to add. Matsumoto said he expected to know the source of the chloroform soon and also found out that someone had seen a white van driving near Houn-ji on the night of the murder, but since they only had a loose time of death, they could not be sure of a connection. Matsumoto's assistant was working on that lead, as well. But so many people in the area drove white vans, it was not promising.

Taitsu had the most intriguing news. In his conversations with some of the parishioners, there was a rumor that a local Buddhist priest had been meeting with members of the *Ehoba* group. It seemed that he was doing Bible study with them. "I don't know who it is and don't have much of a description, but I'm trying to get more information on that. It seems a bit strange to me, but I can probably imagine myself being interested in learning about the Bible and spending some time with local Christians to get a better sense of how they view their religion. There aren't a lot of options for meeting Christians in this area, so it might make sense to meet with members of the *Ehoba* group."

"That's quite interesting, Taitsu-san," said Jack, "I wonder…"

"Wonder what?" said Taitsu.

"Nothing. Just a hunch. I need to piece a few more things together." Until this point in their conversation, Jack had sidestepped saying anything about his big news of having solved the mystery. But he could tell the other men wanted to know what he was thinking. Jack obliged, laying out the details of circumstantial evidence and showing Taitsu and Matsumoto how he had connected the dots and come up with a hypothesis about the motive and perpetrators of the murder. The other men thought Jack's ideas made sense and that there was a good chance he was right, but the evidence was not strong and there were still problems, such as no indication of who the accomplice might be. But if they found the person who bought the chloroform, that would cement it. That was still an "if" and in order to arrest the murderer, it might well require a confession, which seemed an unlikely outcome. Why would someone confess to a murder unless cornered into doing so?

"How are we going to move forward with this?" said Matsumoto, almost to himself.

"I've got an idea," said Jack. "It's a cliché, but we could pull the old murder-mystery trope of getting all of the suspects together and seeing if we can get the murderer to crack. We can do the classic summation, just like Columbo. If we work this the right way, there's at least a chance it might work. We don't have anything to lose. And time is important—I would not be surprised by another murder if we don't move quickly."

"*Sōdesu nee.*" I agree, said Matsumoto. "I really like that show, by the way."

"Me, too," said Jack. "You remind me a bit of Columbo, but you dress a lot better and your car seems to run regularly. You don't have a basset hound, do you?"

"No… But I love dogs, and I think it would be fun to have a basset. But I hear they kind of stink. You always have to clean out their ears."

Jack laughed and Taitsu looked a bit confused.

"Who is Columbo?" he said.

"Oh, it's an old American television show about a police detective who solves all sorts of difficult crimes in LA. It's really good."

"Ah, I see."

Jack brought them back to the murder at hand. "I think we can do this here, tomorrow evening. There's enough space. Matsumoto-san, can you contact everyone and make sure they understand that they are expected to attend?"

"Yes, that's no problem. But I must say that it is not the way we normally work when it comes to interrogating suspects in Japan. A public encounter risks people being humiliated; I'd be much more comfortable if we did this in a private setting at the police department. However, I've also never encountered any crime like these murders and this may be the best way to get a confession. At this point I can't think of an alternative and I don't want to risk another murder taking place."

"I understand, Matsumoto-san. I will work on making sure I've got everything in order in my head so that, perhaps, we can pull out a confession without too much embarrassment or distress among the participants in our little drama."

"Yes, we need to think about how people will feel when potentially being accused of the murders," interjected Taitsu. "It is a narrow line to walk between drama and cruelty. We need to be careful, because this isn't a very Japanese way of doing things."

"Yes, and although I can participate, it needs to be one of you who does the prodding. My language skills are not that nuanced, since Japanese is not my native language. I might get into trouble; sometimes when I'm in unfamiliar linguistic territory, I don't always know the vocabulary."

"We'll be there to help," said Taitsu, to which Matsumoto added, "you seem to do rather well in Japanese, Jack. It took me a while to grasp just how fluent you are. I've never met a foreigner before with whom I could have a natural conversation and even pass the occasional joke or sarcasm. I don't think you're going to have any problems."

"Thanks, Matsumoto-san. We'll see…"

The men continued to plan for the coming evening. When they had finished their beer and *edamame*, about an hour after they came together, the men called it a night and Jack saw them to the door. He felt very nervous about the coming gathering, but also good about his old friend Taitsu and the new friendship he felt he was making with Matsumoto. He had always liked Taitsu and was finding Matsumoto to be an enjoyable ally. He hoped they would be able to maintain a friendship after this was over.

Jack was tired. He stretched and headed for the porch, where he decided to give Saori a call.

"*Moshi moshi*," came the mellifluous voice at the other end. "Hi Jack. How's it going?" Jack proceeded to bring her up-to-date on all of the events since she had left for Tokyo. When he told her about the coming gathering of those connected to the murder, she asked in a worried voice, "Do you want me to come up tomorrow? I can leave in the morning and get there by noon. I can make some food."

"That's really nice, Saori, but it's not that kind of gathering."

"I know, but I feel like I want to do something."

"It's okay. I appreciate the thought, but it may be better for me to be alone on this. I'm not sure what's going to happen, but it's possible that it could turn violent. I'd be much happier if you stay there in Tokyo and hopefully everything will all be done by the time you and Irene head north."

"I guess—" Saori didn't sound convinced, but also decided there wasn't much to worry about, since the police would be in the room. At least it wouldn't be like the States, where it seemed like everyone was armed and dangerous. She was so happy to be safely in Japan, she thought. And then she reflected on the fact that it didn't seem quite so safe with these murders.

"Don't worry. Matsumoto-san will take care of things. He's a good guy and he seems to know his job well. I'll call you after the meeting and let you know how everything went. Hopefully, I'll be able to tell you that we are done with this and when you return we can finally start a quiet, retired life."

"Retired? I'm not planning on just sitting around, you know. I'll still be working and I've got a bunch of other things I want to do."

"I know, I know..." For Saori, retirement would in no way involve slowing down. Unlike Saori, Jack was able to take time to relax and ponder, but he also shared her tendency to always be busy. He just wasn't quite as intense about it. Jack had a laid-back quality that Saori lacked, but that also kept him less stressed about the future. Live in the moment, Jack always thought to himself.

"Jack, I've got to run. I have a big job I need to get done tonight. Sorry about that."

"See? You're too busy to head up here, anyway. No problem. I know you are trying to get things wrapped up there in Tokyo. I'm sure you have a lot to do. Don't worry about anything here. I'll call you tomorrow night."

"I'll be waiting."

"*Oyasumi!*"

"*Oyasumi!*"

23
SOMEONE IN THIS ROOM...

Early the next morning, Matsumoto sent uniformed police to the homes of everyone they wanted at the meeting. Each person was politely informed of their expected presence at Jack's house at 19:00 sharp. He knew the formality of the visits would make it clear that this was not a request, but an order. And if they informed everyone early, there was an off-chance that someone would panic and do something stupid before the evening meeting. Plain clothes officers from the city of Morioka's police department would be discretely monitoring the actions of everyone throughout the day. If someone tried to run, they wouldn't get far. Also, too many loose ends remained, so a mistake on the part of the murderer might help tie those up. The inspector spent the entire day working on a different case—a theft—while keeping close tabs on his assistants in the field.

Taitsu had a funeral to lead in the morning, and that would keep him busy until mid-afternoon. He awoke too early, unable to sleep in anticipation of the evening's events, and spent time doing priestly things like shaving his head. The funeral itself didn't require much preparation—he had conducted the same basic ceremony too many times to count. But as he prepared the *tōba*, the long piece of wood on which one's posthumous Buddhist name was written and which would be placed behind the grave, he found himself painting the characters with even more care than usual. Taitsu was good at calligraphy and enjoyed it. Somehow today, it seemed like it was important to get everything exactly right and to draw each kanji as beautiful as possible amidst the ugliness that had characterized the past several days. Images of the strangled men—and particularly Saitō's neck and body wrapped in the prayer beads—slowly moved through his mind with each stroke of the brush. It was difficult to hold back tears.

He was not one to believe ghosts and spirits, but as he thought about the violent, profane deaths these men had experienced, it seemed understandable how people had come to believe in things like *muenbotoke*. If there were ancestral spirits, how could they find happiness after deaths like these? Both murders seemed to carry an intent to symbolically express a vulgar disrespect for Japanese Buddhism and its emphasis on caring for the dead. He recalled the old saying: born Shinto, die Buddhist. The aphorism pointed to the fact that Shinto was a religion of life for most Japanese; when they turned about three-months old, they would be brought before a Shinto priest for a blessing from the *kami*, the deities of Japan's indigenous religion. And they would marry and go through other rituals of life as they aged, guided by the Shinto priest in their local shrine. Then, at death, Buddhism would take over and a Buddhist priest along with descendants would ritually care for the deceased at the funeral and in regular post-death rituals that continued for as long as fifty years. In recent times, the saying had evolved into: born Shinto, marry Christian, die Buddhist, since so many Japanese tied the knot in Christian wedding ceremonies despite having little interest in the religion from a theological perspective. It was aesthetically pleasing, but not much more than that.

Buddhism was so focused on death rituals, he thought, that perhaps it's understandable how people become frustrated—what do Buddhist priests do to help people live their lives? But the rituals do help with that; they bring serenity to those who have lost loved ones. For the ancestral spirits who were not ritually cared for, it was an eternity of suffering as they wandered around the world of the living, finding no peace and little other than loneliness, made worse if the mode of death had been unusually violent or gruesome. Could it be that the murders had been intended to insure Takahashi and Saito ended up as *muenbotoke*? Or at least to put that fear into their family members left behind?

Jack spent the day sitting on his porch and thinking. It had turned into a four-pipe, one pot of coffee day. In truth, more than thinking, Jack spent the day with nervous butterflies in his stomach that kept distracting him with their annoying flutters. What thinking he managed was more about retirement than about the murders, about which he didn't need to think anything else—either his plan would work or it would fail, no point in rehearsing it all day. Jack realized he was enjoying himself as he tried to solve the murders—enjoying himself immensely. Although he had looked forward to retiring from academic life at the university, he realized now that he had not desired to retire from being an anthropologist. Fieldwork was the most intellectually stimulating thing he had ever done. It made virtually every intellectual conversation he had experienced with colleagues, with the exception of Sam, seem trivial when it came to really learning about the experience of being human. Using fieldwork in an attempt to understand the cryptic dramas that ground the human condition and frame all human social interaction remained both challenging and a powerful way to exercise the mind. Experiencing the complex webs of meaning in which humans spend their lives had a way of bringing one face-to-face with the ambiguous nature of humanity itself. Or, perhaps, more the awareness that the most profound realization about human nature is that there is no such thing—just many different human natures – all of which get played out in the vast array of cultural contexts people collectively construct.

The pipe helped to calm him, but the coffee kept him wired. It wasn't a very healthy balance. Jack didn't feel hungry but still managed to eat a sandwich for lunch. And then as the afternoon rolled in, grey clouds accompanied it as temperatures cooled, leading Jack to put on a cotton argyle sweater in hues of olive and tan—the forecast for the evening was rain, which seemed appropriate. By dinner time, Jack was too nervous to eat, so he turned on the television and watched some local news. Japanese news programs were always enjoyable for their genuine simplicity. The report Jack watched focused on a local elementary school and the excitement kids were having about the cucumbers they had planted earlier in the spring. Jack learned about how the kids were carefully tending to the cucumber patch, being sure to weed and water it regularly. They anticipated a great harvest. From the elementary kids, the news show turned to a look at the activities of people living in an area nursing home. This was a bit more serious, because it raised problems related to residents who rarely received visits from relatives. But overall, Japanese television news lacked the persistent onslaught of criminal violence and political conflict that characterized most of American news reporting. Some Americans he knew thought it was naïve, but Jack found it refreshing that Japanese news programs would often focus on positive aspects of life, rather than endlessly dwelling on the worst examples of the human experience.

A few minutes before seven o'clock, Jack heard the approach of a car. Someone had arrived. It was Matsumoto. Jack opened the slider as the inspector was setting his umbrella in the rack Jack had put to the left of the door for his "guests." He entered the *genkan* and removed his shoes, but the seriousness of the night meant Matsumoto began talking about the day's progress without the usual pleasantries exchanged upon entering someone's house.

"We identified the source of the chloroform and have traced it to the person who purchased it, Jack."

"That's good news. Who is it?"

"I don't have his name yet—just got the call as I was heading over here. My assistant told me she is bringing him to the station for questioning."

"Hmmm. I wonder if it might be better to bring him directly here. It might help us."

"Good idea. I'll call Sakamoto-san now and ask her to skip the station and drive directly here." Matsumoto pulled out his smartphone and punched in the number of his assistant, as he moved into the kitchen. At the same time, he looked in Jack's direction and said, "Jack-san, there's one more thing I need to tell you, so don't drift too far off...*Moshi moshi...*" Another police officer, this one uniformed, had arrived and entered the house with the usual polite exchange of greetings. Jack was surprised, because unlike most police in Japan, this woman was carrying a holstered gun. Police in Japan are generally regarded as community assistants, rather than crime fighters, so the presence of a weapon took Jack aback somewhat.

"Jack-san, this is Officer Wada, she will help with the evenings activities."

"*Hajimemashite*," said Jack with a bow.

"*Hajimemashite, yoroshiku onegai itashimasu,*" replied Officer Wada in a particularly formal style of Japanese. Jack motioned her to the living room and offered her some tea that he had prepared, but the officer refused, instead taking up residence standing in one corner of the room, near the window. Taitsu arrived shortly thereafter and within a few minutes the guests were beginning to appear. Kobayashi was the first, followed by Hashimoto and Itō. They had also requested the presence of Satō Hitoshi, the leader of the local nembutsu cult. He arrived at the same time as Kondo Reiko, who rang the bell at the stroke of seven. Between his furniture and a few folding chairs, there were places for everyone to sit, although Officer Wada, Matsumoto, and Jack remained standing as the others took their seats. The inspector wasted no time, initiating the drama as soon as people had settled in.

The gruff and blunt Inspector Matsumoto had returned. He spoke in a deep and authoritative voice that balanced on the edge of anger and conveyed a clear message that bullshit would not be tolerated. "I'm sure you all understand why you are here. Each of you has been marked as a possible suspect in the murders that took place at Taiyō-ji and Houn-ji over the past few days." A couple of gasps and some very surprised faces indicated that, in fact, they did not all recognize this, which was part of the inspector's plan. He wanted to see their reactions while creating an atmosphere of discomfort in the room.

"Some of you have already been questioned by the police." Jack had not realized that Matsumoto was also conducting an investigation separate from Jack's inquiries, but it was obvious that he would have been doing so once he heard the inspector pointing it out. "I am going to ask a few questions tonight. But I want to make it clear—we know who the murderer is and plan to arrest that person tonight. I also want to thank Riddley-san, who was kind enough to make his house available to the police for this meeting. He is not a suspect." Jack bowed and indicated he was happy to be of help. All faces in the room looked worried, except Kobayashi's—he seemed strangely calm and collected.

Inspector Matsumoto gazed carefully at each face and then began his carefully prepared monologue. They had agreed the previous night that Matsumoto would be the master of ceremonies, given his position as Inspector, and they had even worked on the basic outline of what he would say. "There are several key points of evidence that have allowed us to understand these crimes and identify the murderer. First, each of the murders had evidence that points to a link with the *nembutsu* cult and the *kakushi nembutsu* ritual that used to be performed around here with children." Satō started to look nervous once he heard this as he shifted uncomfortably in his folding chair.

"I believe that the motive for the murder was connected to the cult and that is why burned candles were found in the hands of both victims. It is also the reason the second victim was strangled with the Buddhist prayer beads used by the *nembutsu* cult at the time of funerals. Clearly, the candles must have been placed in the hands of the men after they were killed, and then burned until they extinguished on each man's skin. This was intended to send a message to other leaders in the *nembutsu* cult—and that message was, "I'm coming for you, too." Indeed, as the murderer already knows, both victims were officials involved in the performance of the *kakushi nembutsu* when the murderer was a child. But until yesterday, it was unclear who might have a motive for killing these men. They had done no obvious harm to anyone and were simply quietly leading their lives as members of the community." Jack scanned the room to see any evidence of changes in demeanor. Who looked nervous? Who looked calm? It was difficult to determine, but all three women looked tense, as did Satō.

The inspector continued, "It was not very smart of the murderer to leave such strong clues. But the presence of these symbolic religious objects alone was only circumstantial, therefore, there was little we could gain from these clues. Fortunately, the murderer made a mistake. Yesterday, we learned something interesting," and he turned and looked directly at Kobayashi. "Kobayashi-san!?"

"*Hai*?" Suddenly the calm drained.

"I learned from Riddley-san that you told him the other day about your experiences with the *kakushi nembutsu*. Or, perhaps better, you lied to him about those experiences. Correct?"

"What? No, I didn't say anything. I have no idea what you are talking about."

The inspector looked in Jack's direction to let him know that it was time to join the performance, "When I came over to your place the other day, you told me that you did the *kakushi nembutsu*, but it took you more than one attempt to pass. And then you abruptly told me you had a doctor's appointment."

"Yes, that's right..." Kobayashi said indignantly.

"But you lied," interjected the inspector. "We did some digging and learned that you actually failed. As a result, you've spent most of your life ostracized from the village and looked down upon by your peers among the samurai families."

"*Chigaimasu! Uso desu!*" Wrong! That's a lie!

"It's been a tough life," said Jack calmly, trying to bring down the tension, "we know that you have struggled with alcoholism and depression." Jack heard a soft gasp but didn't know the source because he was looking directly at Kobayashi. It sounded like a woman's voice. "We also know about what your step-mother did when she took control of your family's property upon your father's death. You lost everything, including your heritage and status as a member of the samurai class in this village. It must have been very difficult for you. It's understandable how you would have been in emotional and psychological pain after that."

"But not understandable enough to account for murder," came the terse interjection from Matsumoto. Jack looked around the room and everyone conveyed extreme tension both on their faces and in their stiff postures.

"I did not murder anyone! This is absurd! What evidence do you have?"

"Your fingerprints were found on one of the murder weapons. They were on the prayer beads used to strangle Saito-san. And we also know the source of the chloroform that was used to knock out the victims before you killed them. Here's what happened. You abducted each man by anesthetizing them with the chloroform, dragged them into a white van, and drove that van to each of the temples. At Taiyō-ji you strangled Takahashi-san by hanging him. I think you planned to do the same with Saito-san at Houn-ji, but he awoke before you could finish and you ended up strangling him with the prayer beads instead of hanging him with them, as you intended."

"This is crazy!" shouted Kobayashi. "Why would I want to kill either of those men? I didn't even know them..." The bald head of Kobayashi was lobster red and Jack thought the man was on the verge of erupting into tears. Both of his hands were shaking.

"We struggled with that, at first, but it became clear when we learned that both men had been leaders in the *kakushi nembutsu*. It was simple revenge. You've held a deep grudge for being ostracized from the village, which started when you failed to pass the ritual test. It was years of frustration and anger that built up and you finally took it out on these innocent men who you viewed as having triggered your long journey into suffering."

Kobayashi's hands covered his face as he began to repeat, "No, no, no..." This was very uncomfortable and Jack wished that it would be over. Just as that thought entered his mind the sounds of Kobayashi's melt-down were augmented by an airy gasp from the other side of the room. Jack turned quickly to see that it was Kondo whose face displayed nothing short of sheer terror. Immediately thereafter, a loud commotion came from the *genkan*.

"Why are you bringing me here? I want an explanation! *Yamerō!*" Stop!

Kondo had seen through the window what Jack now could clearly discern entering the living room. It was a slight man wearing wire-framed glasses. His head was cleanly shaven and he wore a black pant suit similar to the one Taitsu had been wearing when Jack encountered him in the garden a few days earlier. For a moment, Jack was unsure of the man's identity, but quickly realized who it was when he limped into the room. There was no mistake. It was the mystery priest from the library and funeral.

As the limping man entered the room, Kobayashi's pained cries continued. His body was shaking and Hashimoto stood from her chair and walked over to him, putting her arms around Kobayashi's shoulders in an attempt to comfort and calm him. She looked at the inspector and with a pained look said, "This is cruel! Surely, Inspector, you don't believe that this man killed anyone!"

"I most certainly do," responded Matsumoto even more gruffly than usual. "And we have the evidence to prove it, so there will be no mistake on this." Hashimoto was concerned that Kobayashi was becoming increasingly traumatized by his ordeal and implored the inspector to stop pushing, to which Matsumoto responded, "Officer Watanabe, please escort Kobayashi-san to the patrol car so that we can take him to the police detention center in Morioka. I'm sure that the long stay there will produce a change of Kobayashi's attitude about his situation."

"Noooooo!" came a scream from the other side of the room. "Stop! Please stop! Stop hurting him, Kobayashi-san didn't do it! He's innocent. Please, stop!" Kondo had dropped out of her chair and was on her knees on the floor.

Matsumoto turned in her direction and with frigidly calm voice said, "Kondo-san, why do you say that?"

"Stop. It was me. I killed them. Just please do not hurt Tetsura-san any more. *Onegai shimasu!*" Please! She used Kobayashi's given name, an unusual move in such a public environment. It told a great deal about their relationship, or at least her perception of it.

"Yes, Kondo-san, we know that you did it. We were not sure until just an hour ago, when we picked up your brother here," Matsumoto pointed at the little man who had hobbled into the room. "What was your motive? Hatred of Buddhism? Or was it your love for Kobayashi-san? Here's what I think. You and your older brother here," and Matsumoto looked directly at the little man with the limp, "shared a mutual distaste for Buddhism and your own anger with the religion was intensified by your feelings for Kobayashi-san, who you knew had been treated poorly when he was a child by the members of the *nembutsu* cult, although he did, in fact, pass on the third try. You attributed his suffering to the cult and to Buddhism in general and wanted revenge. Perhaps you thought it might get Kobayashi-san to realize that you were in love with him. And your dislike of Buddhism encouraged you to locate the murders in places that would show your hatred for the religion and its adherents, while you imagined that the use of Buddhist objects and the location at the temple halls would lead people to think the murdered men would become *muenbotoke*, ghosts that would suffer the same kind of loneliness you felt from your unrequited love of Kobayashi-san for all eternity. But you didn't think that out very carefully, because a person only becomes a *muenbotoke* if there is no-one to care for them in death. Obviously, Takahashi-san and Saito-san were respected members of the community and loved fathers and husbands; you should have realized that they both had dedicated adult children who would care for their ancestral spirits. I'm actually surprised that you made such a dumb mistake, Kondo-san."

"I think I have an explanation for that," interjected Jack. "It's the limp. I suspect that if we look more into the Kondo family history, we will find that her brother was part of the group of children who were being initiated several years ago when a candle was dropped, causing a fire. Several of the initiates were injured and I'd be comfortable hypothesizing that Kondo-san's limp is the result of that accident. It may well be that Kondo-san's fear in the situation led to the candle being dropped and the fire that destroyed the house. It also may well have led to Kondo-san's family be ostracized through *mura hachibu*. Years of simmering rage certainly can form a motive and also can lead to careless errors."

The room was silent, but Jack could see that the elder Kondo was now trembling. He must have hit the nail on the head.

Matsumoto waited to see if there was a reaction, but Kondo-san simply kneeled on the floor in silence. "We suspected you early on, but also realized that the murderer would need an accomplice. It would have been too difficult for one person to suspend even a small man like Takahashi from the rafters using an *onbuhimo*. It was only when we were able to identify the source of the chloroform you used to abduct your victims and found that your older brother had been the one who purchased it, that we became certain it was you—and him. I'm confident that when we have a chance to question your brother, we will find his participation in the *Ehoba* group was accompanied by a growing hatred of Buddhism. I don't know for certain what the source of that hatred may be, but given Jack's hypothesis, I think I have an idea…"

"I think there is more to it," interjected Jack. "I think your involvement," as he turned to Kondo-san's brother, "was motivated by a desire to symbolically purge yourself of the blood of Gutoku— the foolish bald one, Shinran. As you became increasingly involved and obsessed with the *Ehoba* group and, largely, misinterpreted their conceptualization of blood as the soul of life you became compelled to rid yourself of the defilement. You were indoctrinated into the *nembutsu* cult as a child and had become a Jōdō Shinshū priest as an adult, which meant that unlike Zen priests in the area, you were not required to resign from the cult as a priest. My guess is that you thought murdering these two men might somehow resolve the problem that, even if only symbolically, you were one in the blood of another human—which seemed to you a direct contradiction of *Ehoba* doctrine. Perhaps this misinterpretation stemmed from your accident as a child, for which I suspect you have always wanted revenge. For both of you, emotions clouded your own understanding of *Ehoba* and your ideas about the fates of your victim's spirits in death."

As Jack finished, the flashing of red lights from the patrol car that had just pulled up in front of his house began to alternately illuminate the walls of the living room. Inspector Matsumoto motioned to Officer Sakamoto, who escorted the Kondo siblings to the genkan, where two more armed police officers waited. Matsumoto walked in the direction of Kobayashi and bowed deeply and carefully said, "*Sumimasen, arigatō gozaimashita. Hontō ni oseiwa ni narimashita.*" I am sorry. Thank you. You were a tremendous help.

Kobayashi relaxed a little and smiled, "Was I convincing?"

"Yes, Kobayashi-san, you were very convincing," responded Taitsu, and then Jack added, "I actually was getting worried you were having a nervous breakdown."

"I am truly sorry for having to put you through that," said Matsumoto, "but we felt the only way to flush out Kondo-san was to put her on the spot and we felt sure that pointing our finger at you would do that. I truly appreciate your agreeing to help us—I'm sure it was difficult."

Kobayashi continued to smile mildly and responded, "My problems with mental health and alcoholism are known to everyone in the village. It was no surprise, and I have come to terms with that part of my past—and I'm forever grateful to the *Ehoba* group for helping me do that. They saved my life." Kobayashi paused as his face grew quiet and then in a whisper, he added, "I had no idea she felt that way..." He stared through the window in Jack's living room as the patrol car departed in the rain.

"...*daijyōbu desu.*" I'm okay, he said as he turned back to Jack and Matsumoto. "I can understand why you had to take the path you did and I appreciate your trusting me to help. You took a risk, had I known about Kondo-san's feelings." He smiled faintly.

Jack looked around the room and saw that the other members of the group remained in stunned silence. Matsumoto also noticed and turned to the group. "I want to apologize to all of you for putting you through this, but I also want to thank you for your cooperation. Each of you has been more helpful than you might imagine as we attempted to solve these horrid crimes. I sincerely appreciate your enduring this painful evening. Please feel free to go and also to contact me if you need anything." The two-sided personality of Matsumoto kept showing through—the gruff police detective at one moment and the kind, gentle supporter of others the next. He was an interesting man, Jack thought.

24
BORN SHINTO, DIE BUDDHIST

As everyone cleared out of Jack's living room, the three men sat at his kitchen table. Jack brought out some beer bottles—no glasses this time—and placed a bowl of *edamame* on the center of the table. He wasn't sure anyone would eat them, but it was customary to put out something. They were exhausted, but still touched their bottles together in a *kampai* to celebrate successfully ending the case. None of them smiled, however. It didn't feel like much of a victory. Instead, it had been a painful few days punctuated by an evening in which they risked public humiliation of several people who were involved through no fault of their own. It didn't feel good.

They sat for a few minutes and then Jack broke the silence. "There are still a few things I don't understand. Mostly, I really don't get why Kondo-san's brother used the *onbuhimo* and prayer beads as murder weapons. I still think that was meaningful, but I'm blanking on exactly what it meant."

"It was meaningful, Jack-san," commented Taitsu. "It hit me this morning what was going on with that. As you surmised, I think the candles were intended to symbolize the *kakushi nembutsu* and now knowing about Kondo-san's injury as a child, it makes a great deal of sense. Kondo-san was making a statement with this to show his distaste for the ritual and the life-long pain he has suffered, as you rightly suggested, Jack. But the use of the *onbuhimo* and prayer beads I think were aimed at something else. You know the old saying, born Shinto, die Buddhist?"

"Sure," said Jack.

"Think about it. The *onbuhimo* symbolizes birth and the prayer beads symbolize death. He was using these as murder weapons to express his rejection of Japanese religious concepts in general. I think it was part of his conversion to *Ehoba*. By that, I don't mean that the group would have encouraged such a thing, but Kondo-san clearly is very confused. When you question him, Inspector, I think you will find he managed to connect the murder weapons with his own rejection of Buddhism and of the *nembutsu* cult in much the way Jack described in his rejection of his blood discipleship with Shinran."

"That makes a lot of sense, Taitsu-san," said Jack, to which Matsumoto nodded in agreement. The room grew silent again. After another couple of minutes, Matsumoto rose and said he should get back to the station. It was going to be a long night as they dealt with the evening's aftermath. Taitsu stood, as well, and the three were about to call it an evening when Jack asked one last question.

"Matsumoto-san…"

"*Hai.*"

"What was that bit about the fingerprints? You never said anything about that, and it has to have been a lie."

"No, it wasn't exactly a lie, Jack-san. We found the fingerprints of many of Tanohata's residents on the beads—I'm sure his were on them at one time…"

"Damn," Jack replied in English. "You're good!"

The men laughed and bowed as they departed, the tension a little less for Matsumoto's devious response. Jack looked around and thought that the house was a mess, but he lacked the energy to straighten things up. He headed for his bedroom and unfolded the futon on the floor. Not even bothering to undress, he settled on the futon and then realized he needed to call Saori. Fortunately, his phone was nearby and he called her, providing a brief explanation of the night's events and assuring her that he was safe. Indeed, he felt safe for the first time since he had arrived in Tanohata. He fell asleep almost as soon as he ended the call.

25
ONSEN

The next morning, Jack awoke around ten o'clock after a restful sleep. The rain had cleared overnight and although the sky was still grey, there were glimmers of sunlight peeping out from the emerging breaks in the clouds. After some eggs and toast for breakfast, he decided that this would be the day for a trip to the *onsen*. He packed a bag with a change of clothes and toiletries, a large towel for drying himself, and a small towel to carry into the bath. The small towel served the function of covering one's private parts while walking through the showering areas or sitting in the sauna, although the *onsen* Jack had decided on lacked that particular relaxational feature.

The Tesla whirred past wide plains of rice fields, with their muted blue-green hues reflecting the grey morning. The road to Semi Onsen was twisting and narrow—in fact, it was so winding that Irene had experienced motion sickness almost every time they headed there in the past. But it was a favored spot, far removed from anything that might feel stressful. Jack parked the car and walked toward the *genkan* for the *onsen*. Much like any spa, it had a hotel and restaurant in addition to several different baths one could select as a spot for unwinding. He paid his 500 yen and headed for the bath his family always preferred. It was at the top of a long staircase that led to a seating area with drink vending machines—several beer choices—a couple of electric massage chairs, and the entrances to men's and women's dressing rooms. Jack removed his clothes, grabbed his small towel and opened the sliding door leading to the bath. The first stop was a shower in the communal bathing area, because the large pool was for soaking, rather than getting one's body clean, which was the first step in properly enjoying the *onsen* experience. After a thorough wash, Jack headed for the large pool of hot water across from the showering area. There was another man relaxing quietly in the pool so that the water reached his neck.

Jack settled into the water, which was usually between 39°C and 42°C (102°F to 107.5°F). The temperature was guaranteed to turn his body lobster-red after only a few minutes of soaking. As he settled into the steaming water, two more men joined. No words were exchanged; the only sounds being those coming from people splashing as they cleaned themselves in the showers. The water at this particular *onsen* was unusual—it felt slippery on the skin, which was a product of the high sulfur content, which was also evident in the pungent odor that permeated the room. After a few minutes, another man entered the bath area. Unlike everyone else, all of whom were stark naked, this man was wearing a white robe. He sat on the edge of the pool and pulled a *shakuhachi* out of his sleeve. As the man began to play the Japanese flute, everyone turned in his direction and smiles flashed as the gentle melody wafted across the room.

Jack was getting hot.

He stood and walked toward the sliding door that led to the outside part of the bathing area called the *rotenburo*. The mountain air was cool and a gentle rain splashed against the surface of the steaming water as hundreds of circular ripples radiated in all directions. Jack settled in amongst a nook of large rocks and muted Japanese flute refrains from inside drifted across the air accompanied by the tinkling sounds of rain hitting the surface of the water. Jack's body relaxed as he gazed into the celadon grey cloud obscuring most of the myrtle mountain that acted as a canvas across which wispy raindrops cascaded into the steaming pool. It was good to be home, Jack thought. He carefully folded the white towel into a small rectangle and placed it on his head and then settled neck-deep into the warm water's embrace. It may have commenced with a strange dramatic twist, he thought, but retirement was beginning to look very good, indeed.

GLOSSARY OF JAPANESE WORDS AND PHRASES

ah-gyō(阿形), *un-gyō*(吽形) Beginning and end of Sanskrit alphabet, open and closed mouth forms in Buddhism

aka-chan(赤ちゃん) Infant

amida(阿弥陀) Buddha of Infinite Light

anmari omukai ga konai(あんまり　おむかい(＝お迎え)が来ない) I have not yet been taken

ano(あの) Um...

arigatō gozaimasu (ありがとうございます) Thank you (formal)

arigatō(ありがとう) Thank you

bīru mō ippon (ビールもう一本) One more beer!

bento(弁当) Box lunch

Bunmei(文明) Era from 1469-1487

butsudan(仏壇) Buddhist altar

chigaimasu (違います) No, it's different

dango(団子) Rice ball

dōzo ohairi kudasai(どうぞお入りください) Please come in.

edamame(枝豆) Soy bean snack

ehoba(エホバ) Jehova's Witness

fushigi desu nee(不思議ですね) It's strange, isn't it?

gaijin da(外人だ) It's a foreigner.

gambarimashita(頑張りました) I/he/she/ gave it all.

gambatte(頑張って) Do your best.

genkan(玄関) Entryway

gochisōsama deshita(ごちそうさまでした) It was a feast.

go-dai(五台) Five machines

go-hiki(五匹) Five small animals

gokuraku(極楽) Heaven

gomen kudasai(ごめんください) May I come in?

gomennasai(ごめんなさい) I'm sorry

gosenzo-sama(ご先祖様) Ancestors

hai(はい) Yes

hajimemashite, yoroshiku onegai itashimasu(初めまして、よろしくお願いいたします) Pleased to meet you (formal)

hakama(袴) A man's traditional bottom attire resembling a pleated skirt

hisashiburi desu nee(久しぶりですね) It's been a while, hasn't it

hontō ka(本当か) Really?

hontō ni oseiwa ni narimashita(本当にお世話になりました) You were truly very helpful.

hotoke(仏) Buddha, ancestor

ikimashyō ka(行きましょうか) Shall we go?

ikō ka?(行こうか?) Shall we go? (informal)

irasshai(いらっしゃい) Welcome

ittekimasu(行ってきます) I will return (said upon leaving the house)

itterasshai(行ってらっしゃい) See you later. Have a fun. Said in response to ittekimasu.

jichikai (自治会) Self-government association

jichikai-chō(自治会長) Head of self-government association

jizō(地蔵) Statues of the Bodhisattva protect children and travelers

jyaa...oisogashii tokoro wo(*ojyama shimashita*)...*soro soro*(*shitsurei shimasu*) (じゃ....お忙しいところを(お邪魔しました)....そろそろ(失礼します) Terms indicating imposition on one's time

kakure nembutsu(隠れ念仏) Secret nembutsu

kakushi nembutsu(隠し念仏) Secret nembutsu

kami(神) Deity

kamoshika(カモシカ) Serow

kampai(乾杯) Cheers

kanreki(還暦) Ritual of transition into old age/retirement

karaage（唐揚げ）Chicken nuggets

kashikomarimashita（かしこまりました）Certainly!

katsudon（カツ丼）Rice with pork and egg

katsudon onegai-shimasu（かつ丼お願いします）Katsudon, please!

komainu（狛犬）Lion-dog

konbanwa（こんばんは）Good evening

konnichiwa（こんにちは）Good day

kotatsu（炬燵）Heated table

kura（蔵）Storage building

mata ashita（また明日）See you tomorrow

mata asobi ni kite kudasai（また遊びに来てください）Please visit again!

mata kitte kunansei（またきって（来て）くなんせい）Please visit again!

mochiron desu zenzen mondai nai（もちろんです全然問題ない）Sure, no problem

moshi moshi（もしもし）Hello (on telephone)

moshikashi（もしかし）Perhaps, maybe

muenbotoke（無縁仏）Sandering spirit

mugicha（麦茶）Barley tea

mukoyōshi（婿養子）Adopted adult son

mura（村）Village

murahachibu（村八分）Ostracism

naamu aamidaaa buuutsu（南無阿弥陀仏）Prayer to Amida

nda nda（んだ、んだ）Yes

nemawashi（根回し）Laying groundwork

nembutsu（念仏）Form of Buddhist prayer

nembutsuko（念仏講）Buddhist prayer group/cult

obaa-san denwa-desu（おばあさん　電話です）Grandma, telephone!

oban de gasu（お晩でがす）Good evening (local dialect)

obon（お盆）Summer festival of the dead

ogenki desu ka（お元気ですか）Are you well?

ohayō gozaimasu（おはようございます）Good morning

ojyama shimasu（お邪魔します）I'm in the way (said upon entering a house)

okaa-san（お母さん）Mother

okaerinasai（お帰りなさい）Welcome home

ombuhimo（おんぶ紐）Cloth strap to tie an infant to mother's back

onigiri（おにぎり）Rice balls

on-nomi（オン飲み）Online drinking gathering

onsen（温泉）Hot spring

osewa ni narimashita（お世話になりました）You were very helpful

otsukaresama deshita（お疲れさまでした）Thank you for your hard work. You did a great job.

oyasumi（おやすみ）Good night

rotenburo（露天風呂）Outside area at a hot spring

sake（酒）Rice wine

shakuhachi（尺八）Japanese flute

shinkansen（新幹線）Bullet train

shokupan（食パン）Japanese white bread.

soro soro（そろそろ）Indicator that it's time to leave

Sō desu nee（そうですね）I see

sumimasen（すみません）I'm sorry

sumimasen, arigatō gozaimashita（すみません、ありがとうございました）I'm sorry, thank you.

sumimasen-deshita（すみませんでした）I'm sorry (past tense)

tadaima（ただいま）I'm home!

taihen desu nee（大変ですね）It's difficult, isn't it.

tasuke tamae（助け賜え）Save me.

tōba（塔婆）Board on which posthumous Buddhist name is placed

torii（鳥居）Shintō Gate

ue-sama（上様）The Head Person

un-gyō（吽形）Closed-mouth form (Buddhism)

uso desu（嘘です）It's a lie

utsubyō（うつ病）Depression

yamerō（止めろ）Stop!

yasashii nee（優しいね）Kind

yoroshiku onegai shimasu（宜しくお願いします）Please favor me

yurushite kudasai（許してください）Please forgive me

zūzū-ben（ズーズー弁）Local dialect in northern Japan

Made in the USA
Monee, IL
30 November 2021

83464161R00132